SCULLY'S LUGS

Stewart Hutchinson

Scully's Lugs

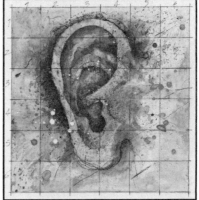

STEWART HUTCHISON

CHAMBERS

First published by W & R Chambers Ltd 1979

Printed in Great Britain by
Morrison & Gibb Ltd Edinburgh

ISBN 0 550 20402 4

Part One

ELEMENTS

Boreland *1*
Scully's Lugs
   MALCOLM LESLIE *8*
36C
   DAVID SINCLAIR *25*
A Tree in the Well
   MALCOLM LESLIE *35*
Greek Fire *44*
Double-sided Sticky
   JOE O'ROURKE *51*
Four Bells
   SANDY SYME *63*
The Garden of Earthly Delights *80*
In the Footsteps of Marie Grosholtz
   JOE O'ROURKE *94*
Slug Road
   MALCOLM LESLIE *104*
Measurements
   MALCOLM LESLIE *113*

Part Two

THE THIRD OFFICER'S STORY

KG5 *123*
London–Dakar *133*
Dakar–Durban *142*
Durban–Djakarta *149*
File Cards *154*
Manila *162*
Hong Kong *171*
Three Days Plus *188*
Up in Nagasaki . . . *198*
Tweendecks *208*
Glass *217*
Atonement *224*

Part One
ELEMENTS

Boreland

Malcolm Leslie stood, legs apart, on the sleeper-paved track beside the railway, almost exactly mid-way between the new metal footbridge at Dysart and the old wooden one at Boreland, but slightly to the Boreland end. The six strands of rusted wire which set apart the realms of British Railways from the rest of the world supported his bicycle, but so half-heartedly that the front wheel revolved idly disturbing the yellow grass at the base of the fence. The wind added to the problems of the grass, hummed through the telephone wires overhead and whipped in vain round Malcolm's stocky red knees before tangling with the smoke from the Francis Colliery chimney and slanting it south west across the roofs of the town.

It was seven thirty in the morning and Malcolm had been waiting five minutes. There had been no difficulty in getting out so early. His father, who was an electrician at that time engaged on installing lighting in schools and other County Council establishments in rural districts, was obliged to leave home at six. Thus Malcolm had already had breakfast and packed his stained, green canvas gas-mask case with such books, jotters and sandwiches as would be necessary for his day at school. The case now hung over a British Railways fence post and swayed very gently in sympathy with the grass.

Malcolm narrowed his little, closely spaced eyes to slits and peered across the monochrome landscape. What was he looking for between the telegraph poles that spaced themselves out, sixty paces apart, along the horizon formed by the Randolph Road? Behind his back, behind the railway and the sidings and behind the chimney of the Francis Colliery, the Firth of Forth was greyer than the sky. Had Malcolm turned round, he would have seen three blue buses creeping along the edge of the water towards the smoking chimney, bringing the clean, tired day shift to the colliery. Further out in the greyness, he could have identified the steamship *Marga* (ex *Louise Williams*), 7200 tons and registered in Monrovia moving upriver with bauxite ore for Burntisland. There was no hope of her catching the tide. She would have to lie off. He would have had more difficulty recognising the motorship *Franz Reinhard*, 800 tons and registered in Bremen, chugging downriver with general cargo from Granton. Had Malcolm turned round when the dark grey silhouette of the *Marga* superimposed itself on the light grey one of the *Franz Reinhard*, he would have seen the three blue buses creeping away from the chimney, taking the dirty, tired night shift from the colliery. But Malcolm did not turn round. He narrowed his eyes, pushed his hands deeper into his pockets and peered between the telegraph poles until the front wheel of his bicycle gave up and stopped turning.

As it happened, David Sinclair did not appear between the telegraph poles on the Randolph Road. He came over the metal footbridge from Dysart. He crossed the red painted bridge awkwardly, for he was carrying his old black bicycle over one shoulder with his arm through the frame. From his other shoulder a huge grey newspaper bag hung almost to the ground, threatening to trip him as he came precariously down the steep metal steps. Malcolm must have heard him coming, heard him bumping down the steps and the clatter as he reached the bottom, for he turned his attention away from the telegraph poles and adjusted his stance just sufficiently to bring David Sinclair, by then mounted on his bicycle and approaching rapidly, into his field of vision.

There were two remarkable things about David's bicycle. The first was its age and blackness, which went together. It had been bought fourth-hand by David's brother who was away in Germany on National Service and David had taken advantage of his brother's enforced military activity to appropriate the machine. He bore his classmates' criticism of its narrow, upward-curving handlebars and total lack of chromium plating with annoying stoicism. Its second unusual feature was a sheet of heavy cardboard, cut to a rough triangle and covered on both sides with white paper, which was fixed to the bar by loops of wire and hung down between the knees of the rider. This home-made appendage was not really David's doing. It was the work of Mr Ballantine, the newsagent in Gallatown, for whom David delivered morning papers and who had a flair for publicity.

Every morning at six-thirty when his four delivery boys arrived at the shop, Ballantine would take a pinch of snuff, open the bundles of newspapers, and study the front page of each rival publication deeply. Finally deciding on a headline which took his fancy, he would move over to a table on which six triangles of paper lay ready and while each boy sorted out his quota of newspapers, would inscribe the chosen slogan six times in thick black ink which he kept in a jam jar. Only six times, because Archie Tulloch, the youngest and by far the smallest of Mr Ballantine's newsboys, was obliged to use his mother's bicycle which, being a ladies' model, was devoid of a crossbar from which to suspend a placard. Consequently, he had to forfeit the extra three pence which Ballantine added to the wages of those who proclaimed the news of the day from between their knees.

Had Malcolm wanted to, he could have made out the words 'Grace to marry Prince of Monaco' between David Sinclair's rotating legs. Perhaps he did, but by the time David had dismounted and let the bicycle and newspaper bag topple into the grass, Malcolm's back was turned once more and his eyes fixed on a grey plume of smoke which was swelling from between the fourth and fifth telegraph poles, where the railway lines passed under the Randolph Road.

'Where have ye been, Davie?'

'I had some left over, so I sold them at the Dubby.'

David Sinclair was almost seven months older than Malcolm Leslie, half-a-head taller, and like everyone in Dysart and Gallatown and even in Kirkcaldy, called the Francis Colliery the Dubby because its seams and galleries stretched right out under the Forth, and it was a very wet pit indeed.

The cloud of smoke was being propelled towards them by a black steam engine which, for some reason, was going

backwards and pulling a dirty grey brake van from its front
end. Try as it might, the thin white wisp emerging from the
brake van's chimney was totally engulfed by the grey smoke of
the engine. David shifted position, leant over the fence and
closed his grey knitted gloves round the top strand of wire. It
was a small, antiquated tank engine with six wheels, large
cylinders and a disproportionately long chimney, in fact a J88
Class designed by Mr W P Reid and introduced to the North
British Railway Company in 1904 for light freight and
shunting duties. Its fuel supply was carried in a high-sided box
behind the cab and it was from this that the fireman, whose
grimy form was just distinguishable through his self-inflicted
pall of smoke, took a lump of coal. His throw was so half-
hearted that the missile fell well short of the two figures by the
fence. David Sinclair raised his voice.

'That's the pug. What's it doing out here?'

His companion addressed him with the condescension of
an expert.

'Going to the harbour, of course. Did ye think they kept it
at the harbour? It goes to Thornton every night and they bring
it down in the morning.'

To be truthful, David had never noticed the engine
passing before although he had cycled along this length of
track many times before school. If Malcolm said the pug was
going to the harbour, he would be right. Malcolm knew
everything about the harbour. This was because of Hook.

Hook was Malcolm's maternal grandfather. He was never
away from the harbour, where he did odd jobs, helped to
operate the dock-gates and sometimes crewed the little black
pilot cutter when it was necessary to give assistance to a vessel
which was unfamiliar with the channel. Hook had both his
hands. His nose was not even particularly curved. He was
called Hook because of his rank. He had run away to sea when
very young and by the time of the Battle of Jutland, had
already been four times round the world and held the rank of
leading seaman on the cruiser HMS *Warrior*. Later, in another
cruiser, he had sailed to America and the West Indies and had
finally been caught in the ice at Murmansk where he had been
just in time to fight against someone, he was never very clear

whom, in the Russian Revolution. Everyone called Malcolm's grandfather Hook and almost everyone knew that Hook had a howff at the harbour.

The howff consisted of an old wooden deck-house removed from a coaster long since towed to the breaker's yard, and re-erected against the gable end of a shed on the side of Kirkcaldy harbour basin. In this howff, Malcolm's grandfather kept all the lengths of rope, nails, old lamps, oilskins and tarpaulins necessary for his line of business. He kept an old cage, but no parrot, some barrels to sit on and an armchair with the stuffing hanging out for himself. He kept cards and rum to while away bad weather, and he kept something else, which was why David Sinclair was standing that morning among smelly wisps of smoke beside the railway line.

'Did ye ask him about it?' He spoke into the smoke, away from Malcolm Leslie.

'Who?'

'Hook.'

'I didna' see him.'

The pug whistled as it passed under the metal bridge.

'But did ye get some anyway?'

Malcolm considered. He pushed his hands deeper into his pockets, almost withdrew one, then pushed it deeper still and narrowed his eyes.

'Hook disna' chow.'

To be sure, Hook was seldom seen without his pipe, which was short and worn, its rim caked in tar and carbon. And Hook was never without tobacco because he made his own pricks in his howff. The boys had often watched him. He got the tobacco leaves from friends on ships which called from time to time at Kirkcaldy, and when a fresh stock had arrived, he would stride purposefully to the howff with his rolling, sailors' gait, close the door behind him and set to work. Sometimes Malcolm or one of his friends was allowed to look on, but they never spoke, for making a prick was a serious business that demanded total concentration. Under the yellow light of the lamp if it was dark or in the dusty daylight if it was not, Hook would open the lid of his chest, consider the contents and eventually extract a thin strip of brown, stained canvas.

This he would lay to one side and lighting his pipe, settle down to trim the bundle of tobacco leaves one by one. When the shape of the leaves was satisfactory, he would close his pocket knife and lay them one by one on the canvas strip. He would then return to the chest for his bottle of rum and carefully decant a small measure into the bottom of a tea cup, or glass, or indeed any vessel that happened to be to hand. Hook would sniff the rum. Sometimes, but not always, he would treat himself to a swig from the bottle before returning it to the chest. Then he would sprinkle what remained in the cup over the trimmed tobacco leaves. But Hook had another secret to flavour his tobacco. On a shelf, indistinguishable to all but the keenest eye from the tins of nails and glue that surrounded it, stood a well-rusted tin of curry powder. It, in turn, was taken down and a liberal sprinkling of the damp, yellow powder dusted over the rum-stained leaves. The canvas was then wrapped carefully round the leaves and the whole affair lashed up extremely tightly with a length of thin rope, several of which Hook kept specially for this purpose. He would then hold up the cocoon-like sausage, examine it closely, weigh it first in one hand then the other and finally stow it carefully into his chest. Hook always had three pricks, one newly made, one maturing, and one which was ready, from which he would cut black chunks of tobacco to see him through the week; for one prick lasted a month and required two months to mature.

David Sinclair knew all this. He also knew, however, that when working hard splicing rope, or on a dirty night when the rain cut your face and the waves came over the sea wall, Hook would forsake his pipe and leave it on the bench in his howff when he went to take out the pilot cutter. On such nights, Hook would cut several small pieces from his oldest prick, put some into his pocket and pop one into his mouth before setting off down the quay. This is why David looked angrily at Malcolm and said,

'Aye he does. I've seen him and so have you.'

Malcolm hunched his shoulders against the wind and stared at the ground.

'Are ye sure ye want to try it?'

David Sinclair nodded. Slowly, Malcolm withdrew his hands from his trouser pockets. His fists were clenched, but when he opened them there was no lump of curry-flavoured tobacco. He went over to the fence and opened the flap of his gas-mask case. His hand slid down between *First Year Algebra* and *An Approach to English*, hesitated for a moment, then found what it was looking for beneath *Scottish History*. He extracted the little twist of greaseproof paper, held it up between thumb and forefinger, then dropped it into David's outstretched palm.

David unwound the paper in one quick movement, saw a little square block nestling in his hand, closed his eyes, conveyed it quickly to his mouth and bit hard. For a moment his eyes remained shut, then they opened and simultaneously a glaucous trickle of dark brown liquid ran from his mouth over his chin and on to his knitted, grey jersey. His twelve-year old teeth had closed not on a quid of spiced tobacco, but on an old, gritty Oxo cube. David looked up, trying hard not to choke. He flailed out with his fists, but Malcolm Leslie was not there. He was on his bicycle, heading for Gallatown and over his shoulder he was shouting 'Scully's Lugs' into the wind.

Scully's Lugs

MALCOLM LESLIE

Scully had only one name. At least, if he ever possessed a
Christian name, pet name or nickname, it has been forgotten
during the years. He has passed into history as Scully. The
gulls know about Scully, because over harbours, over wharfs,
quays and tidal basins, over flow-tides and ebb-tides, over
spring tides and neap tides which often, despite the sand bags
supplied by the Town Council, flood cellars and basements in
the lower part of the town, the gulls are watching and
remembering.

The gulls know that then, just as now, before Mr
Gladstone had begun his second term as Prime Minister,
before work had begun even on the foundations of the Forth
Bridge to carry the railway across the upper reaches of the
river, and years and years before Mafeking had been relieved,
the most direct route from Kirkcaldy harbour to Sinclairtown,
where the linoleum factories of Mr (later Sir) Michael Nairn
were only just beginning to spread an aroma of boiling linseed
oil through the ozone-filled air, was by a narrow, twisting
gradient called the Path. Then, as now, the name of this six-
hundred-yards-long municipal thoroughfare was misleading.
Only in the dimmest past had it consisted of nothing but a path
up the steep slope of hill and cliff which surrounded the
harbour. The gulls know that when they swooped and dived
over Scully's head, the Path was well cobbled and wide
enough for two carts to pass, provided they kept well in. No
doubt the gulls know that today the Path is surfaced in
tarmacadam, widened at the expense of landlords whose
property adjoins it to accommodate the largest motor vehicles,
and bereft of its more tortuous curves. But at the time of which
I write, when the gulls were just beginning to find that it was
more profitable to flock round the sewerage from the new pipe

near the end of the pier than to wait for the fishing boats, and when Dave Sinclair could scarcely tempt two of them with chunks of dry bread, the Path was much the same as in Scully's day.

Scully was a carter. Six days a week, he and several dozen others would bring their carts to the harbour, fill them with whatever commodities were being unloaded at the time and transport them slowly but surely to their destinations in the town or indeed anywhere in the country. Unless the route lay westwards, leaving the harbour necessitated a steep climb and the steepest route of all was the Path. It was the policy of the Fife Forge Company, who had to haul by far the heaviest loads, to keep four trace horses at the foot of the Path, and I am reliably informed that in Scully's day, as many as fourteen trace horses, under the charge of a one-armed man, who had been at Balaclava, could be found waiting to assist the heavily loaded wagons up the gradient.

There is no record of Scully ever having had difficulty getting his cart to the top of the Path. Whether carrying timber or barrels of fish, bales of jute or loads of bricks, his two horses, with the assistance when necessary of a couple of Clydesdales from the one-armed man, seem to have been entirely competent to haul any load to the top.

It was on a dry day near midsummer when coming down the Path that things went wrong for Scully. Nobody seems to know exactly what caused it. Perhaps a traction engine was in the vicinity, on its way to power a threshing mill at a local farm, or perhaps the presence of a barking dog was enough to startle Scully's horses. The gulls will know. There is no doubt that Scully's horses were startled and that they bolted at the top of the Path.

It must not be imagined that Scully was a bad driver. Today, if a motorist finds his vehicle going into a skid, he at once adopts certain procedures to retrieve the situation, or at least to come out of it with minimum damage. Similarly, Scully used every ounce of his skill as a carter to avert disaster. His attempt to rein in the team having failed, he spun the handle and clamped the brake-shoes tight against the steel-tyred back wheels of the cart so that they locked and sparks flew from the cobbles. Perhaps if the cart had not been so heavily loaded all would have been well, but as it happened, the weight of the bales of oil-cloth added to the energy of the uncontrollable team and provided sufficient momentum to render the effect of the brakes useless. It was the practice in those days to carry two large wooden chocks on most carts to provide extra security when parking on hills. In the heat of his predicament, Scully seized one of these chocks and swung himself out over the side of the cart with the intention of ramming it in front of one of the wheels. Did his foot slip, or did one of his horses jerk on its rein and hurl him from his seat on the cart? Only the gulls know. One moment Scully was on top of the squealing, skidding wagon, the next he was beneath it, his foot helplessly ensnared in the heavy, leather reins.

Scully's team did not stop when they reached the foot of the Path. They passed by the harbour as if it had not been there. Only when they came to the beach on the west side of the harbour and the salt-pans where women were scraping up the white crystals into sacks, only when the wheels cut so deep into the sand that they stopped turning did Scully's team pull up and stand foaming and quivering before the crowd. The dozen or so salt-wives, sailors and dockers did not lift Scully from under the cart. The one-armed man, who came riding up astride one of his Clydesdale trace horses did not call for a stretcher. Scully was not borne away on a door. He crawled out from under his cart and stood up. His trouser knees were beyond mending and his jacket was dusty and torn, its collar stained with blood. The rough granite cobbles of the Path had shown no respect for human flesh and hair. They had remodelled Scully. They had smoothed him down and rounded him off. Scully no longer had any ears. I have been told that a young fish-wife at the back of the crowd removed her blouse and covered herself with her shawl, and that it was with this white cotton blouse that they first wrapped Scully's poor, bleeding head and covered the messy red holes where his ears had been.

Plastic surgery is not a pleasant topic. Even today, if I chance to come across an unfortunate person whose features have been reconstructed, albeit extremely skilfully, by cosmetic surgeons, I experience a sense of horror which is most upsetting. How much more disturbing it must have been for the people of Kirkcaldy to find Scully, who was always a quiet, dignified and inoffensive man, in their midst devoid of ears through no fault of his own. Although medicine at that time lacked the necessary sophistication to restore ears to Scully's curiously smoothed-down head, the people who lived near the harbour and who saw Scully every day during his convalescence, decided that something must be done. A collection was made. The Guild of Waggoners contributed the balance required, and sent to Edinburgh for a saddler who specialised in intricate leatherwork. Within a week, the worthy craftsman had fashioned a magnificent pair of substitute ears from the finest leather. They were light tan in colour, double-stitched round the edges and tooled all over with complicated whorls and volutes designed to represent the contours of everyday ears. Perhaps they were a trifle larger than one would expect, but nobody objected to this because they were so splendid and had cost so much money. A slim leather strap connected the ears, and to fasten it under the chin the harbourmaster himself contributed a buckle of solid silver.

I have no reason to believe that Scully was not completely satisfied with his new ears. He wore them in his quiet, dignified way for the rest of his life. If the weather was fine he wore them with the strap under his cap and when it was windy, he quite sensibly wore them with the strap passing over his cap. Hook can remember Scully when the carter had retired and taken to strolling round the harbour in a velvet smoking cap, speaking to the horses and passing the time of day with the stevedores and dockers. Perhaps the old carter befriended the young lad with aspirations to seamanship, who was never away from the harbour. How else could his ears have found a permanent place on a nail driven into the wall of my grandfather's howff between the bird cage and the tin of curry powder?

A cloud passed across the late September sun. The ray of light slanting through the half-open door of the howff moved over, left the ears in peace and settled languorously on the dusty floor. Dave Sinclair threw his last piece of bread to the gulls, who packed up and flew off to join the white flock at the end of the sewerage pipe. We were sitting outside the howff looking across the tidal basin. We were not at school because, for one week, there was no school to go to. Our old school, in the centre of town, which was comfortable and mostly made of stone and too small, had been replaced by a new school which was uncomfortable, mostly made of glass, too large and set among fields and woods behind the town. So for one week, while removal contractors transported the desks and chairs, blackboards and vaulting horses to their new, paint-smelling location, we were not at school.

Dave was fifteen then. I had seven months to wait. As far as I remember, no thoughts of great consequence were occupying my mind. I was lazily keeping an eye on a group of bathers who had appeared outside the ramshackle hut on the other side of the basin, which served as the headquarters and changing rooms of Kirkcaldy Swimming Club. Sandy Syme, who swam like a fish despite his club foot, had said that the girl might be there and I wanted Dave to see her. One by one, the two dozen bathers donned white bathing caps and teetered, bare footed, down the slimy slipway towards the water. One by one, they tested its temperature with their toes or with their arms and one by one they launched themselves into the grey, oily water beside the seaweed and lumps of dirty cork. Their squeals and laughter were louder than the cries of the gulls, but not nearly as loud as the coal hoist, which was tipping a wagon load of coal into the bunkers of a grubby little steamer somewhere behind the howff.

Dave lit a cigarette. He had a packet of twenty Senior Service. He inhaled deeply and shaded his eyes, for the sun had come out again. I'm sure that he would have given me one had I asked, but I didn't ask, for frankly at fourteen-and-a-half, Senior Service made me feel ill. I didn't need to follow Dave's gaze to know what was attracting his attention. A dumpy, grey dredger had emerged from behind the harbour wall and was steaming above its reflection towards the mouth of the estuary.

For a whole year Dave Sinclair's mind had never been far

from the sea. Ever since the previous October he had insisted on accompanying me every time I visited Hook. He had watched quietly while Hook painted lifebuoys and fenders. He had looked on while rope was being spliced and the cables of one or other of the steam-cranes being repaired. Time and time again he had requested Hook to repeat his stories until I became quite bored and wandered off to watch lobsters being sold further down the quay. He had followed Hook about, always quietly, always politely and consequently had been introduced to masters and mates, deckhands and engineers of numerous coasters that called at the harbour. Whenever there was something he did not understand, he would get Hook to explain; and gradually, without anyone noticing but me, he had begun to help Hook with his duties. But he never got out on the pilot cutter.

The pilot's name was Mr MacBeth. He was an elder of the Old Kirk, always wore his uniform and was a very grave man indeed, which was only fitting, because a pilot's job is a very serious one and necessitates an orderly and sober outlook on life. It was one of Mr MacBeth's cardinal rules to have only the authorised personnel aboard his pilot cutter, and though the authorised personnel consisted only of Hook and there was easily room aboard for another three, no amount of pleading would persuade him to offer a place to a young, land-locked sailor who had never been on a boat.

I had sailed with Hook aboard the pilot cutter, however. Every year, when Mr MacBeth went away up north for a fortnight to stay with his sister and a substitute pilot came from Methil, Hook would call at our house, make my mother wrap me up well and despite her protests, take me with him when a ship needed assistance in the Forth. He had done this for five years, ever since I was nine, and during the last two years, we had gone out at night when the sea was really rough and you couldn't see the lights of the town for waves. The last time had been particularly splendid. The substitute pilot, who had a beard and was much younger than even a substitute pilot should be, asked me to come aboard the ship with him. Even Hook was surprised at that, but he let me jump from the wet, heaving deck of the cutter and watched as I struggled up the quivering rope ladder after the pilot. Then he sailed the cutter ahead of us towards the lights of the harbour mouth.

The sailors were amused when my bedraggled form emerged on deck behind the pilot. They laughed and slapped me on the back and took me into the smokeroom while the pilot went off to the bridge to meet the master. As the vessel got underway once more, the sailors made me take off my duffle coat and lay it over some hot pipes to dry out. I was brought a mug of coffee with condensed milk in it and then someone gave me a glass of aquavit, which burned my throat and made my eyes water. The sailors laughed and joked all the time, but I couldn't understand them because they were Finns. I drank two more glasses of aquavit, which didn't burn my throat so much, and smoked half a cigarette. One of the Finns was the biggest man I have ever seen. He had a beard as well, but a much fairer one than the substitute pilot's. Just as we were approaching the harbour mouth this particular Finn left the smokeroom and returned a few seconds later with a little book. I had never seen a book like this before. It was full of pictures of men and women without any clothes. They were doing things which, till then, I had only half imagined possible. Some were indoors, some outside and some were even in the snow, gathered round a little wooden hut. They did not seem the least bit embarrassed to have been photographed like that. They were smiling and looking at the camera just as people do when snapshots are being taken at a party or after a wedding. The girls all had long blonde hair, but they had other hair too, which was not always blonde. Both indoors and out, the men were always completely naked, which made the women look extremely soft and round, but indoors, some of the girls had put on long black stockings, which I thought very attractive.

Of course the sailors laughed when I looked at the book. They seemed to find everything I did amusing but this didn't worry me. The book was too fascinating and I went on turning its glossy, worn pages until we had almost berthed and the pilot shouted for me to come out on deck. Before I left, I asked the giant Finn if I could keep the book. What would the boys at school think of it? But he did not understand me and took it away. Then he gave me a packet of cigarettes instead, which wasn't half as good because they weren't even foreign ones. However, Dave Sinclair asked me to tell him about the sailors and the book again and again. I have a suspicion that Dave would also have been allowed to come out with Hook and the substitute pilot to go aboard the Finnish ship, but he was in bed with 'flu at the time.

A month after my escapade with the Finns, Dave took the only step open to a young, land-locked sailor who couldn't get a deck under his feet as he still had a year to wait before sitting his Highers. He joined the local unit of Sea Cadets. This body of thirty or so youngsters, tenuously associated with the Royal Navy, met in a huge old mansion with a mast and yard arm outside it, tucked away between mills and factories behind the harbour. Under the more or less watchful eye of several retired officers and petty officers, they were given instruction in the more rudimentary aspects of seamanship, signalling and service regulations, between the hours of six-thirty and nine on Tuesdays and Thursdays for ten months of every year. The cadets were also issued with uniforms left over from the war, cut down and altered to fit their often dim-inutive wearers. As the older cadets grew, broadened out and generally acquired a stature more fitting to members, however part time, of the Senior Service, their old uniforms were repaired, cleaned and handed down to smaller boys who had more recently been recruited to the organisation.

Dave spoke very little about the Cadet Force. In fact, I don't believe he enjoyed it very much, because for every hour the cadets spent boxing the compass or tying bowlines, sheep-shanks and double and single Matthew Walkers, two hours were spent marching and countermarching, dressing from the right and from the left and cleaning antiquated .303s whose firing mechanisms had been removed. Dave Sinclair joined the Sea Cadets for one reason only. They had a boat.

So his mind was not on the bathers. It was on the dredger, disappearing behind the pier. It was on the steamer under the coal-hoist. It was on *MFV 129*.

'The wheelhouse needs painted,' he said almost to him-self. 'I'll ask CPO Armstrong about it.'

The wheelhouse was about all that was visible of the Sea

Cadets' motor fishing vessel, berthed in the harbour between the pilot cutter and the steamer. *MFV 129* was larger than the pilot cutter. It was $64\frac{1}{2}$ feet overall, $17\frac{3}{4}$ feet in the beam and, according to Dave, displaced fifty tons. He was probably right because he knew almost all there was to know about the boat, though at that time he had not yet succeeded in making it his exclusive preserve. In accordance with the regulations of the Sea Cadet Unit, he was allowed on board only on one night of the week ... Tuesdays, if I remember correctly, when Starboard Watch underwent training in seamanship. On Thursdays, the vessel was given over to Port Watch, while Dave and his fifteen or so comrades-in-arms were instructed in drill and signals practice at the shore headquarters. Of course there were occasional weekend exercises when, if the weather was fair, the older cadets and the more energetic officers would venture as far as Port Edgar or North Berwick; but this situation was evidently unsatisfactory to a boy who spent almost every moment of his free time at the harbour, within stepping distance of *MFV 129*'s gang plank.

Needless to say, Dave soon put matters right. Over the year that followed, he rose rapidly to the rank of leading seaman, won several awards for proficiency in nautical matters and attached himself to CPO Armstrong, a rather rough, retired Petty Officer who was responsible for looking after the maintenance of the Sea Cadets' boat. I am sure that right up until Dave Sinclair left the Unit, CPO Armstrong deluded himself that he was taking advantage of the boy who was only too keen to give up his evenings to chip and paint and to clean the brightwork on the dowdy little vessel. He got into the habit of relying on Dave's assistance whenever some form of heavy work was required to be done, or when it was necessary to strip down the single shaft Kelvin diesel. Soon Dave was in possession of keys to the boat's deck houses and cabin, and had permission to go aboard at any time to carry out maintenance duties.

Over the course of that year, the little boat metamorphosed under Dave Sinclair's hand, from a standard, drab little Admiralty packet expended after war service to a Sea Cadet Unit, into a showpiece worthy of mention by the Flag

Officer himself. The paintwork and trim were immaculate. The wooden deck boards were scrubbed and sanded as smooth as ivory. CPO Armstrong modestly accepted credit for the notable transformation, but Dave did not mind. He had already gained his satisfaction from doing the job and had learned a lot in the process. But that sunny, late September afternoon, as I sat watching the bathers, Dave was far from satisfied. He regarded the wheelhouse of *MFV 129* with considerably more anxiety and apprehension than I did the girl who had just appeared outside the hut on the other side of the tidal basin.

I had first noticed her two days previously in the dreary, cream-painted, chromium plated establishment on the sea front which went by the name of the Clock Café and was favoured at that time by the senior pupils of our school because of its recently installed espresso coffee machine. I must admit that, to this day, I have never been a regular habitué of cafés, restaurants or public houses. Somehow, I find the familiarity between staff and customers, which becomes noticeable after you pay two or three visits to any particular establishment, rather uncongenial. It is therefore my practice as often as possible to eat and drink in places I have never been before and am unlikely to be again.

Whether or not this particular foible in my make-up existed when I was fourteen-and-a-half is doubtful, but I am convinced that it was a particularly ominous turn of fate that made me park my bicycle against the railings that day and make my way into the sticky, airless interior of the Clock. Several boys from my class were there, sitting in an alcove, empty coffee cups and Coca-Cola bottles with bent straws before them. Nearer the counter, where the glittering espresso machine hissed and gurgled threateningly, the leading lights of our second rugby fifteen were engaged in a highly secret, incredibly boring discussion about tactics for the coming season. They treated the boys at the other table with studied disregard and conversed in hushed tones, lest any treachery befall them. Taking a place beside my classmates, I ordered a coffee and listened absent-mindedly as George Black explained the intricacies of a new engine he had bought for his model aircraft. No one was really interested in model aircraft, but as the little petrol motor had cost six pounds, we made the necessary exclamations of awe, and privately speculated on how such an expensive item had been within George's means.

The girl did not make a spectacular entrance. She was there before I arrived, though I had not noticed her sitting at the counter between two other girls on high, chromium-plated stools. Indeed, it is quite likely that she would never have attracted my attention at all had she not dropped her coffee cup. The crash made everyone look up and there she was down on one knee, picking up pieces of broken crockery out of the wet, brown pool on the floor while the fat woman of Italian extraction who ran the Clock shouted angrily at her from behind the counter.

The girl had very short, dark hair and a pretty face. She was unusual because, in contrast to the uninteresting school uniforms of her companions, she wore a wide, red skirt with white, frothy petticoats bunched beneath it. I cannot remember the colour of her pullover, but I have no difficulty in recalling its shape, or rather the shape which the remarkable contours of her body forced upon it. When she got up and turned to face the Italian, the singular, or more correctly, duplicate features to which I refer were temporarily removed from view. Their effect on the group at my table was not. Someone, probably Jimmy Barrie, whistled softly through his teeth. Little Sandy Syme went red in the face and pretended to study the lettering on his empty Coca-Cola bottle. Only George Black, who was always slow on the uptake, was left unmoved and continued to flick the propeller of his little engine round and round and to make through his nose a ridiculous buzzing noise, intended to simulate that of an aircraft in flight.

The girl was unusual because, when she turned to face the Italian, our eyes rested on stockings with seams which made her curved calves seem even more curved. The pale flesh and white socks of her companions faded to insignificance and though the lettering on the Coca-Cola bottle could not embarrass anyone, Sandy Syme's face grew a shade redder.

The girl deposited the shattered fragments into an ash tray

on the counter with her left hand and at the same time held her right one, palm uppermost, under the Italian woman's indignant nose. We could not see what rested in the small, upturned hand, but the Italian could. The girl said in a tone neither of complaint nor of accusation, 'Can you give me another cup of coffee, please? The handle snapped off when I lifted it up.'

We knew the Italian woman would scream. She always threw a tantrum when a customer hinted at the slightest fault or discrepancy on her part. But the girl who was unusual, whose hair was short, whose legs were in stockings and whose back was much less interesting than her front, stood her ground.

'Then if I can't have another cup,' she said firmly but not angrily, 'please give me my money back. I didn't get a sip of the last one.'

Every eye that blinked in the steamy atmosphere of the Clock Café was now focused on the confrontation. The second rugby team interrupted its discussion of scrum tactics against a heavier pack, bus drivers and conductresses drinking a quick cup of tea near the door looked on, even George Black, who had sensed that his aero-engine no longer formed the centre of attention, peered inquisitively at the little scene by the counter. The girl's companions, acutely aware of the spectacle in which they had become involved, slipped timidly off their perches and made towards the door. But the girl did not follow. She did not walk the half-dozen yards from the counter to the door, through which sunlight streamed temptingly, until the fat woman had lumbered muttering to the cash register, withdrawn a threepenny bit and banged it down on the brown plastic counter top. The girl lifted the small, twelve-sided coin, slipped it casually into her handbag, turned and walked after her friends out of the café.

There was not a boy at our table who did not notice how she walked. Her steps were regular and even, despite the high-heeled shoes, and had a deliberation about them that I had never previously associated with a girl. She held her head up and looked those who had not by then averted their gaze straight in the eye with such candour that a lump formed in my throat and I found myself, despite everything, displaying a hurried, totally sham interest in George Black's engine. Nevertheless, the five seconds or so which elapsed between the girl leaving the counter with her refunded money and my sudden, involuntary desire to concentrate on something else, were sufficient to allow two images to form indelibly on my awareness. The first and more surprising was that at most she could have been only a year older than I was. The second and more exciting was that every step she took towards the sunlit exit of the café caused the bipartite attraction within her pullover to bounce quite independently of the rest of her body and to bestow an animation between her neck and her waist which conjured up but one memory in my mind.

Why do men find it necessary to describe a woman feature by feature like a landscape or a piece of furniture? Liberationists could point out that nowhere in this narrative have I mentioned the colour of Dave Sinclair's hair, or whether Hook was fat or thin, ruddy faced or of sallow complexion, but no sooner is the first female character introduced than she is visually dissected and her physical features analysed even down to the characteristic motion of a very personal part of her anatomy. My only defence is a desire for accuracy. There, in the Clock Café, I came across for the first time someone who promised as much as, and possibly more than, the delightful young Finnish ladies whose photographs I had studied aboard ship.

Sandy Syme was too red in the face. Although he pretended to study the engine, even asking to hold the little metal object for closer inspection, the colour which flooded his cheeks always gave away his secrets. It was quite clear that he knew more about the girl than we did and it was not difficult to persuade him to part with the information. When you are small for your age and are obliged to drag a grotesque, built-up shoe on your left leg, people do not often pay so much attention to what you say and tell George Black to shut up into the bargain.

'I don't know her name,' Sandy said slowly. 'I saw her a couple of days ago at the Swimming Club. She was applying for membership because she just came to live here last week.'

Jimmy Barrie looked interested. He said, 'In that case, how does she know the other two?'

The girl's companions had been immediately identifiable as locals because they had been wearing the uniform of our school.

'Maybe she lives near them,' I volunteered, hoping that the conversation would not be steered too far from the topic of the Swimming Club.

Sandy made the most of it. He whispered the date of the next meeting of the club. First he said she would be there, then changed his mind and said she would not and finally admitted that he did not know for sure. And just when everyone was becoming thoroughly disgruntled with his behaviour, he let slip the choicest piece of news as if by accident.

'She starts at our school next Monday.'

Conversation immediately turned to the relative merits of the new and old schools. I helped things along, conjecturing on the number of desks there would be in each room and on whether the staff would wear gowns as they had done in the old school. I am pleased to think that my stratagem worked. Within a couple of minutes, I can guarantee that only two boys remembered the date of the next swimming meeting. Perhaps it had even slipped Sandy Syme's memory eventually, for from my position against the dusty wall of the howff, I could not discern his thin, awkward figure among the white bathing caps.

Nudging Dave Sinclair with my elbow, I pointed to the girl on the other side of the basin and asked his opinion. In a single movement, he removed the cigarette stub from his lips, flicked it with his fingers and sent it arching over the edge of the quay into the water.

'She's a' right if ye like big cans, I suppose.' Every schoolboy in Fife knew that girls like Eva had 'cans' under their jerseys.

The slipway could not have been to the girl's liking. She walked to the top of the slimy, concrete ramp, watched one or two bathers totter precariously down it into the water and retreated along the top of the basin with her pale arms clasped round her as if for protection. Every twenty yards or so, metal rungs were set into the face of the harbour basin for the convenience of crab and herring fishermen who frequently berthed their boats along its sheltered wall. It was down one of these rusty iron ladders that the girl finally entered the water and struck out, on her back, towards the centre of the basin. For a few moments, her white cap joined the flock of white caps whose squeals rivalled the gulls'. But the white cap tired of the splashing, tired of the squealing and soon broke away, drifted and grew larger as it pushed itself backwards through the oily water towards our side of the basin.

I was amused when Dave got up and strolled over to the edge of the quay. I was surprised when he crouched down to get a better view of the girl in the water beneath. But when he shouted 'Hey, Eva, come up here for a minute,' I almost overbalanced with astonishment and he had to catch me by the shoulder to prevent me from joining the smiling, white-capped figure in the water.

Dave took the wind out of my sails. I had intended showing him the girl from a distance, awakening his interest, then mentioning what had happened in the Clock, perhaps inventing for myself a fictitious role of rescuer of a damsel in distress. Now all hope was lost. She was standing before us bare footed, dripping, the white rubber bathing cap covering her short hair. Dave introduced me, but I was obviously a complete stranger to her. How could I have known they had met in the local dance hall the previous evening? Seven months' difference in age was nothing at school, but when it came to staying out late and getting past the doorman of the Palais, it made all the difference in the world. I had to play second fiddle while Dave chatted about the quality of the band which had provided music at the dance. I could only look on when he invited her to sit down on a flat-topped metal bollard and propped himself up, one foot on the quay, one foot on the bollard beside her.

The role of silent observer has compensations. Without having to utter a word, I discovered that the girl was called Eva Cameron, that her father had something to do with insurance and had only just been transferred to our town from Stonehaven, where she had been born. I learned that, from an early age, she had been a keen and proficient swimmer and that she found the facilities available for this sport in Kirkcaldy rather disappointing. I permitted myself a smile when the girl confessed she could not remember Dave's name. He was losing ground and talking very rapidly about all manner of trivialities. He spoke about swimming, described the new school buildings, enumerated the cinemas in our town, listed the films currently showing and left me to watch how the sun was already causing Eva Cameron's clinging black bathing costume to dry in uneven patches. Cement dust from the quay had left white crusts between her stubby little toes. The tightly stretched woollen material covered but could not conceal her remarkable figure. The white bathing cap made her head smaller, making the rest of her seem more curved. There was absolutely no reason why I should run over to the howff to fetch Dave's cigarettes. Which one of us suggested that we all go?

To the best of my knowledge, no female had ever before set foot in Hook's howff. Although my grandfather held the superstition common among seamen of his generation that women were bad luck aboard ship, I do not believe it was for this reason that he never entertained female company in the old deckhouse. There was quite simply nothing among the tar and ropes and dust to tempt any of the fair sex to pay a visit to Hook's place of business. For this, I imagine, Hook was extremely grateful. His own wife had died when I was very young of some wasting illness that nobody mentioned, and since ever I could remember, his domestic affairs had been in the hands of Jeannie Dease, a buxom widow several years younger than himself, who called daily at his house to put things in order and to cook his evening meal. If ever Hook had a desire for further female company, it was always available in the Snug Bar of the Harbour Tavern, to which he would repair perhaps once a fortnight with one or two of his cronies.

I walked behind Dave and the girl as we crossed the quay and was interested to observe how skilfully he slipped his arm round her waist to assist her over the railway lines and how equally adroitly she removed it.

Eva Cameron's feet made damp, grey prints across Hook's

dusty floorboards. Eva Cameron's fingers slid gently over the surface of the work bench, lingered on coiled hemp, hesitated over glue brushes, rattled against the empty bird cage. She refused a cigarette. I took one. Lit up. Did not cough. Dave tried to go one better, to find a prick and cut off a quid of tobacco and chew it, but Hook's chest was padlocked. He had to make do with a Senior Service. The girl scarcely spoke. She questioned with her fingers, traced patterns in the dust. It was inevitable. The bird cage swung due to the attention of her fingers. The tin of curry powder had been moved through forty-five degrees. What was between them? What hung from the nail just out of her reach?

'That's just an old pair of horse's blinkers Hook fished out of the harbour one time.'

Why did he say it? He knew as well as I did what they were. He even tried to get in my way, but I dodged past and reached up to the nail. Eva Cameron came closer. Squat, bare feet, big, swelling cans, little head smoothed down and rounded off by the white bathing cap; she knew to hold out her head and jut her chin forward till I fastened the strap.

36C

DAVID SINCLAIR

'Until 1773, British power in India was left in the hands of the East India Company, a great chartered company whose charter gave it the monopoly of British trade in India and the East. India at this time was divided into a large number of states under the nominal rule of the Mogul at Delhi. Underline "Mogul", we'll hear more of him later.'

Thirty-one pens drew thirty-one lines of varying straightness under the Mogul. Seventeen boys and fourteen girls knew they would hear more of him later. Mr Prosser, whose watch must have been faulty, interrupted dictation for the fourth time, wiped his glasses on the sleeve of his gown and peered obliquely through the single pane in his classroom door. The electric clock was just visible at the end of the corridor. Thirty-one pupils shifted position. Thirty-four legs in grey flannels and twenty-eight bare legs in white socks crossed or uncrossed. Sixty-two shoes of varying colour and design scraped on the linoleum tiles. Someone yawned. A pencil was dropped and picked up.

'The East India Company had to defend itself against attacks from the French, who also had great trading interests in India, and from various rulers of Indian states. To secure itself against such attacks, the East India Company took over control of territory, to begin with mainly in Bengal.'

Mr Prosser scrawled 'Bengal' on the blackboard, which was actually dark green and for good measure added the word 'Mogul', but forgot to underline it.

'Clive, for example, greatly increased the territory of the East India Company. Yes, yes, take it down and you may write EIC for East India Company.'

Thirty heads bent over notebooks. Thirty pens wrote EIC for East India Company. The thirty-first pen remained in the

groove provided for pens on the desk. Its owner could not lift it
to inscribe EIC because his hands were struggling behind his
back, caught up in folds of denim. Malcolm Leslie, whose
watch kept perfect time, knew that only three minutes of the
history period remained and was struggling to change his
appearance from grey to white. It is difficult to put on a white
boiler suit while seated at a desk among thirty blue and grey
clad classmates and remain inconspicuous. Malcolm's whiteness unsettled several of his sixteen grey and fourteen blue
companions. Restlessness spread through the rows of desks.
Fewer and fewer pens concerned themselves with the territory
of Bengal, and Mr Prosser, whose senses had been sharpened
by forty years as an educator, brought his myopic gaze to bear
directly on the source of the distraction and simultaneously
emitted a roar by which the culprit was given to understand
that he should rise to his feet.

When Malcolm stood up, a million particles of grey,
kaolin dust released themselves from the folds of white denim
and hung suspended in the air around him. A million particles
of the finest terracotta dust descended on desk tops and
notebooks. A million particles of pulverised Siporex cement
flew from the white folds to form a silver aura around their
master. Mr Prosser's chalk dust could not compete. It fell half-
heartedly from his gown when he waved his arms and rapped
his desk with a blackboard ruler. It settled round him, barely
noticeable, as his voice was drowned out by the electric bell
signifying the end of the period, and the noise of thirty pupils
vacating the classroom. It mingled inconspicuously with
Malcolm's dust when he detained the boy firmly but not
painfully by the arm to issue a final warning with regard to
behaviour and dress in class. Neither was under any illusions.
Mr Prosser administered the standard penalty of five hundred
lines, knowing full well that he would be required to repeat it
the following week. Malcolm accepted the censure, fully
aware that the history teacher would never understand the
importance of ten minutes gained by changing in the last few
moments of class rather than in the locker rooms before a
double period of art.

Malcolm was a favourite among the three teachers who

had charge of our school's art department. He applied himself diligently to every subject they had to offer and excelled at most. Mr Forsyth, the robust, tobacco-stained head of department who taught drawing and art appreciation though he looked more like a bookie in his loud, checked tweeds, would often take Malcolm's work as an example for the less talented members of our class and hold up his still-life and draped-life sketches, proclaiming, 'You see before you the result of a great gift and constant application.' We were appropriately impressed.

The design teacher, mousy and forty, who always wore woollen stockings and a canvas smock was called Miss McDougal. She treated Malcolm's creative attempts at wallpaper patterns and multi-coloured lino-cuts with greater reserve, but when assessment time came she was obliged to pin them in first position on the brown hessian adjudication wall, despite her usual preference for the work of female pupils.

Had Malcolm excelled so obviously over his classmates in any other subject on the curriculum, he would no doubt have aroused their jealousy and dislike. Had he applied himself with such unfailing dedication to mathematics, English or history, he would have stood the risk of being branded a swot and suffered the ridicule that this entailed. In the event, his performance at every other subject in his timetable was only average and he was notoriously bad at mathematics. Outstanding achievements of an artistic nature, however, tended to be regarded in the same light as spectacular prowess at rugby or on the athletic field.

To be frank, most of Malcolm's classmates regarded the hours we spent painting with water and poster colour, drawing in pencil and crayon and making grotesque little models in clay if not as a waste of time, then as an amusing, unnecessary lark, a 'skive', as we called it. While any form of artistic appreciation was beyond us, we nevertheless had an uneasy regard for anyone who allowed himself to be regularly penalised in order to pursue any academic subject for ten minutes longer than scheduled. Thus Malcolm's reputation as an artist was established in our eyes and we did not mock the products of his hours at the easel. Jimmy Barrie, Sandy Syme and I would let him expound on the subjects of Rembrandt and Rubens, though we had intended discussing football on the way home from school. Girls were particularly impressed by his knowledge of the more subtle aspects of design and good taste, and would frequently consult him with regard to colour-schemes or before buying dress material. And 'Cans' Cameron: we all knew, or professed to know, what happened with her. Was this the reason that Malcolm Leslie, in his penultimate year at school, became leader of something of a cult among certain of the senior boys? Was this why an unusually large number of sixteen-year-olds visited the permanent exhibition at our local art gallery and even made the train journey to Edinburgh to see the annual exhibition of the Society of Scottish Artists? It became fashionable to describe perfectly commonplace characters as 'Breughelian'. Television actors and actresses were referred to as 'impressionist' or 'rococo' and we impressed one another by calling girls whom we had taken home from the local Palais as 'pre-Raphaelite' or 'of Titian beauty'. Malcolm's artistic leadership lasted exactly a year at our school. I am sure his influence has stayed with us all much longer.

Why did Malcolm set so much store by the ten minutes he gained fastening a dirty white boiler suit over his regulation grey flannels and jersey in the history class every Tuesday afternoon? It was because of the potter's wheel. Our school was new and thus was fitted out with all manner of equipment which but a few years previously would have been thought of as unnecessary extravagance. We had a library, separate classrooms for physics and chemistry and the girls' and boys' gymnasia were separated by a diminutive but serviceable swimming pool, sufficiently large to instil the basics of self-preservation in water. In the art department, this outpouring of municipal largesse had manifested itself in an electrically-fired kiln and two potter's wheels. A third art teacher who knew the secrets of throwing, glazing and firing ceramics was taken on to the staff and timetables were re-arranged to allow every senior pupil half-an-hour's instruction every four weeks on one of the wheels.

Malcolm, because he specialised in art, was already

officially permitted twice as much time as we were at the
wheel, but it soon occurred to him that most of our class
regarded the periods spent messing about with damp, slippery
clay as dirty, frustrating and wasted. He soon worked out a
system of exchanges, whereby any of us who wished to could
allow him to take over our half-hour at the wheel, leaving us
free to make coil or thumb pots, model little figures in clay, or
simply gaze through the plate glass window at the first girls
netball team practising near the bus-park four floors below.
Joe O'Rourke did not complain. It satisfied him to see the
wheel being used to some purpose, so he let Malcolm have his
way.

Joe didn't look like a teacher. He was really quite small,
perhaps five-feet-six at the most and had a massive chest and
shoulders. He was rumoured to take part in amateur weight-
lifting competitions and quite possibly he did. Joe had a beard
which was huge and black and always filled with powdered
clay. Beards were unfashionable and Joe's caused raised
eyebrows and adverse comments among the more conser-
vative teachers when they met him in the corridors and staff-
rooms. And of course there were the books. Joe had a passion
for reading which far surpassed Mr Forsyth's craving for
tobacco. Whereas the head of department only indulged his
pleasure in tobacco after the bell had sounded end of period,
Joe made no similar attempt at self-control and would quite
blatantly sit throughout a period immersed in a paperback,
only occasionally casting a thoughtful eye over the adolescent
potters in his charge. It must not be imagined that the
paperbacked and case-bound books which littered his tiny
office in the corner of the room were concerned with the art of
pottery. No treatise on the chemical properties of ceramic
glazes with a bus ticket for a bookmark found itself on Joe's
window sills. His preference was for science fiction, spy stories,
westerns, sex revelations, murders, detectives, whodunnits.

And so, while Joe O'Rourke followed Maigret from the
Boulevard Richard Lenoir to the Quai des Orfèvres and we
made tedious, irregular coil pots with one eye on the clock,
Malcolm Leslie got on with the job. He took great handfuls of
clay from one or other of the bins at the end of the room. He

pummelled it, kneaded it, rolled it, stroked it. He divided it up into little cone shapes and threw it on the wheel. He raised thick walled and thin walled cylinders, bowls of varying shapes, vases with wide and narrow necks. Over the period of three months, he completed a small earthenware tea service, making one or two items each Tuesday. When he was not engaged at the potter's wheel, Malcolm sculpted in terracotta. His plump stubby fingers pressed and moulded. He seldom employed a modelling tool. Jimmy Barrie and I often looked on as he conjured the pliant, red-brown clay into shape. Like all artists, he had favourite subjects, but why did so many of his projects follow the same initial pattern of construction? Why, regardless of what the end result would be, did he so frequently begin by moulding from a shapeless lump of clay two smooth, convex mounds? Why did he stroke them, cup them between his hands, weigh them and size them up before separating them and swiftly prodding them into the form of a matching pair of seagulls, a rabbit or a sleeping cat? I believed he was practising for later, anticipating what would happen perhaps half-an-hour after school closed. I was not alone in my belief, but no one came out with it and asked him.

During our final year, Malcolm made at least a dozen terracotta models of seagulls — gulls in flight, gulls on the water, sleeping, fighting, dead gulls. In several instances, the wings were too delicate and cracked during firing. He was unconcerned. I was not present when he embarked on the only project which seemed beyond his talents. Because of a letter sent to our headmaster by the Commanding Officer of my Unit, I was permitted to absent myself from school for two days that spring. An exercise for senior sea cadets had been arranged aboard a submarine depot ship in the Gareloch, so that particular Tuesday I was involved with watertight bulkheads and the mechanics of steam and electric winches miles away from Joe O'Rourke's classroom.

I only saw them a week later, lying on a shelf near the kiln, unfired, dried out, cracking up, already covered by a fine layer of dust. Malcolm had chosen grey clay, perhaps with the intention of adding a more natural glaze. Their shapes matched perfectly and he had decorated the edges with cunning indentations to represent stitching, but he had clearly been unable to devise a suitable method of suspension. Twisted, abandoned pieces of wire were strewn over the shelf; a little wooden stand had been partially completed, then rejected. Joe O'Rourke had misinterpreted Malcolm's intentions. The boy had remained silent when asked to explain the inspiration behind his efforts and Joe had concluded that the flat, rounded shapes with raised edges and complicated grooves were intended as twin ash trays. He made a joke, pointed out the impracticability of their design and suggested that if Malcolm wished to make ash trays, he should have thrown them on the wheel. Malcolm abandoned the project forthwith, deposited the results of his fruitless labours on the shelf and left them to gather more and more dust until a janitor disposed of them once and for all in the course of biannual cleaning operations.

Dust. I always tend to associate it with Malcolm. For eighteen months at senior school he carried dust with him in his hair, in the folds of his blazer, in the turn-ups of his grey flannels. Everywhere he went, he collected more dust. He sought after it. The municipal planners had sited our new school at the southern edge of a large public park, which had originally been part of a private estate. To the north and east of the building, playing-fields, rugby and hockey pitches had been laid out as far as the low wall that bounded the main road. On the western side of the art and commercial block, there was a small, tarmac playground used by junior pupils and beyond this, a netting fence and a dense strip of pine trees formed the boundary between our school and the adjacent establishment. The trees formed good cover. Even in midwinter, the bare branches obscured most of the red brick building that stood a hundred yards west of the playground. But the square, short chimney reached higher than the pines and cast its shadow almost to our fence. The chimney frightened the youngest pupils with its smoke, but it tempted Malcolm with its microscopic, virtually invisible dust. The chimney belonged to the Municipal Crematorium which stood in its Garden of Remembrance one hundred yards through the pines. Of course it was out of bounds. There was nothing among the tailored lawns and fragrant shrubs to interest us. Who wanted to go near the decorative pool with the low, marble walls like a fountain? Who was interested in the names and dates on the little brass plaques set into the marble? From the northern playing-field, it was just possible to misdirect a cricket ball over the boundary of the Garden of Remembrance. In such an eventuality, a master always retrieved the offending object and the pupil responsible for its loss was so severely censured that such occurrences were rarely repeated. But we knew, or thought we knew, who was no stranger to the consecrated lawns and pathways. And 'Cans' Cameron: we all knew, or professed to know, what happened with her.

Schools are breeding grounds for nicknames. Labels and tags are added at primary school, others develop only at secondary. In certain cases, the nickname supersedes the actual name and its bearer is known by it for the rest of his life. Nicknames can be flattering or derogatory, ingeniously amusing, or merely stupid corruptions of real names, but at our school, nicknames were seldom applied to girls. Eva Cameron was an understandable exception. She could not carry things like those around under her blouse and go unnoticed. She could not hope to play tennis or netball and fail to attract attention. She could not be a member of the girls' swimming team and expect to be regarded with indifference. She had to have a nickname and her nickname was obvious. Who first substituted a four letter word for the three letters of her Christian name? It may have been Jimmy Barrie or Sandy Syme. Possibly I was first to use the expression. It was definitely not Malcolm Leslie, for he disapproved strongly. Few people used the nickname when he was around unless they wanted to annoy him, though he was never known to have fought with anyone over the matter.

There is no doubt that Eva was well aware of the epithet universally applied to her by the senior boys. I have had ample opportunity to discuss the subject with her. On each occasion she behaved rather frivolously, laughed a lot and claimed that the name had amused her ever since our schooldays and that she had not minded it in the least. We once sat late into the night, let neon lights reflect their exotic messages into our iced gin, and compiled a list of colloquial expressions for human mamillae on the back of a paper napkin. We began with the vulgar 'tits', added 'titties' then the variation 'diddies', which was in vogue at the time. We included 'knockers', 'headlamps' and the more derivative 'Bristols', all English terms, unknown when we were at school. She mentioned the Scots' word 'doos', an expression I had forgotten, which was probably inspired by its original meaning of 'doves'. We lost interest with a series of American origin which included 'bazoomas' and the horribly commonplace 'boobs'. She had to agree that the four lettered name used from the mid-fifties until the early-sixties along the Fife coast, but which enjoyed little popularity elsewhere, was by far the best. When we left, she insisted on amending her name to 'Cans' in the visitors' book just for a joke.

You may be surprised that under such confidential circumstances I did not mention the subject of municipal crematoria or bring the topic of kaolin or terracotta dust into the conversation. Some things are impossible. Besides, I already knew, or professed to know, what had happened between 'Cans' Cameron and Malcolm Leslie.

Sandy Syme could not have noticed the label. His handicap precluded gymnastics, so he was obliged to take extra periods of maths while we hazardously sweated our way over and under beams, up parallel bars or across vaulting horses. It must have been Jimmy Barrie or perhaps even George Black who, in the changing room, drew our attention to the tiny strip of white cloth inexpertly stitched beneath the genuine label on the inside pocket of Malcolm's blazer.

'Silhouette. 36C. Hand-hot wash. Rinse well.'

We read it quickly, jokingly. He might have come through the door at any minute. I chuckled and poked fun like the rest, but the evidence was there. He could scarcely have expected it to go undetected. Already the label bore a fine coating of powder which had not all been collected from the dusty lining of the regulation blazer. It had fallen from his hair. It had rubbed off his stubby fingers half-an-hour after school when, with a thin barrier of cotton sometimes beneath, more often above his hands, Malcolm practised moulding, stroking and conjuring with something other than clay. It had been applied during preliminary operations, just before the label's parent garment had been unfastened to afford greater scope to his talents. Why had he seen fit to detach the tiny strip of artificial silk and reposition it so unnaturally? There was no need. We all knew that after school, on the dry, secret lawn of the Garden of Remembrance, Malcolm Leslie mixed his grey kaolin dust with consecrated crematory dust through the medium of Eva Cameron's sweet saliva and even sweeter sweat.

A Tree in the Well

MALCOLM LESLIE

No sooner were the Higher Leaving Certificate examinations completed in the assembly hall of our school than preparations began for the end of term play. Janitors and junior boys were still removing rows of desks and chairs when I took my sketch pad and accompanied Mr Forsyth and Mr O'Rourke into the glass-walled auditorium. For the staff as well as the senior pupils, the time of stress was over and Mr Forsyth considered the atmosphere sufficiently relaxed to light a cigarette. His colleague thrust his hands into his pockets, lounged against a convenient pillar and directed his narrowed, artist's gaze at the stage. Adopting what I believed to be a sufficiently man-to-man attitude, I propped my foot on a chair and rested the sketch pad on my knee. In the top pocket of my shirt, a folded, official note stated that Leslie, Malcolm, 6th Year was henceforth excused attendance at all classes for the final four weeks of term, in fact for the rest of his school life, and was answerable only to the head of the art department. It was my responsibility to design and supervise the construction of scenery for the forthcoming production of *A Midsummer Night's Dream*.

Throughout the duration of the final examinations, the standard issue pocket edition of the play had never been far from my side. Although I was not taking part, I studied the work as thoroughly as any of the performers. My copy was by now hopelessly bent and earmarked. Smudged ball-point marks, which changed from blue to red opposite Hippolyta's lines, formed jagged lines in the margins. It had not previously been regular practice in our school to redesign the scenery against which the junior and then the senior dramatic societies were to render up their offerings. The makeshift store behind the gym in the old building had, during its hundred years' existence, acquired sufficient drapes, flats and props to enable the most elaborate effects to be created with minimum bother. Granted, the dimensions of the stage in our new, glass-plated assembly hall differed greatly from those of the old one, but the trouble went deeper than that. The old scenery, except for a few worthless props, had gone missing during the removal and its loss had only become evident several months after the event. Rumour had it that enquiries had been made and allegations lodged by the head janitor against Mr O'Rourke, who had reputedly ordered the whole lot to be scrapped. More enquiries were to be made before the end. They came to nothing. Suffice it to say that for the second production in the new building (as an emergency measure, the first had been performed against angular white drapes) the art department resolved to spare no effort in creating an environment which truly reflected the outward-looking modernity of the school.

Palace walls and tombs were no problem. It was agreed that the junior woodwork classes should construct flats to my design as an end of term exercise. From time to time I visited that department to check on progress. Everything was well in hand. I was constantly annoyed by my lack of control over costume. Frequent visits to the public library had filled me with ideas, but in vain. The rotund matron who supervised sewing and home-management classes regarded my concern as precocious and insubordinate intrusion. With careless ease, she succeeded in turning the courtiers, gods and goddesses into down-at-heel Elizabethans and the rude mechanicals into a decrepit Victorian football team.

I should have known better, but at the time it seemed such an obvious thing to do. No harm could possibly have come of it. Besides, Eva had been worrying so much about her lines. In the normal course of things, between the hours of twelve forty-five and one forty-five, pupils were allowed in none of the school buildings except the refectory. Because work was in progress in the assembly hall, however, its side door had been left unlocked. It was an easy matter to climb the fire escape behind the bicycle shed and gain access to the back of the stage. At first Eva was reluctant to come. She made excuses. She said she had left her book in class. I produced my copy from a blazer pocket. My reasoning won her over in the end. I was convinced that her nervousness stemmed from the fact that she had never before faced an audience from the stage. Moreover, I soon discovered that she had not even been given the opportunity to set foot on the stage of the new auditorium.

Eva climbed the steeply sloping metal steps in front of me. Like several other senior girls, she had taken the opportunity afforded by more relaxed restrictions and the cancellation of gym classes, to adapt her standard school uniform by wearing nylons in place of the prescribed white socks. I remember seeing their dark tops as she reached the assembly hall door.

'A Wood Near Athens.' What unsavoury memories these words bring back. Through arrangements made with the head janitor, I had acquired several dozen broken, but still leafy branches and arranged them along the light blue backdrop to create what I considered a suitably sylvan impression. The other scenery was still in the course of construction, so it was against this background that Eva spoke her lines timidly and too softly at first, later with more assertiveness.

> Four days will quickly steep themselves in night;
> Four nights will quickly dream away the time;
> And then the moon, like to a silver bow
> New bent in heaven, shall behold the night
> Of our solemnities.

Something was wrong. Something was lacking. From my position near the front of the stage, I realised what was preventing Hippolyta, Queen of the Amazons, from manifesting herself in the form of Eva Cameron. She was being suffocated. She was being held back and shut in by blue serge and white cotton. How could anyone have acted in our school uniform? No costumes were to hand on the empty, leaf-fringed stage. I had to improvise. Again Eva made excuses, but this time they were half-hearted. She knew the source of her inspiration as well as I did. Rather than discard her tie, she fastened it round her waist like a sash. A good touch, I thought. One button, two, three, four. Carefully, she folded back the white cotton and tucked it behind her straps. Hippolyta was free.

I was with Hercules and Cadmus once,
When in a wood of Crete they bay'd the bear
With hounds of Sparta: never did I hear
Such gallant chiding; for, besides the groves,
The skies, the fountains, every region near
Seem'd all one mutual cry: I never heard
So musical a discord, such sweet thunder.

We turned together, she away from, I towards the noise which beat louder than my heart. Her confused fingers could not cope with the elusive little buttons. My mind could not cope with the bare, empty hall and the regular, sarcastic slapping. He was in the balcony, right in front against the parapet. The massive chest heaved silently, the massive arms were folded.

'Your lassie's fine, but your wood looks bloody awful.'

His voice resounded in the emptiness. The top two buttons defeated Eva. Tears welled up. She found shelter in the wings. My voice was thin as a reed.

'They were the only branches I could get, Mr O'Rourke.'

His entire frame was shaking with laughter. All he said was, 'Look.'

I followed his outstretched arm to the unescapable glass wall. What was outside? Only a playground. Only a strip of grass ending in a pine wood.

There was no way out. It had to be done, though all that afternoon I tried to put it out of my mind by working on the papier-mâché mask required for Bottom's head. Such a subject should have posed few problems, but my efforts were awkward and futile. I know a lot about heads and even more about what should surmount them, but Bottom's head defeated me. Eventually, Miss McDougal constructed a bizarre monstrosity out of felt and wire.

Ten minutes before the final bell sounded, I made my way to the woodwork department and spoke secretly with two of the boys who worked there. Persuasion was required, but at last a cupboard was opened, the requisite tool removed and an appointment arranged for the following morning after break.

I favoured a quick dash across the deserted playground

and lawns. Sandy Syme believed it would be wiser to go out on to the road and enter the wood from the hidden side. While we argued behind the technical block, George Black settled the matter by strolling off across the tarmac and grass with the axe on his shoulder. We had no choice but to follow. No teachers noticed us through their classroom windows. No janitor bellowed from the steps of the quadrangle. We simply walked across the grass, climbed the fence and picked a tree small enough to move but large enough to leave no doubt of its authenticity on stage.

. . . to give and not to count the cost,
To fight and not to heed the wounds,
To labour and not to seek for any reward
Save that of knowing we do Thy perfect will.

Sandy Syme had no cause to pray. People pray when consecrating a cathedral, burying a relative, launching a ship, perhaps, but not when cutting down a tree, even if it is in a Garden of Remembrance. Nevertheless, Sandy prayed and as we still felt embarrassed to hear words of prayer with open eyes, George Black and I bowed our heads and clasped our sweaty, nervous hands. Felling even a small pine was considerably more difficult than we had foreseen. We started too near the ground and had to begin again a couple of feet further up. Taking turn about, we hacked and chopped for almost an hour before the remaining section of trunk eventually splintered and the tree slowly toppled over, roughly in the direction we had intended.

It was necessary to recruit another five boys to drag the pine tree along the edge of the wood and into the school grounds beside the tennis courts. With the tree carefully concealed behind a wall, I surveyed its fine, solid trunk, imaging the effect its abundant foliage would create on the stage. Was it Jimmy Barrie who said we'd never get it up the stairs? Arguments followed, measurements were taken. He was right.

To make my predicament clear, I must explain something of the layout of our school. The assembly hall was situated on the first floor and could be reached either by the twisting fire escape previously mentioned, or more usually by a long corridor which ended in a modern, glass-walled staircase. Like many stairways in new buildings, this one ascended in short, right-angled flights round an open well. The tree was clearly too long to negotiate the bends. I was reluctantly preparing to have the trunk cut into several sections when Dave Sinclair, who had been watching for a while, hands in pockets, but not helping, said, 'I'll get it up there for you in one piece.'

No one jeered when he turned and wandered pensively off across the playground. We left the tree as it was.

It's my guess that he had the equipment delivered from the Sea Cadet Headquarters during the lunch hour. A friend of his in the Unit who was an apprentice garage mechanic had use of a battered pick-up truck. In any case, at the commencement of the first afternoon period, I slipped out of school by way of the woodwork department and found a stout, fourteen-foot plank, upper and tail blocks with well-oiled sheaves and a considerable quantity of neatly coiled rope lying beside my pine tree. It was none of my business. Dave had agreed to organise the operation and I wanted none of it. Besides, on my way through the woodwork department, I had noticed that the long-awaited flats were complete. It was now time for me to instruct the rest of my classmates, who had a double-period of art that afternoon, how to apply paint to the wood and canvas frameworks. Joe O'Rourke was nowhere to be found. When Dave appeared in the classroom asking for six volunteers to help him, I could hardly object. The remainder of our class followed me to the assembly hall, where we got on with the painting.

So I only arrived on the scene after the commotion had started. I only made my cautious way along the corridor after Mr Forsyth and two janitors, followed by our portly, asthmatic headmaster, had run past the glass doors of the assembly hall with unseemly haste. From the end of the passage, all that was visible was a mass of greenery through which second year girls were vainly trying to struggle from the commercial to the domestic science departments. All that I could see from behind the crowd of excited youngsters who blocked my way were the uplifted arms of our headmaster. He bellowed and roared, then suddenly spoke very quietly when he noticed the legs dangling forty-five feet above his head.

Dave's reasoning had been perfectly sound. He had carried the plank to the top floor, pulled the cords which opened two panes at the top of the glass wall and with considerable ingenuity, not to mention strength, swung the wooden batten out over the stair-well until one end rested on the metal window frame and the other on the railing of the fourth-floor landing. Suspending the two blocks from the centre of the plank in the form of a double-whip purchase had been child's play for him. Carefully, effortlessly, he had edged his way along the plank over sixty feet of nothing, rigged the tackle and tested its strength. The tree had been dragged to the bottom of the stairs and the rope secured to the base of its trunk. There was absolutely nothing to prevent it from being hoisted successfully into the upper part of the stair-well and then having its narrow, lower end swung gently into the corridor leading to the assembly hall.

If only the foliage had been a little less dense, Dave would not have had cause to climb for a second time out on to the batten to control the six diminutive figures heaving on the rope and the seventh one hopping excitedly about on a club foot, four floors below. If only the electric bell had not ended the first afternoon period, forty squealing, thirteen-year-old girls would not have had their stalky, bare legs scratched by branches which were already engraving a fine tracery on the paintwork of the staircase. If only the commercial teacher's spectacles had not been whipped from her scrubbed, spinsterly face by a twig releasing itself from the railings, she might not have screamed and rushed towards her internal telephone. If only the headmaster had not interrupted his weekly meeting with heads of departments, a telephone call would not have been made to the local fire brigade.

The firemen arrived, laughed, became serious and shrugged their municipal shoulders. The solution was patently obvious—Dave Sinclair was in complete control. Teachers and prefects shepherded the blue and grey spectators to their destinations by alternative routes. Because of my official note,

I was permitted to stay. Four helmeted firemen and two bare-headed janitors replaced the six boys at the end of the rope. Somehow, Sandy Syme remained unnoticed at the bottom of the stair-well, while sixty feet above, Dave Sinclair straddled the beam, calmly superintended his first exercise in cargo handling and brought the operation to a successful conclusion.

Committees of Inquiry are as ridiculous as their name. It did not occur to the panel of representatives from the local education authority who convened shortly after the events described above, to question the origin of the instrument with which, in their eyes, the offence had been perpetrated. They disregarded the fact that *A Midsummer Night's Dream* had been a great success. Admittedly, Bottom had become confused and forgotten his lines when an ear detached itself from his asses head, but Hippolyta had performed outstandingly. Further-more, mention was made in the local newspaper of the ambitious, imaginative scenery. The Committee of Inquiry failed to acknowledge the considerable initiative and skill required to suspend a twenty-five foot pine tree upside down in a sixty-foot stair-well. They were only concerned about slightly scratched paintwork. They trembled at the thought of what might have happened, accidents, liability.

Dave Sinclair's expulsion was never officially announced before the whole school. He just stopped attending classes and was never seen around. When prize-giving time came on the last schoolday of our lives, the chair from which he should have risen to collect the third prize in mathematics was left conspicuously vacant. His name was not read out. It must not be imagined that expulsion during his final month at school in any way affected Dave's career. It was a symbolic gesture, the futile action of people who considered something must be done. Dave had already sat his final examinations and in the course of the summer that followed, received adequate passes in every subject. His application for admission to the pre-sea course for deck officers at Nautical College in Edinburgh was immediately accepted. I had to wait longer before an official, buff-coloured circular informed me that I could take my place as a first-year student at the College of Art in the same city the following October. Tides ebbed and flowed. Gulls still flew over the tidal basin and *MFV 129*. Nothing disturbed what hung between the bird cage and the tin of curry powder. Only Eva Cameron changed. From the day Dave Sinclair hung a tree in the stair-well, nothing could persuade her to take my hand and wander into the pine wood. Her feelings cooled as the summer grew warmer. I often lay awake at nights.

Greek Fire

All through August and well into September, a little Greek
merchant vessel lay alongside the quay opposite Hook's howff.
No cargo had been loaded or discharged. The ship was
completely empty and her grey, rust-stained hull rose high
above the slate-grey water. There had been trouble with the
Board of Trade. An inspection had shown that seaworthiness
regulations were not being adhered to. Consequently, the ship
had been impounded until the defects were made good. For
weeks now, scarcely any activity had been noticeable aboard
the sorry little vessel. The rust patches had widened, bent bow
plates had not been repaired, the rigging, through lack of
attention, had become even more slack and chaotic. Sunday
afternoon strollers and amateur fishermen, who cast their lines
from the point of the pier, passed by the ship with curiosity,
joking among themselves about its dilapidated condition. The
harbour master, worried about payment of harbour dues, was
prompted on several occasions to telephone the London agents
of its owners. About the same time, a series of break-ins and
petty thefts occurred round the harbour area. Naturally,
suspicion rested on the Greeks and scarcely a week went by
without police boarding the impounded ship, from which
several stolen articles were recovered amid frenzied protestations of innocence. So, with one thing and another, the
little ship's crew gained an unenviable reputation in the town.
People who worked at the harbour went out of their way to
avoid them.

It was most unusual, therefore, that one Sunday evening
towards midnight, a Greek seaman should emerge from the
darkened fo'c'sle and commence to ring the ship's bell with
great urgency, while his companion dragged a fire-
extinguisher down the gang plank and across the quay

towards the howff, which had inexplicably burst into flames. Had the extinguisher functioned properly, it would have been quite sufficient to quell the flames licking round the windows and out beneath the door. Alas, it proved to be in no better condition than the ship's other equipment, emitted a pitiful dribble of watery foam and gave up with a gurgle, though the Greek banged it repeatedly on the ground and only withdrew when the heat became unbearable. Few people were about the harbour so late at night. Several minutes elapsed before the assistant harbour master appeared at the end of the quay with two other men, uncoiling a hose between them as they ran. When water eventually came through, they confined themselves to spraying it over the gable end of the shed against which the howff was built. Greedily, the fire consumed creosoted boards and tar-paper roof. Flames flickered in the faces of the growing crowd of onlookers. Bright red sparks burst spectacularly, shot high into the night sky, or arched like tracer bullets into the placid water of the harbour. Everywhere was bathed in a lurid, red light. It conjured a reflection from the forlorn, grey plates of the Greek ship. It mirrored itself in the water and set the whole harbour ablaze. It found its way across the basin and behind the swimming club hut, where Malcolm Leslie was contending with stifled sobs while his fingers fumbled beneath St Michael suspenders. Redder than red-lead, the glow from the fire penetrated the engine-room skylight of *MFV 129*, casting polychrome illuminations over David Sinclair and causing him to abandon his lead-filled paintbrush and climb up on deck.

Later David Sinclair and Malcolm Leslie stood side by side with the dying light of the fire reflected in their eyes and said nothing. There was nothing to say. Eva Cameron pressed her head against the flaking paintwork of the swimming club hut until the last sparks drowned themselves in the tidal basin, crossed the swing bridge by the dock gates and slid a small, warm hand between five, red-lead stained fingers.

Although Hook had heard the bell of a fire engine above the sound of his television set, he knew nothing about the disaster that had befallen his howff until the harbour master called at his home early next morning. It would be wrong to

say that the loss scarcely affected him, but he showed little
emotion on hearing the news. He went at once to the harbour
and sadly picked his way through the ashes in company with
the assistant fire master, a police sergeant and his artistically
inclined grandson, who had not left the scene all night. David
Sinclair was there too, but he declined to enter the charred
deck-house. He was content to watch while a severely
scorched, though otherwise intact sea chest, a twisted, mis-
shapen bird cage and several battered tins were dragged from
the wreckage and arranged on the dusty quayside.

Things could have been worse. Although the old deck-
house was a total loss, the fire brigade had succeeded in saving
the shed. It was generally agreed that the fire had been started
deliberately and, of course, the Greeks were blamed. Surprisingly, Hook tried to intercede on their behalf, but the harbourmaster was adamant. Within the week, a tug arrived from
Leith and towed the ship, heaven knows where, out of the
harbour. Within the week, David Sinclair resigned from
Kirkcaldy Sea Cadet Unit in preparation for taking up his post
as officer cadet in the merchant service. Within the week,
Hook compiled an inventory of articles salvaged from the fire
and had it pinned up on the noticeboard outside the dock
office. The list included sea chest and bird cage, paint tins and
tool box. All the rope had perished and with it the rolls of
canvas and tarpaulin, but no mention was made of what had
hung between the bird cage and the tin of curry powder. A
small, scorched silver buckle was not found among the
smoking, tarry ashes.

Scarcely a month later, Hook shocked his relations and
delighted everyone else in the town who knew him by
suddenly marrying Jeannie Dease, his housekeeper. To someone who had been shipwrecked off Valparaiso in 'ninety-eight
and again in the Mersey in 'eighteen, the loss of a few,
transient possessions held little significance. He put his house
up for sale, withdrew his savings and that November, took
passage for New Zealand, where Jeannie's only son owned a
road-haulage concern. He frequently corresponded with his
friends in Kirkcaldy and in one letter, he enclosed a coloured,
Polaroid photograph of an old metal deck-house erected

against one of his stepson's warehouses on the Auckland waterfront. On the back of the picture, he had written two words—'Fully insured'. He still carries on business as usual.

Two days after Hook's wedding, David and Malcolm had their first drink together, not, as Malcolm had hoped, in the Harbour Tavern, but in a new roadhouse on the outskirts of town, as it was more convenient for Eva Cameron, who was to join them later. Malcolm arrived first, flushed and out of breath. He had run all the way from the bus stop, determined to put up the first pints. He knew next to nothing about pubs; still, the calculated comfort of the lounge bar made him uneasy. Having dressed with particular care in blue suit, white shirt and cuff-links, Malcolm was understandably abashed when David appeared in a jerkin and tee-shirt. David casually threw his jerkin on to a bar stool and knocked it over. It was that sort of evening. Despite the tartan curtains and plaster claymores on the walls, the establishment was not sufficiently affluent to provide music free of charge, so they decided against putting a sixpence in the carefully camouflaged juke-box. In hushed voices they discussed Jeannie Dease, New Zealand and fire-fighting, and traced patterns with sodden beer mats on the red Formica bar top. The only other customers were two middle-aged men who leant over the bar and made the barmaid giggle. On several occasions, Malcolm had to ask David to repeat what he had said. When, towards eight, the bar filled with people, they moved over to a table near the window. Malcolm ordered a whisky, though his second pint was scarcely half finished. It was thus a slightly hazy vision of Eva Cameron that met his eyes when she squeezed her way towards their table.

Eva's parents, who were considered to be comfortably off, had celebrated the successful conclusion of their daughter's school life by bestowing on her a complete new wardrobe of coats, dresses and costumes. Over the last two months, she had adopted the habit of paying weekly visits to the best hairdresser in town. From where he was sitting, Malcolm detected the mingled, but not unattractive scents of perfume and hair lacquer. He permitted himself a brief moment of resentment that such a stylish young lady should see fit to twine her arm round the waist of someone in a tee-shirt. Nevertheless, he insisted on buying them both a drink although it was not, strictly speaking, his round. On his way back to the table, he surreptitiously took a sip of the vodka Eva had ordered and was pleasantly surprised by the taste. Someone had taken his seat.

Malcolm would have been quite content to stand, but David made an issue of the matter. The thin, spotty youth in the leather jacket, who probably did not even own a motorcycle and was barely half David's size, beat an ungracious retreat, muttering under his breath. When order had been restored, and Malcolm had taken his place once more within Eva's aromatic vicinity, she announced that in ten days she was leaving town to begin her course at Teacher's Training College in Dundee. Clearly David was already aware of this, but Malcolm, who had always assumed that Eva intended to study in Edinburgh, was quite taken aback and could scarcely conceal his regret. During her eighteen months at school in Kirkcaldy, Eva had made few female friends. Some women are happiest in the company of men and thus inadvertently arouse jealousy among others who are less popular. It was chiefly for this reason that Eva had elected to study with her old school friends in the north rather than take the course at Edinburgh along with half a dozen other girls from her class. Her only complaint was that her parents had insisted she spend the first year in a hall of residence. David and Malcolm agreed that a private flat offered much more freedom, but secretly Malcolm felt relieved to know that her activities would, to some degree, be restricted.

As far as David was concerned, the question of private accommodation did not arise. In accordance with standard procedure, he had applied for a room in the Seamen's Mission adjacent to the nautical college. He was to find it completely satisfactory throughout his year of pre-sea training. Malcolm had not devoted much thought to where he would stay during his four years of further education. In common with most young people, he did not always see eye to eye with his parents. Nevertheless, he had taken it for granted that, while at college, he would stay in his home town and commute to his studies by rail. It was not long before the disadvantages of such an arrangement became evident. At the start of his second year, together with several fellow students he moved into digs and by the time his third year commenced, he was able to afford the rent of a small flat. In the lounge bar of the roadhouse, however, in the haze of whisky and the scent of hair lacquer, he felt a sudden panic that he was being left out. From his inside pocket, he withdrew a battered little diary with a pencil in the spine and painstakingly noted down the addresses which Eva and David respectively offered. Next day, he found them incredibly difficult to decipher.

The bell signifying last orders had begun to ring. Neither of the boys was prepared to elbow through the impossible crowd to the bar, so they did without, leaned over, and exchanged promises to meet regularly throughout the coming years. Eva was quick to agree, though she could scarcely make herself heard above the incessant electric bell. Presently, she allowed David to take her arm and lead her towards the door. Malcolm followed on. His sleeve upset an empty glass as he passed one of the tables.

The whisky bottle fragmented six inches above Eva's elaborate, scented coiffure. The glass container from the hand of Leatherjacket ended its life exactly one foot in front of Malcolm Leslie's eyes, which were not yet accustomed to the darkness. Leatherjacket shouted as he threw, 'Gett im Deke.' Leatherjacket's bottle knocked pebbles from the outside wall of the roadhouse and powdered the scented hair with sharp-edged fragments. Eva screamed, 'Oh, David. Oh, David.' Leatherjacket bore a grudge and with an empty whisky bottle struck from the pleasantly intoxicated character of Malcolm Leslie a spark of creative anger. Flying glass gave life to a soldier-artist. Not Michelangelo, hammer and chisel, nor Leonardo, war-machines. Malcolm Leslie's plump fists became those of Mathis Gothardt Nithardt called 'Grünewald'. Figures whirled in a gothic landscape. Sharp, high-heeled sounds. 'Run Eva.' Torn nylons. 'Kick is bliddy teeth in.' Eva ran and disappeared round a pillar. Sanctuary. And from the empty space in the darkness where she had been, a merchant adventurer bore down on Leatherjacket's henchman.

'Behind ye, Deke.' But Deke was caught in a broadside neither from Raleigh nor Drake. Deke's metal-studded leather hull bent before the fury of William Jardine. 'Oh by Christ.' Opium wars. British interest. Deke was taken by storm, cut his cables and ran across the concrete sea. With long, loping strides, William Jardine was after him. Mariner's eyes narrowed. Bearings were taken by the stars. Deke was chased into the Canton Estuary and driven aground against a black pile of beer crates. His junk was raked with grape-shot. Timbers split before knees and boots. He abandoned ship. Up the black mountain of crates. 'Let go my fit.' Torn trousers. Over the wall that was much too high. Down into bushes and oblivion.

Battle won. British interest protected. Power balanced, but the sailor was worried about the artist and tacked his way towards the noise of chopping. His concern was needless. Mathis Gothardt was making a woodcut. A bas-relief was being formed against a pebble-dash wall. 'Grünewald' was painting the Isenheimer Altar with Leatherjacket as model. He worked in the dark and found his colours by touch. Although his subject was by nature black, 'Grünewald' had made the face white. Blotches of blue were added and from the nose and mouth, the master's hands drew more and more red. The sailor stood back and became the critic. 'That's enough.' William Jardine extended an arm. 'Leave it at that.' The altar was finished. Artist and sailor withdrew, for pilgrims who could no longer ignore the electric bell were filing slowly through the pool of light by the doorway. Happy, laughing, noisy pilgrims. On their way to cars and buses, they would stop to admire the artist's creation. And on the far side of the car park, Eva Cameron held out her arms and welcomed sailor and artist with kisses. What a combination. William Jardine and Mathis Gothardt Nithardt called 'Grünewald' linked their arms through hers and savoured, in turn, the impartial scent of her hair.

Double-sided Sticky

JOE O'ROURKE

I didn't want to go to the party. To be more precise, I would
have preferred to spend the rest of the evening alone with
Naomi, but they were her friends after all, so I went along with
the idea. Naomi offers compensations that a man at my stage
of life thinks twice about foregoing. Because she knew I was
disgruntled, she made a special effort to be bright and
amusing, which soon caused several of the younger men in the
company to regard me with ill-concealed envy. My annoyance was replaced by rather conceited self-satisfaction, just
as she had planned. I bought a couple of bottles of Newcastle
Brown and followed her to the battered little Citroën.

It was one of those affairs that happen so easily during the
Festival. What had started with a few afternoon drinks at an
exhibition degenerated in the course of the evening into a
pub crawl. Someone knew of a party and the Chinese artists
who had given the exhibition would be there, so Naomi could
not possibly be left out. Eastern art, mythology and religion
formed one of the few discernible passions in her uncon-
ventional existence. She was a vigorous campaigner, a righter
of wrongs, a collector of funds for every lost cause east of Cairo,
yet she regarded current events in the west with such alarming
indifference that she frequently gave the impression of being
pitifully ill-informed and dangerously naive. I have no reason
to believe that she applied a different attitude towards the
men in her life. Then, as now, Naomi offered compensations.
When I followed her to the little grey Citroën, my feet had
climbed the twisting stairway to Naomi's flat every weekend
for two years. I had become used to sitting cross-legged on
rush matting and behaving politely to the young men from
Persia or Japan who sometimes passed me on the stair. Naomi
offers compensations.

From my point of view, the exhibition was a damp squib. Naomi had promised that, in addition to the main event of the afternoon, several fine examples of Chinese ceramics would be on display. Perhaps she intended to whet my appetite. In any case, school had not yet re-opened. I had no excuse for staying away. When we arrived, the gallery was already fairly full of the types who usually fill galleries where unique exhibitions are to be staged. Connoisseurs inspected loftily, reporters drank determinedly and intelligent people, who talk loudly, ignored everyone else.

As soon as we came in, the owner of the gallery spirited Naomi off through the crowd with a torrent of charmingly broken English and a gold-plated smile. Edging my way round the seven or so pedestals which lined the sides of the room, I confirmed my original impression of the second-rate ceramic offerings and indicated my preference for whisky rather than sake which was, rather inappropriately, being served by a person of quite indecipherable sex and age.

Apart from his diminutive stature, the neat young man standing next to me made no impression until he touched my arm and said:

'Good afternoon, Mr O'Rourke. Perhaps you remember me.'

His face was certainly familiar. I made a noncommittal noise and confessed to having forgotten his name.

'Archie Tulloch,' he said excitedly. 'I was in your class five or six years ago. Never thought I'd see you here.'

I never thought I'd shake your sweaty little hand.

'Of course, I don't know much about this art thing. I'm a linguist, you know. Final year now at the University. Actually, they invited me along as interpreter. Specialise in Chinese, you see.'

'I see. What do you hope to do?' Apart from go away.

'Commerce. Very interested in the commercial aspect of linguistics. Don't know much about this art thing, of course.'

'Of course.'

And off he went to be linguistic to Wilson, Keppel and Betty who had appeared in the centre of the floor at the sound of a gong. I thought the Wilson, Keppel and Betty joke sufficiently good to make it known to Naomi who, true to form, was in the front line of spectators. She shot me a dirty look, but nevertheless had to bite her sleeve and turn away. Indeed, the display which unfolded before us certainly owed as much for its inspiration to the music hall as to creative fabric design. With ample doses of eastern formality, Wilson and Betty unwound yard upon yard of white calico and whirled it about over our heads and under our noses while Keppel, crouched beneath the billowing cloth, succeeded in erecting a highly polished, medieval primus stove. The quantity of flame which this contraption was eventually induced to belch forth, not only sent the front rank of onlookers two paces backwards with great despatch, but seemed to exceed the wildest expectations of Keppel, who beamed with delight, and the gallery owner, who inched his fire-bucket two feet forwards.

The fabric painting commenced. With the cloth between them like a newly laundered bed sheet, Wilson and Betty swung to and fro, passing the billowing fabric dangerously close over the flame. Keppel, who was by now firmly established as the star, sprinkled a clear liquid, probably water, from an oriental coffee percolator, on to the calico with his left hand and with his right tossed handfuls of multicoloured powder-paint into the air in such a fashion that at least half of it landed on the cloth. By manipulation of heat, water and powder, Keppel succeeded not only in spreading blotchy patches of colour over the hitherto inoffensive material, but also in creating alarming clouds of polychrome steam which puffed out heartily above the flame, chose a generally purple hue and drifted lazily into critical eyes, up intelligent noses and down the throats of ladies who would normally have been too well bred to gag in public.

Before the perfumed steam reached the elaborate stucco ceiling, before educated and well bred handkerchiefs found their way back to carefully tailored breast pockets, the gong successfully drew attention away from the pyrotechnical activity towards an elderly bead curtain, which swept aside to reveal a single bar electric fire and a naked, fleshy, European girl standing in classical pose with her face and fore-parts turned demurely to the wall. Voices rose. Elbows jabbed into backs. Flash bulbs popped at the dappled backside. Wafting fabric over flame for the last time, Wilson and Betty bunched up the material, conveyed it rapidly across the room, and employing the skill of the window-dresser rather than the couturier, draped it in a style somewhere between that of sari and toga, round the painfully unclad mannequin. Keppel knelt in supplication before the flame, the gallery owner let the handle of his fire bucket fall with a clatter and led the applause while the freshly-robed young lady turned, presented her amply endowed front to the audience and performed a series of pirouettes and rotations designed to display the creation to advantage.

Everyone spoke at once. The press jostled. Archie Tulloch interpreted. Ringed fingers were clapped under a golden smile. For the benefit of the press, the exhibition was to be repeated in five minutes. Those who wished to stay were cordially invited to do so. Otherwise, buffet and refreshments were at our disposal. To the bar, hang the buffet, arm round Naomi's waist.

'What did you think?'

'Lousy.'

'Great fun.'

The words 'symmetry of movement' were mentioned. One of Naomi's friends kissed her, onions on his breath.

'Who's the girl?'

'Dunno.'

The fat man pushed past.

'Sure I've seen those three in Limehouse,' he said, wheezing a laugh into his insipid sake.

Naomi, head on my shoulder, twisted round.

'Let's get out of here. Freddy can come too. The others will be in the pub.'

So you see, I didn't want to go to the party, but four hours later I bought a couple of bottles of Newcastle Brown and followed her to the battered little Citroën.

We climbed the stairs. Every party in Edinburgh takes place in a top flat. This one was a substantial, Georgian top flat in the New Town. Fords, Austins and a Jaguar parked beside the Citroën. On the stairs, a man with hand made slippers, a dachshund and a plastic dustbin passed us disapprovingly. The brass name plates changed to plastic ones at the third floor. There were two doors on the top landing, one blank, one with a calling card pinned off-centre. Naomi read the name. We were at the right place. The noise on the other side of the calling card left little doubt. We waited for onion-smelling Freddy, puffing with his huge carry-out, before stepping through the doorway into darkness punctuated by red light bulbs. Everyone was at the party. The people from the gallery. Critical and well bred people. People of both sexes and of neither sex. Gold teeth flashed, offered red wine. Ringed fingers extended for Naomi's arm, which withdrew and closed more tightly round my waist.

'Let's go into the living room. Not so crowded.'

In a corner of the living room, I pressed against Naomi, carefully unscrewed the cap from one bottle of Newcastle Brown and tried to block out the adjacent argument about the performance of the Morgan Plus 4. Naomi didn't want Newcastle Brown.

'What about whisky?' she said. 'Mark will have plenty. He's a lecturer at the University. It's his flat.'

Good for Mark. I didn't want whisky. Naomi reconsidered and stayed beside me to watch the passing show. Synchronised gyrations emanating from the centre of the crowd led me to believe that some people were dancing. It was difficult to be certain. Wilson, Keppel or Betty appeared from time to time, distributing paper flowers. After the third attempt, Naomi reconciled herself to the fact that one would not stay in her hair. From somewhere amidst the dancers, Gold Teeth clapped his hands again. Keppel had agreed to give an impromptu demonstration in the kitchen. Murmurs of approval were made. Critical and well bred fingers snatched up glasses and beer cans. The crowd moved towards the door. The dancers dwindled from twelve to six to two. More room. More space to breathe.

'... Nonsense, old boy. The gearbox ratios are 12.85 7.38 5.24 3.73 and 12.85:1 in reverse.'

We reversed towards the window and the cigarette spattered fireplace. Directly opposite us, two Germans matched the creases in their light grey suits and behaved charmingly to an intelligent young lady with spectacles. Biedermann presented the cigarette, Bummelmeier applied the light. Biedermann filled the glasses, Bummelmeier passed round a plate of peanuts and cigarette ash. Someone came between Biedermann and Bummelmeier. Someone gave the intelligent young lady cause to move aside. Someone pushed past and stood in the middle of the room.

Why the hell was I uneasy? It was not an unlikely meeting. In a way, it was inevitable; nevertheless, he had taken me off guard and I had to think fast to catch up. The contents of critical reviews are not entirely unknown to me. Despite the self-imposed restrictions of the field in which I practise, magazines and periodicals on the arts frequently find their way into my possession. I knew everything about him. I was well informed. Why the hell was I uneasy?

His career had been, from the outset, controversial and unique.

'A new, long-awaited star has burst in the darkness of contemporary Scottish painting. Whether or not it is to progress to nova and ultimately supernova is, considering the age and relative inexperience of the artist, a matter for conjecture. Nevertheless, the four works which I viewed in the St Giles Gallery were of such quality that few attributes of the shooting star manifested themselves in ... '

He had been very lucky. Rather than allow the disciplines enforced by the prescribed art college curriculum to channel his energies into any single compartment of academic activity, he contrived, throughout his entire period of training, to cover the widest spectrum of subjects while his contemporaries were neatly shunted into good, safe classifications such as painter, sculptor, ceramic or graphic designer. Malcolm Leslie was all of these and more.

'Seldom in my experience as a critic have I encountered so much vital talent within so many diverse fields. It is doubly remarkable when one realises that Mr Leslie is not yet twenty-three. ... '

As early as his first year of training, influential members of staff claimed to have discovered a rare talent. He applied himself diligently to drawing and painting and effortlessly gained a number of minor awards. Reconsidering, he took advantage of tuition in sculpture and within a year had two works exhibited in a national competition.

'The primitive boldness of Mr Leslie's *Seagulls* left me with the profound impression that sculpture among our young contemporaries is no longer the barren desert...'

Scholarships and the Royal College had been mentioned. In his postgraduate year he had gone off on another tangent. In tiny local theatres at first, later in full festival productions, his bizarre designs had been applied to scenery and stage sets.

'Large, multi-coloured ceramic cylinders, the work of Malcolm Leslie, are already well-known to connoisseurs of Scottish creative pottery. In his remarkable set for the Empire Theatre Group's production of *Romeo and Juliet*, he has attempted to break down the barrier against ceramics as major items of stage furnishing by employing vast concrete and earthenware drainage pipes set against spartan backdrops. He has succeeded magnificently. ...'

'My enjoyment of the Empire Theatre Group's ambitious *Romeo and Juliet* was utterly spoilt by the monstrous set designs of the young Scottish artist, Mr Malcolm Leslie. At a stroke, he succeeded in reducing the quarrel between the noble houses of Montague and Capulet into a squabble among Indian refugee drainpipe-dwellers. Even the permissively bare-breasted Juliet (Julia Hawthorn) had little opportunity to impress the audience when forced to deliver her classic balcony scene from the mouth of a vessel designed to carry vast quantities of municipal effluent. ...'

Yes, in ten years Malcolm had stirred them all up. Ten years. Not such a long time. Ten years had made Malcolm famous in a restricted, claustrophobic way. Ten years had given Malcolm a receding hairline, fashionably tinted spectacles and a silk suit. Ten years had taken Malcolm to London and Italy. Ten years had brought Malcolm on to television and into the post of senior lecturer at the College of Art. But ten years had not once led Malcolm Leslie up the long-repainted glass-walled stairway of a provincial secondary school.

Malcolm Leslie was twenty-six and three-quarter years old. Malcolm Leslie's arm was round the shoulders of the fleshy mannequin who had forsaken her recent orientally inspired drapery for a pullover and jeans. Malcolm Leslie's voice was ten years louder.

'Little did I think, when I agreed to drop in on this little party, that it would reunite me with Joe O'Rourke. You see, Doris, Joe was my earliest artistic mentor, my first pedagogue in matters ceramic. If it were not for Joe, I would not be where I am today.'

Ten years had put two gold rings on Malcolm Leslie's fingers and eight inches on his waistline. My introduction of Naomi was deliberately vague. Despite the cigarette smoke, despite the tinted spectacles, I sensed that little would be necessary to distract his eyes from Doris towards my impressionable companion.

'Nonsense, Malcolm. You did not need anyone to point you in the right direction. In time, you would have found it for yourself. Why did you never call to see us at school? I regret that Mr Forsyth was deeply hurt when you declined to present our end of term prizes. He has retired now, so no matter.'

Had I thrown him off balance? Inwardly, I chuckled at his violet-glazed eyes.

'As far as I can remember, I was out of the country. In Canada, I think. There was some trouble over a piece of sculpture commissioned over there.'

'An angel, I seem to recall. The clergy, whose transept it was intended to decorate, rejected it on the grounds that its wings were thought to bear an embarrassingly close resemblance to a huge pair of ears.'

His laugh had not changed.

'Was that story in the newspapers over here? As it happened, the government bought the first angel and I did a second one in sandstone on the spot.'

It is not beyond the power of a middle-aged, Scots-Irish secondary school teacher to summon embarrassingly prominent beads of sweat to a prematurely cultured brow. By its very nature, our profession bestows on its more perceptive members a unique facility to moisten expanses of flesh that lie between receding hairlines and tinted spectacles.

'What,' I asked politely, 'has befallen your acrobatic accomplice? How has life treated the juggler of sanctified pine wood?'

Before Malcolm Leslie spoke, Biedermann had time to pour another drink for the intelligent young lady. Before Malcolm said a word Naomi had time to steer Doris into a conversation about printed calico. Before Malcolm replied, he placed a familiar hand on my shoulder.

'People such as we,' he said, 'employ the frailest of materials—clay, powder, dust—yet make an indelible impression on the world which sets us apart from other men. Is it not ironical that David, whose soul was never devoid of artistic spirit, should have chosen steel, potentially the most powerful medium of all, merely to incise transient furrows on the face of the ocean? What a self-defeating preoccupation. There is nothing surer than a wave to bring disorder to harmony and chaos to worthy intentions.'

I took issue with him; saw through his cover of riddles; sniped behind the tinted spectacles.

'There are those of us who have not placed ears on the back of angels. There are those of us who have not set bronze seagulls in the prairie, where salt breezes shall never play on their wings. Because our vision remains unfiltered by the violet lenses of Messrs Zeiss and Co, our world is not a meaningless monochrome. A silver wake across an emerald ocean can never offend us. We are not appalled by the chaotic irregularity of the tides.'

I counted two crowns in his smile.

'Surely you are in a better position than I to chart the subsequent courses of your countless adolescent charges. Unless I am mistaken, your position has remained static since we last met. Neither advancement nor demotion has infringed on your reading time. I can't believe that, between the pages of Alistair Maclean, your thoughts have not, from time to time, been drawn back to fingers that once soiled their nails with institutional clay. Come on Joe. You're holding out on me. You know the score. Where's Sandy Syme with his club foot? Who is George Black boring these days? What has happened, say, to Eva Cameron? Your eyes lingered on her long enough never to forget.'

His hand left my shoulder, found his pocket and a cigarette. He did not give me the opportunity to refuse.

'You must remember Eva, Joe. The one who ...'

'Ah, yes. Your Hippolyta.'

'The one with enormous ...'

'Equipped for childbearing. Superlatively fitted out for regeneration.'

'Some sort of endocrinal derangement, I suppose. There are operations these days.'

'Nonsense. Time has inflamed your imagination and dimmed your perspective. Her proportions followed a classic canon, perhaps not of this culture, but just think, Malcolm, of Flying Gandharvas. Someone of such obvious sensuality would never have recourse to the scalpel. Eva Cameron has not reduced herself to the mean.'

'You know what she's doing, where she is?'

He was trying to be off-hand, but my glance caught his fingers trembling and followed his powdered cigarette ash to the carpet. What had brought this barely discernible convulsion to fingers that had made feathers from stone? Was it the meaning of what I had said, or had the mere mention of her name opened an intriguing gate within him, which he had never really locked? It was in my power to prolong his consternation or to cut it short with one word. Inwardly, I called him a fool: nevertheless, behind his fashionable artifice, beneath his studied, corrosive scepticism, I sensed something akin to an anguish whose symptoms were all too familiar. I did not administer the coup-de-grâce. My advice was of a purely geographical nature.

'Our town,' I said, 'is, by road, barely thirty miles from this city. If one projects a straight line across the Firth, the distance is reduced to seven. Even allowing for some slight delay at the ferry, it has always been possible to negotiate the journey by car in well under two hours. Since the construction of the new road bridge, the journey can be done in less than an hour, despite the additional inconvenience of toll fees. In short, Malcolm, it has never been impossible for you to visit the homes of your former schoolmates. Addresses are easily forgotten. Notebooks get lost, but not streets, bricks and stones. Memory doesn't wipe out a path it has taken on numerous occasions after the final school bell. The mind doesn't erase lilac bushes or bus shelters.'

He shook his head.

'I've been home frequently, ever since I went to college. Admittedly, there's little to attract me to the place, but, since my parents still live there, I feel a certain duty. At first, I could seldom walk along the Promenade from the bus station to my parents' house without encountering a familiar face. Often, I'd stop for a coffee and listen while one or other of my friends told me the latest news. In time, however, these occasions became few and far between. Recognition seldom dawns these days on faces by the waterfront. My friends of former days have become scattered, have left town, or worse, settled smugly into Wimpey self-complaisance, with families and mortgages round their necks.'

'Have you any reason to suppose that a similar fate has not overtaken David Sinclair, or for that matter, Miss Eva Cameron? The proportion of female teachers who marry within three years of completing their training is alarmingly high and seamen are notoriously domesticated when they come home.'

Perhaps I can be accused of having behaved unkindly. I admit to taking a mildly malicious joy in the discomfiture of others, but Malcolm Leslie needed no prompting. It was unnecessary to goad him deeper into the mire of self-pity in which he had chosen to wallow. He glanced momentarily at Doris and Naomi, whose laughter was louder than the music, then turned to me once more. Violet tinted glass filtered all expression from his eyes.

'Years ago, when she had just started training at Dundee, we exchanged a few letters. She made no mention of her parents, but I discovered quite by chance that they had moved back to Stonehaven barely a year after we left school. Now there is probably no reason for her to visit either Kirkcaldy or the capital.'

'And David?'

'I don't know. When he was studying at Nautical College, we met occasionally. Even then, we had less and less in common. Points of mutual interest diminished until the only common denominator was the beer, and when it began to taste bad, we lost touch. I arranged to meet him when he returned from his first voyage, but he didn't turn up.'

There was no more to say. Malcolm Leslie withdrew from his pigskin wallet a small, white rectangle three inches wide by two-and-a-half deep. The typography was immaculate.

'My card,' he said. 'It will very definitely be in your interest to keep in contact, old friend. At present, I am engaged in certain negotiations which, if successful, will put a completely different aspect on my creative activities. Finance is no object. Have you never longed to read a thriller without forty eyes to note the turn of every page?'

My uneasiness had returned. What could I do but take the card? Where could I look to escape the blank, violet spectacles? My eyes sought a new point on which to focus. They found it in the dimpled navel that punctuated Doris's quivering, flaccid belly. They found it halfway between the frayed waistband of her jeans and the rumpled edge of her pullover, which she had pulled up to afford a better view. The room rang with Naomi's laughter. The sound cut through the smoke, came between Biedermann and Bummelmeier, threw the Morgan out of gear and fixed a smile beneath the tinted glasses. Naomi laughed till tears welled up in her eyes and coursed down her cheeks. She seized my arm and drew me across the room towards the navel and the pale bulge of flesh. Thin red lines intersected on Doris's belly. Vivid pink weals criss-crossed as if plaster had recently been removed. Naomi steadied herself against my shoulder and pointed with a finger which shook with delight.

'That's how they did it. That's how they stopped the robe from falling off. Double-sided sticky!'

Four Bells

SANDY SYME

I had plenty of warning of the battle. For the past five days, the straggling little village and muddy, sluggish river had been constantly in my mind. With considerable difficulty I had acquired both historical and contemporary maps of the region and committed their undulating contours to memory. On more than one occasion, Mr Willoughby, in his jocular, patronising way, has criticised my intense preoccupation with detail. I cannot agree. No commander worthy of the name would ever embark on an operation which required complex, sophisticated troop movements, intelligent siting of artillery and positioning of reserves without a thorough knowledge of terrain. Furthermore, when the action to be fought is a defensive one, on home territory, so to speak, such an omission on the part of a commander should render him liable to the most severe censure. No, Mr Willoughby spoke out of envy as I have already eroded his reputation in the field. Junior commanders and beginners, who can seldom raise more than two or three companies, are pleased to put their men at my disposal, acknowledging that it is better to ally themselves with a general totally committed to winning at all costs rather than with one whose strength is directly related to numbers and whose manoeuvres seldom stray far from the text book.

Please do not assume, however, that a keen desire to foresee any military eventuality, coupled with a deep conviction to win the day, automatically indicates invincible self-confidence. My responsibility had never before extended over 120 000 men and 640 guns. This was, in fact, my first major action; my first really grandiose battle, in which the course of history could possibly have been changed. Such immense responsibility brings with it a supreme elation which, as the day of battle approaches, gives way at first to desolation and, ultimately, to great inner calm. Similar feelings, I expect, are experienced by athletes and sportsmen before a vital confrontation, but as I have been handicapped from birth by a talipes, I was denied personal experience until, relatively recently, I embarked on a military career.

Mr Willoughby drew the white piece of paper from the buff coloured envelope, unfolded it with two fingers, puffed his pipe as he read the contents, and addressed himself to twelve people across the baize covered table.

'We have been invited by the Perth Club to fight the action which took place at Borodino on September 7th, 1812. Rules will be as usual. Action will commence with the opposing forces disposed as of 06.00 hours on the 7th. The battle will last for six hours, or until such time as a decisive result has been achieved by one or other side. A draw has been made. We, gentlemen, will have control of the Russian Army. A meal and refreshments will be provided. Are there any questions?'

Numbers of troops were mentioned. It was agreed that if both clubs pooled their resources, sufficient men and guns would be available.

'We have decided that British Light Cavalry will be used to represent Russian Cossack units,' announced Willoughby.

'Who has decided?' I asked.

Willoughby puffed his pipe and ignored my question. Instead he continued, 'Now, gentlemen, shall we count the ballot for C-in-C?'

More pieces of paper. Scribbling with Biro and fountain pens. Mr Willoughby's hat was the receptacle. Slowly, the Adjutant unfolded piece after piece and whispered to Willoughby.

'Congratulations, Alec,' he announced.

Fists thumped the table in approval. I shook extended hands. Willoughby coughed.

'Well, that's about it for tonight. If you other gentlemen would like to choose your posts as field officers from the list that Peter's pinning to the board, we should be in time for a last pint across the road.'

In the homely, overheated pub, I bought half a pint

of beer and accepted the whisky which, oddly enough, Willoughby saw fit to press into my hand.

'Hang Alexander the First.'

'What's that?'

'Oh, nothing.'

On August 17th, 1812, Tsar Alexander the First gave in to ill-informed, malicious criticism and relieved Barclay de Tolly of his command of the Russian Army. Barclay de Tolly; of Scottish-Baltic descent, a splendid soldier, architect of the 'scorched earth' policy that eventually broke the Grand Army. Without Barclay de Tolly, there would have been no retreat from Moscow. Without Barclay de Tolly, would Tchaikovsky have had cause to write the 1812? Despite myself, I can't help identifying with those whose decisions actually framed the outcome of such great battles. Somehow, I want to understand their thoughts, smell the smoke, to some degree, even, adopt their personalities. But the man I had to understand was not the eminently understandable Barclay de Tolly. On August 17th, 1812, Tsar Alexander the First relieved him of his command and appointed Prince Kutuzov in his stead. Kutuzov, sixty-seven years old. Kutuzov, breathless and overweight. One-eyed Kutuzov, who in 1805 lost the Battle of Austerlitz. How can one become attuned to a man like him? If it had not been for Tsar Alexander the First, there would have been no Kutuzov. If it had not been for Kutuzov, there would have been no Borodino.

The following Tuesday afternoon, I telephoned Napoleon, my opposite number, at an estate agent's office in Dunkeld. We had met only once before, at Bannockburn as I remember, and he had made little impression on me. My attitude towards him warmed, nevertheless, when he referred to the impending battle as 'Moskova'. My opponent's predilection for accuracy was clearly equal to my own. After some polite discussion of the topographical details to be included on the gaming table, I brought up the subject of mounted Cossacks, which had been troubling me for some time. Napoleon agreed with me wholeheartedly. Aesthetically, the uniforms of any British cavalry unit would look totally out of place on the field of Borodino/Moskova, albeit that, for the purpose of the game, they would have been regarded as Ural, Don or Kalmuk Cossacks. He regretted that neither his club nor my own had at its disposal any authentic miniatures of this most interesting branch of Russian irregular cavalry. How imposing, how noble they would have looked on their hardy little steeds, in skirmishing order on the flanks of my army. When I offered, time permitting, to supply and equip the required Cossacks at my own expense, he was overjoyed. Our conversation ended on extremely amiable terms.

My professional career in banking has progressed steadily, if in no way spectacularly, along the channels of advancement. It affords me a style of living which is adequate for my needs and, indeed, since my recent promotion to branch manager, has allowed me certain luxuries which few unmarried men of my age enjoy. Being in a natural position for favourable investment, I have over the years put my modest salary to good use. My little flat, in an area of the city in which the value of property appreciates daily, is now well on the way to becoming my own. Last year I visited the battlefields of Waterloo and the Somme, and this summer it is my intention to inspect the remnants of the Lines of Torres Vedras. In short, my pocket was well able to withstand the outlay on a couple of dozen twenty millimetre mounted figures. Whether or not the figures were available and whether I could complete the necessary painting within the three days left to me, was another matter. By a remarkable stroke of luck, one of the suppliers whom I telephoned in London had a travelling salesman leaving for Edinburgh that very night. They agreed to make up my order at once and arranged for me to collect it at the shop where I bought my regular supplies. By Wednesday lunchtime, twenty-four mounted Cossacks in white metal were in my possession. That night and the night that followed, the light in my sitting room was not extinguished until 4 am.

Have you ever studied a twenty millimetre wargaming figure? The amount of detail which can be moulded into such a tiny format is truly amazing, and considerable dexterity with a paint brush is necessary if a satisfactory finish is to be achieved. In this instance, my concern was not over the quality of my paintwork, but rather over the historical accuracy of the colours I was applying. It is a common fallacy to assume that, because the Cossacks were a volunteer force who usually supplied their own weapons and equipment, they did not adhere to any standard uniform during the Napoleonic period. Of course, by the very nature of the Cossacks themselves, and through exigencies of the war in which they were engaged, individual units frequently modified their style of dress. Nevertheless, a basic pattern did exist. They followed eastern fashion by wearing baggy trousers. Headgear was often altered to suit the particular penchant of the wearer, but in the main, fur caps were worn, often with a red busby bag. Except for the Bug regiment, which dressed in green, and Cossacks of the Guard, who adopted red jackets, all Cossack units wore blue. At one point, identification colours were introduced for collars and cuffs. Thus, by applying flesh tones, blue, black and red paint, I was able to recreate the uniforms of a section of Don Cossacks with fair authenticity. Choosing green as a base and adding white to cuffs and collars, I introduced two members of the Bug Regiment. Selecting carmine from another tube, four blue-painted white metal figures took on the identity of Cossacks from the Ural region. An element of doubt crept in only when I completed the entire set and was applying the finishing touches to whips, swords and lances. Each figure on the table before me had a black cross-belt over the left shoulder, on the front of which was mounted what I had taken to be some form of ammunition container. In my haste and eagerness to complete the series, I had assumed that these containers would be of tin, or some other white metal and had accordingly painted them silver. Why had I done so? For all I knew, they might have been made of brass. Nowhere in my extensive military library was there a reference on which to draw. I pored over books and drawings until sleep overcame me.

With the problem still on my mind, I worked impatiently through Friday at the bank and when it closed, put on my overcoat and went to consult Willi Zakrewski, an elderly gentleman from Poland, who is probably not a Jew and lives in

Leith without a telephone. For a living, Willi makes exquisite little jewellery boxes out of wood, cardboard, leather and satin. Last year, I commissioned him to construct ten leather-covered, velvet-lined boxes to dimensions somewhat larger than those to which he normally confined himself. Within a fortnight, I took possession, at a very fair price, of ten excellent containers in which to store my military figures. When Mr Willoughby enquires how I came by such sumptuous objects, I answer evasively. He must never meet Willi for, though Willi does not play wargames, though Willi paints neither twenty nor fifty-four millimetre white metal figures, his knowledge of military minutiae is the most remarkable I have ever encountered. Granted, his familiarity with uniforms which have originated west of the Rhine is scanty, but entirely from memory, Willi can describe with complete accuracy the facings of an 1812 Schwarzburg-Rudolstadt infantry officer's tunic. He can enumerate the gaiter buttons of a grenadier from Frankfurt, serving in 1806 with the army of the Confederation of the Rhine. Pausing barely to wrinkle his brow, he can itemise the badges of every regiment within the Imperial Russian Army with less difficulty than I can my laundry list.

I took the bus to Leith with complete confidence. If Willi Zakrewski did not know the answer to my question it did not exist. At the door of the little flat, a smell of glue mingled with that of Polish cooking. Mme Zakrewska was apologetic. Willi had gone out for the evening. She was entertaining a few lady friends, but I was welcome to stay until he returned about ten. Not wishing to intrude on the company, I wrote my request on a slip of notepaper and bade Mme Zakrewska be good enough to ask her husband to telephone me from a public call box on his return. With considerable disappointment, I made my way downstairs. When I reached the street, the force of the wind quite took my breath away. Gusting from the sea, its December iciness cut through my coat like a knife. My constitution has never been robust. All my life I have been prone to take chills and fevers at the slightest exposure to inclement elements. It was, therefore, to safeguard myself from being indisposed on the day of the battle that I fought my

way against the wind to the street they call the Shore, and
entered the first bar I chanced upon.

You don't need to tell me the perils of drinking in a
dockside pub. Though, in the general course of things, I
seldom have occasion to visit Leith, a week rarely passes
without some mention in the evening paper of a fight or
robbery or stabbing that has taken place in just such an
establishment as I had now entered. Looking neither left nor
right, I walked straight to the bar and attracted the attention
of one of the barmen. Without taking his eyes from the
television set, which was perched on a shelf over the toilet
door, he moved to the row of bottles and measured out a large
whisky. When he grunted and waved away my hand, my first
thought was that I had not offered enough small change to
cover the price of the drink. For an instant, the barman's eyes
left the television set and he nodded towards a figure propped
on a stool at the far end of the bar.

'That fella's paid for it.'

A feeling of extreme uneasiness, very close to panic,
overcame me. My eyesight has never been good, and though I
always wear spectacles, the light was so poor that I could
barely discern the features of my benefactor. Like the half-
dozen other customers, he was hunched over the bar and
seemed to be directing his entire attention towards the quiz
show. At first, I considered refusing the drink and taking my
leave at once, but well aware of the possible result of the
offence I might cause, I took my courage in both hands,
approached the man, and raised my glass.

'Hello, Sandy. What the hell brings you in here?'

In my surprise, my hand trembled and spilt some whisky
on the pitted wooden bar top. Dave Sinclair turned and
slapped me heartily on the back.

'Good heavens, Dave,' I shook his hand. 'How long has it
been . . .?'

'Must be twelve years at least. I wouldn't have recognised
you if it hadn't been for the foot.'

'Of course.'

He was well dressed, even expensively so, and over the
years, had both grown taller and broadened out; or so it

seemed to me, whose last recollection of him was as a lanky schoolboy in an ill-fitting uniform, astride a precariously balanced plank. A docker, who had been studying racing results nearby, folded his newspaper and left the bar. With some difficulty, I climbed on to the vacant stool. The barman put up another two drinks.

'Are you still at sea? I mean ... '

'First mate with Blair Lines. Got my Master's four years ago. I paid off in London this morning, but I have to look into the Company Office here tomorrow before going on up north.'

His use of 'up north' with reference to Fife, as I thought, was rather unusual, but I made no mention of it at the time. Apart from Dave, I don't think I had ever spoken to an officer in the merchant service and I found myself plying him with numerous, probably boring questions, about places he had visited and ships on which he had sailed. He took it all in good part, listened attentively and related a few very amusing anecdotes about the Far East. In contrast to his career, I failed to see how my own mundane history could be of the slightest interest to him. Nevertheless, when six empty glasses were before us, I fell to discussing accounting systems, rates of exchange and savings schemes with as much detail as he had harbours, cargoes and navigation. When Dave found it necessary to visit the toilet, he laid a little plastic folder on the bar.

'One or two snapshots. I'll be back in a moment.'

Nothing in the world can say so much, yet remain so mysterious, as a photograph. Whether posed or completely natural, a studio print or an ill-composed amateur snap, a photograph affords the viewer an image of complete reality, petrified like a fossil in the spectrum of history. I have always regarded being allowed to study other people's photographs as a special privilege, not to be taken lightly. I cleaned my spectacles carefully before picking up the little album. Dave had mounted his photographs in a series of transparent plastic holders, fixed edge to edge like one of those postcards that disgorge a strip of pictures when a paper flap is lifted. There were nine holders in all, each one containing a different photograph. Some were black and white, but the majority were coloured. A few had been cut down with scissors to make them fit the plastic frames more easily. I started from the top, holding the folder at an angle where most light would fall on it.

First came a coloured shot of a harbour scene. In the foreground, the huge bow of a ship loomed impressively alongside the quay. The letters *Blairgowrie* were clearly marked on the bow. From the barely visible signs on cranes and warehouses, I recognised the port as being European, but not British. Perhaps somewhere in Holland. Yes, definitely in Holland. Further down the quay, in the middle distance, a group of stevedores was unloading, or perhaps loading, bales of cargo wrapped in hessian. Apart from two tiny figures on the fo'c'sle, they were the only people in the picture.

But Dave was in the second photograph, in the middle of a group of men and holding a half-full beer mug towards the camera. His mouth was open, as if he was shouting or singing. Though they were not in uniform, I assumed the group to consist of officers from his ship in some night club. The quality of the print was very poor. It was taken with flash, which had added even more glaze to their shining eyes. On the extreme right of the composition, a woman in an extremely low-cut dress was leaning forward to look at a young man who had slumped over the table. An unsavoury picture, not to be dwelt upon, but indicative, perhaps, of how seamen all too often while away their off duty hours.

'That's Hamburg. I forget what they call the club.'

Dave was once more beside me. Swiftly, I passed on to the next photograph. A carefully composed study, this time in full colour against a brilliant blue sky. Dave was in uniform, standing on the plinth of a bronze statue, which was half as tall again as he was. I saw by the rings on his sleeve that, at the time the photograph was taken, he held the rank of second officer. The statue was unusual and very modern. Although it looked like an angel, with overscaled, clasped hands, the wings were oddly curved, reminding me more of twin parachutes. I did not need to ask the location. Across the bottom corner of the print, the word 'Vancouver' was written carefully in biro.

Another group photo, in colour and the tiniest bit out of focus, which lent a muted, impermanent atmosphere to the composition. Once more, the group was centred round a table, but this time it was a frail card table that had been temporarily erected between holystoned planks and canvas awning on board ship. An almost symmetrical arrangement, consisting of two men and a young lady seated on three sides of the table and one man standing directly behind the lady, forming the axis of the triangle. Dave Sinclair was on the left. His face was in profile, as if his attention had been distracted from the camera by an amusing remark made by the young lady. I made a quick comparison with the earlier group photograph and discovered that Dave was the only person to feature on both. There was no doubt they were in the tropics. The men were wearing shorts and white shirts with their rank indicated on the shoulder strap. To protect herself from the heat, the young lady wore sunglasses and a wide-brimmed straw hat, which cast a shadow over her face. But she was smiling, and something indefinably familiar in that smile stirred my memory.

'My wife,' Dave said, in anticipation of my question. 'She came with me on a voyage about a year ago. The snap was taken off Singapore. You can just see some land on the horizon.' His finger jabbed over the shoulder of the standing man.

Dave married. It should have occurred to me that, like most of my contemporaries, he would probably have a wife by now. I felt confused, almost thought I should apologise for not having inquired before.

'Your wife?'

He misunderstood my confusion.

'Most good companies let senior officers take their wives with them once in a while. You've no idea of the shortage of qualified men. They've got to keep us happy, or we'd just walk out.'

I flicked over the next slip of plastic. An odd photograph. In a wide expanse of dusty concrete, bordered by a high wire fence, stood two or three lorries and articulated trailer units. Masts and ships' funnels pierced the skyline, and in the middle, at the door of a white, flat-roofed hut, an old man was standing with arms folded and a short stemmed pipe in his mouth. I searched for the purpose of the photograph. Not one of the distant funnels bore the distinctive marking of Blair Lines. The dust was of no interest. At first, I took the old man to be an Indian, but though his face was tanned dark brown, his eyes were blue and the thin bands of white where he had rolled up his sleeves gave him away. What age could he be? The tan was deceptive. Though the eyes and neck indicated an old man of eighty, this estimation was called into question by the solidity of the arms, whose prominent biceps suggested an age of less than fifty. Likewise, the location was equally difficult to establish. While everything pointed to the photograph having been taken in a warm country, the buildings and vehicles seemed to be of British origin. No matter. Dave was not interested enough to enlighten me. I imagined the old man to have been a docker or fisherman, whose photograph Dave had taken to please him, or, perhaps in return for some favour.

I applied myself to the sixth print in the folder.

This photograph did indeed demand considerable application if anything was to be understood from the pattern of light and dark patches that mottled its surface. From top left to bottom right, a jagged beam of light dissected the picture, and was itself criss-crossed by thinner lines of darker tone. Only when I recognised the boom of a derrick and the head and shoulders of a Chinese stevedore silhouetted within the patch of light, did I realise that the shot had been taken from the bottom of a hold, looking upwards towards the open hatch. Dave was apologetic.

'A wee bit too abstract, that one.'

Number seven. A young woman in a walled garden. Her head was too near the top of the photograph. Her bare feet were placed further apart than usual on the close-cropped lawn, for they had to support what was hidden above tennis player's calves. They had to bear the weight of what had grown out over swimmer's thighs and provide a firm foundation for that which had taken temporary residence beneath the accordion pleats of a bell-shaped smock. Sunglasses and straw hat were absent. Her expression was docile enough, but there was a hint of amusement in her eyes, which were ever so slightly lowered as if to survey the impressive, though transient, metamorphosis nature had imposed on her body. The penny dropped. I remembered the Clock Café, the Swimming Club, *A Midsummer Night's Dream*. Dave supplied the name that still eluded me. I could not bring myself to pronounce the nickname.

'Eva in front of our house in Stonehaven, just before the kid was born.'

'Eva Cameron.'

'I haven't seen the baby yet. It arrived about a week after I sailed. Just my luck.' His fingers fumbled for the next photograph. 'There it is, you see. A wee girl. She's being christened on Sunday. I want to call her Eva, but the wife prefers Margaret. She'll probably end up with both names.'

I assumed the last two pictures had been posted to him aboard ship. Baby pictures, differing in no way from those of countless other tiny beings, displayed before the camera for the fond perusal and future reminiscences of their parents. The child was neither handsome nor ugly, only wrinkled and incredibly small, with the faintest wisps of hair on its bullet-shaped skull. Although no resemblance was evident, I said the baby was remarkably like its mother, which seemed to please him.

'Do you really think so?' he asked proudly.

Two more whiskies, large ones this time. We had to wet the baby's head. Before serving us, the barman pressed a switch below the counter. The last bell drew customers, anxious not to miss their final drink, towards the bar. To avoid being jostled, I relinquished my stool and discovered, to my surprise, that my balance was by no means as steady as I had anticipated. Dave drained his glass.

'Let's go up to my hotel. I'm a resident, so we can drink all night if we feel like it.'

Regretting that I had not seen fit to bring my walking stick that evening, I followed him to the door. Within the last three hours, the icy wind had changed to snow. Huge, damp flakes whirled in the sodium lights and flurried over the dismally grey water, challenging the windscreen wipers of cars and buses on the bridge. Wet snow, horrible snow, slippery snow. I fastened up my collar as far as it would go. Grey snow, blinding snow, Russian snow. On the bridge, Napoleon was turning back from Moscow. Thick snow, unexpected snow, military snow. I shouted against the deafening whiteness.

'I'd better go home. I'm expecting a phone call.'

Flakes came to rest on Dave Sinclair's hair and nose and lips. He did not lick them off with his tongue.

'Why don't you come to my flat? I think there's some beer left.'

He shook the offending whiteness from his collar.

'Right you are. We'll take a fast black.'

What is more alone than a taxi in a snowstorm? Our tracks were covered as soon as we made them. Slowly, the diesel engine slid us uphill towards the city, changed gear, idled and ticked over under the glass roof of the railway station.

'What's the idea? My place is up ...'

'I must get something out of my case in left luggage. Won't be a minute.'

The neon lights above the bookstall flickered and went out. A man pulled down the shutters with a long pole. When Dave got in again, an icy blast of air accompanied him. The taxi lurched once more across the rutted carriage way. Dave plunged his hands into the pockets of his overcoat and pulled out two bottles.

'Four Bells Rum. Good stuff. We always get some when we pay off.'

With fingers trembling as much from excitement as the cold, I withdrew the cork and applied the bottle to my lips. The driver's eyebrows rose in the rear-view mirror.

The sound of my telephone met us at the front door. Zakrewski's voice was thin as a reed, as if the snow had deadened the wires.

'What an interesting question, Mr Syme.' He pronounced my name with a peculiar inflection of the vowel. 'You almost had me baffled, then a statement from one of your own officers came to my mind. Does not Robert Ker Porter, who visited Russia before and after the Corunna Campaign, for which he is better known, describe the Cossacks he encountered on his travels in 1812? I think he said: "Their principal weapons are a pike about eight feet long and a pair of pistols. A black belt crosses their left shoulder to which is attached a sort of tin cartridge box, holding ammunition, and surmounted with a ramrod" ... which seems to indicate you have chosen the proper colour for this feature of the mounted Cossack's equipment. We cannot overlook the possibility that the tin might have been lacquered to prevent corrosion, but for your purposes, my friend, a silvery-grey finish is quite in order.'

I thanked him profusely and not without relief. Had I been obliged to repaint my figures at that stage of the evening, the result hardly bore thinking about. My guest had settled himself on the sofa. While I took his coat and fetched glasses, I mentioned Mr Zakrewski's remarkable talents and drew his attention to the collection of military figures displayed about the room. Dave Sinclair did not mock the results of my extra-mural endeavours. He examined several of the figures with great care and listened as I outlined the action at Borodino, which the French call Moskova. Curiously, however, he seemed more interested in the containers in which the minia-tures were displayed, regiment by regiment. Perhaps it is natural for someone, whose profession embraces as many practical as intellectual skills, to show more regard for the functional than the decorative. In any case, he was not satisfied until every box had been examined and I had parted with the address of their maker.

What do two people, whose only common denominator is their birthplace, talk about in a snowbound flat when the level of the first bottle of rum has crept well below the label? We covered various topics, embarked on numerous lines of dis-cussion, but could not escape the inevitable. Our conversation took a geographical turn, ranged along the coast of Europe, rounded the Cape, plumbed the Strait of Malacca, bypassed Manila, put in at Kaoshiung, but with unavoidable regularity ended up between playing fields and a municipal crema-torium.

'Remember old Prosser. Never could tell the time. Should have been pensioned off years before.... What about the time he lost his ...'

'And McNaughton. How he ever managed to teach maths when he could hardly ...'

'Wait a minute. You must have heard about the scandal. That butch art teacher, McDougal was her name, got caught touching up one of the second year girls in the bogs and had to leave. Must be about eight years ago now.'

'You don't say. Always reckoned she was ...'

The flow of names grew thicker than our voices.

'Remember Andy Peterson, the one with the sister? Went out to Zambia or somewhere. And George Black, when he chopped the top off his thumb with that aeroplane engine? Christ, the blood. Archie Tulloch fainted.'

'No. It was Jimmy Barrie.'

'He joined the police. Bound to be quite high up by now.'

'If he had the brains.'

'Don't need brains. Just stay there long enough and keep your nose clean. What about Willy Arnott? Used to pinch books from the pottery teacher and slip them back again when he'd read them. And Angus Proudfoot ... and Tom MacManus ... and Malcolm Leslie. Hell, there's a guy. Saw him on television last week. "Magnet"—one of those arty programmes on a Sunday. He had this bloody plastic seagull on waterskis, size of a fucking plane, no kidding, and they towed it into the sky with a speedboat. Only got about half a mile and crashed. But all the cameras were there, and reporters, and crowds of people. Couldn't tell if he took it seriously or not.'

'Could you ever?'

'Right enough. Remember how he used to muck about with that clay? Bloody obscene, if you ask me. And the rumours he spread about the cemetery; made out it was haunted and scared half the young ones out of their wits. And remember when he sewed his mother's bra label into his jacket, just to make us think he'd been ...'

'That's enough.'

'What?'

'Forget it. You haven't seen him lately?'

'Hell, no. He moves about all over the place. London. The States. He's got it made, man, and all out of this art business. A load of crap, in my opinion. Mind you, he's got his head screwed on all right. Bought quite a bit of property in town.

Runs a gallery near George Street, but he's never there. Still teaches at the college as well. Guest lecturer, if you please. Couldn't teach you how to blow your ruddy nose. He's bound to be in the papers again soon, 'cause he always pulls some sort of stunt at the Art Students' Ball. Went there myself once, about five years ago. You could hardly move for people. I got covered in beer and I'd hired the fancy dress costume too. Not my cup of tea. Not my idea of ... '

Not my idea, in fact, of how to spend the prelude to combat; but events were to prove otherwise. The bedroom light pierced my brain before I opened my eyelids. Dave thrust a glass under my nose.

'Rum. Oh, Lord. I'm going to be sick.'

'Rubbish. It'll set you up for the day. When you flaked out, I dumped you in here. Hope you're all right.'

The noxious brown liquid passed over my gullet with the fluidity of sand.

'What time is it?'

'Nine thirty. Still pretty dark outside.'

120 000 men and 640 guns.

'Perth. The train leaves at ten fifteen.'

The action that took place at Borodino on September 7th, 1812.

'You broke your glasses.'

'What?'

'You fell over a table and stood on your glasses. One of the lenses is completely smashed.'

One-eyed Kutuzov.

In the taxi, I gave up counting ten boxes of figures and twenty-four mounted Cossacks to gulp frozen air through an open window.

Breathless, muddle-headed Kutuzov.

After a brief argument over the fare, Dave took my arm and assisted me to the barrier. Words of parting were mumbled hurriedly, and with a gentle push, he injected me into the throng of passengers crowding towards the train. How was he to know he had succeeded in doing the impossible? How could he tell that, by letting Four Bells ring through my brain, he had transformed a shabby, unshaven ex-schoolmate limping down a railway platform into Prince Kutuzov, Commander-in-Chief of the Imperial Army of All the Russias? Kutuzov ignored the eyes of a person who called himself Willoughby. Kutuzov surveyed the field with the insight which only a clouded vision can bestow. Kutuzov issued orders with a speed and alacrity which taxed his aides to the utmost to ensure their execution. Kutuzov eschewed liquid refreshment and ate only sparingly when obliged to dine with his subordinates. And after six hours had passed, when the fifth bell sounded, Prince Kutuzov cast his good eye over a field on which lay 86 000 French casualties and 327 captured cannon. My Napoleon would never reach Moscow.

The Garden of Earthly Delights

Fourteen days later, David Sinclair announced to his wife that the shipping company which employed him required him to call once more at their crew department office in Edinburgh. He travelled to the city by rail and as soon as he had left the train, went to the station washroom, where he hired a cubicle for threepence and there transformed himself from an officer and gentleman into a figure of fun. At least, such was the impression he intended the long Chinese dressing gown, baggy white trousers and conical hat to convey. Something in the way he had added black outlines to his inexpertly whitened features, however, gave his clown's face an unsettling mephistophelean expression, which caused curious passers-by to turn away in embarrassment as he made his way to the scene of the festivities. A sizeable crowd of variously disguised merrymakers was already alighting from cars and taxis and picking its way through the snow towards the main gates of the College of Art. Rather than join this throng, David stood for a moment, watching the procedure being followed by the commissionaires at the door. He must have resigned himself to the impossibility of gaining admission to the function without a ticket, for he turned abruptly, crossed the narrow side street that separated the college from neighbouring buildings, and passed through the frosted glass doors of a little bar, frequented by art students.

At the best of times, if more than twenty customers were present, the diminutive size of the establishment made it extremely difficult to attract the attention of the bar staff. On the night of the Arts Ball, a clamouring mass of grotesquely costumed figures, eight or nine ranks deep, completely hid the bar from view, effectively preventing any latecomers from being served. Drink, however, was not what David was seeking. He pushed his way forward, surveying the tables ranged along the wall opposite the bar, until his eye lit on a young couple seated in the shadow of the corner. By the manner in which the young man was slouched in his seat, an upturned beer glass before him, it was evident that the effects of alcohol, or perhaps some other soporific drug, had taken their toll of him before he had reached the ball. The girl, blotchy tearstains on her make-up, was shaking her partner's shoulder, but could not in any way bring him to life. When David sat down, suspicion was clearly marked on her face, but the tightly rolled bank notes, which he produced as if by accident from beneath his disguise, soon brought quite a different sparkle to her eyes. A few words were mumbled, the girl leaned carefully forward over her partner to extract the tickets from his inside pocket, and on the understanding that she and David part company immediately entrance had been gained, followed her newfound escort out of the bar. The commissionaires, by now hard pressed by revellers arriving for the ball in various states of sobriety, admitted them without question. The girl planted a wet kiss on David's make-up and disappeared, leaving him on the threshold of a scene more bizarre than he had ever imagined could exist.

For the theme of their revel, the students had chosen *The Garden of Earthly Delights* and based their decorations on the central panel of the well known triptych by Hieronymus Bosch, which goes under that name. But in contrast to the original, which is bathed in a pleasant, almost warm light, the adaptation of gothic fantasy which met David Sinclair's eyes was in semi-darkness, illuminated only where coloured spotlights shone through the grotesque tracery. At the far end of the vast, glass-roofed hall, huge forms, partly architectural, partly organic in conception, rose like fortresses till their turrets, sprouting like artificial plants, lost themselves in a web of metal rafters. In the centre of the dance floor, a circular platform had been constructed to represent a pool, and round this there revolved a grotesque cavalcade of mechanical animals, cats, fish, pumas, boars, each bearing a reveller on its back, like the wooden horses of a merry-go-round. From the centre of the pool, a beat group sent forth wild, deafening music over the heads of a thousand twisting, writhing dancers, to every corner of the hall. And what dancers! The figures that twined and wrestled round this fountain of youth showed little of the innocent, nude enjoyment envisaged by the master. Fantastic helmets mixed with wildly dyed hair. Bare legs vied with those in Roman togas. Devils and angels danced together, tramps and concubines, jesters and bishops, soldiers and gypsies. Setting his fool's cap squarely on his head, David Sinclair brushed a gauze curtain, designed to catch out unwary newcomers, from his eyes and entered The Garden of Earthly Delights. What overpowering motive led a first officer in the merchant service into this hellish menagerie? Fingers with vermilion nails thrust out from a giant, globular fruit to clasp at the cord of his gown. 'Come on, sweetie, in here.' Magicians and cowled nuns nudged his shoulders. He narrowly avoided jackbooted legs, which thrashed in the jagged cavity of a huge, broken egg shell, carving white ladders in the fishnet tights of a recumbent apache dancer. An angel took his hand. 'This way, this way', only to be lured from him by a cowboy smoking a purple cigar. David wrested his cap from the grip of a forty-year-old harpie, who dangled by the knees from an overhanging vine, fended off a drunken vampire and pressed towards an ornate portal through which yellow light streamed invitingly. He found himself in a spacious anteroom, with sufficient air to breathe and light to take stock of his surroundings. This room was less liberally decorated than the main hall. Down one wall, trestle tables were arranged, from whence refreshments were being served to those dancers overcome by heat, thirst or desire for alcohol. The sweating barman, for whom only the money was real, poured whisky into a plastic beaker. David paid, treated himself to a large shot of soda and was about to turn away when a gryphon standing nearby touched his elbow and said, 'Though the face is whitened, the eyes give you away. Only David Sinclair would present himself in black and white.'

Taken aback, the seaman regarded the gryphon with embarrassed curiosity. A cunningly constructed mask completely covered the other man's face. It was connected to a feathered jerkin which, in turn, descended to fur-clad lion's legs, already mottled by damp beer stains. Between jerkin and trousers, a black sash was stretched tightly round the waist. Between feathers and fur, David Sinclair found the clue to the gryphon's identity. The sash was not quite wide enough to prevent three inches of a cheap, paperbacked novel from projecting above its upper edge. In view of this unexpected encounter, David sought words to explain his presence. Joe O'Rourke waved him to silence and with the accomplishment of a stage manager, beckoned his former pupil to follow him through the crowd to where a globular, transparent hemisphere was suspended from one of the arches that lined the main hall. A young woman, clad in a disguise more convincingly oriental in conception than David's makeshift costume, was already standing under the dome. Joe O'Rourke ushered his companion to a place beside her, and raising both hands, drew the hemisphere down around them until it encompassed their bodies as far as the waist, effectively screening its occupants from the hubbub of the crowd and the loudest excesses of the beat group.

'This, Naomi, is David Sinclair who, for one night, has shaken the rings from his sleeve and assumed his former character. For one night, the sailor desires to leave the world of material things and sample the deception of art.' The gryphon turned to David Sinclair, bright eyes twinkling behind the feather mask. 'You will not be disappointed. Presently, the object of your excursion into this expensive land of make-believe shall begin his charade and set forth an act of folly which will immediately convince you of the hollowness of his existence. You shall return to your ship with no further thirst for culture.'

'I'm not so sure about that,' said David with a smile. 'Surely this entire affair exists only to allow all these jesters, tramps, angels and gryphons to forget their colourless daily occupations and behave, for one night, with the reckless abandon they quite wrongly associate with those who practise art for a career.'

The gryphon's beak turned through ninety degrees. 'Experience seems to have taught you little. Don't you realise that art does not lie in imagination alone? To visualise the branches of a pine spreading over the heads of adolescent players is nothing but an extension of reality. But to raise the tree, to suspend it upside down in a tower of glass transcends the boundaries of mundane imagination and renders the original conception of the designer as stale as that of the gardener who first planted it in consecrated earth.'

David Sinclair would dearly have liked to extend this discussion, but Naomi, who had been quietly peering through their transparent plastic shroud, seized his arm and drew his attention to a figure moving slowly through the crowd, whom a spotlight had suddenly picked out and thrown into relief. At first he took the man to be a naked hunchback, laboriously edging his way between the bewildered dancers towards the circular bandstand. The dancers stood aside, clearing a path for the curiously encumbered figure, and as he passed by, began to applaud and urge him towards his goal. All lights were dimmed save for a single spotlight, and with the aid of its fluorescent beam, David realised that the awkward, lumbering figure was neither naked nor, indeed, deformed in the way he had first imagined. A skin-tight, flesh-coloured costume clung to the paunchy figure. Where it met genuine flesh, at the wrists and collar, puffy red marks had formed and patches of sweat stained the thin, pink cloth. As the man reached the stage and turned round, as the press photographers, who are never far away at such events, peppered the darkness with blue flashes, as the light glinted on violet spectacles, David Sinclair beheld the burden that bent the back of his former classmate. On his back, between his shoulder blades, reaching from neck to waist, Malcolm Leslie carried a gigantic mussel shell. Like all mussel shells, it was constructed in two parts, hinged at one end. Like all mussel shells, it was coloured grey-black and lacquered to a fittingly shiny hardness; but something about it was unique. Something set apart Malcolm Leslie's mussel shell from all other shells, delighted the spectators and attracted the pressmen. From the open end of Malcolm Leslie's mussel shell, where the upper and lower lips parted, projected two pairs of legs, and by the way they flexed, writhed, crossed and intertwined, there was absolutely no doubt that the legs were alive.

Four legs, two and two. Two legs, hard and angular with a covering of curly brown hairs, two legs soft and hairless with an inward curve to the thighs. Two pairs of legs so small they could fit into the mouth of a mussel shell. Slowly, Malcolm Leslie rotated, displaying his burden to the expectant crowd. Slowly, then faster and faster came the drum roll from the bandstand. Slowly, Malcolm eased the object from his back, then a crash of cymbals, a gasp from a thousand painted lips and he whisked the shell away to reveal two tiny, perfect lovers locked in a sensual embrace. Unshelled and exposed to the light, the midgets made a great pretence of embarrassment. Though both were clad in flesh-toned suits similar to that of the giant who had transported them, the little gentleman made an elaborate show of covering his private parts while the little lady clasped her hands to her bosom and fluttered her eyelashes till the audience roared with delight and pressed so close that the tiny performers were temporarily screened from David Sinclair's view.

How easy it would have been to remain concealed behind the glazed anonymity of the hemisphere. How easy it would have been for seaman and gryphon to part company and wait for the mid-day editions of the local newspapers to furnish them with a selection of half-tone photographs accompanied by a neatly précised account of the night's events. But this would have been too easy an escape for the seaman; too obvious an admission of defeat. Hurriedly, David grasped the lower rim of protective plastic and raised the hemisphere above their heads. The gryphon and Chinese lady waved, clapped, shouted out over the music of the band, until they succeeded in making Malcolm Leslie turn his violet gaze in their direction. He brushed aside those reporters whose attention was not yet fixed on the acrobatics of his midget companions, and strode towards them through the sea of spectators. In silence, Malcolm and David mixed their perspiration in a handshake, and as gryphon and Chinese lady withdrew, sought common ground in names from the past.

'Dave Sinclair. Where have you been all these years? How did you know to come tonight of all nights?'

'I ran into Sandy Syme. He let the cat out of the bag. ... '

'Good Lord. Haven't heard of him for ages. Remember when he tried to ride a bike . . .? Funny he should have known about tonight. Anyway, how are you doing?'

Between pauses occasioned by the noise of the band, David Sinclair navigated from London to Japan, Capetown, Durban, Singapore, Manila, Hong Kong, Kaohsiung, Pusan, Kobe. And behind violet spectacles, Malcolm Leslie listened, interrupting from time to time in an attempt to steer the conversation towards the concrete car park of a not-so-modern licensed roadhouse. William Jardine and Mathis Gothardt Nithardt called 'Grünewald', what a combination. In the centre of the bandstand, the midgets, who had completed their act, were posing for photographs, while around them, the cavalcade of mechanical animals once more jerked into motion.

'This way. You must meet Doris, a soul that lives in the company of angels.'

Together they approached the ring of gaudily decorated beasts and Malcolm pointed to a plump, white faced girl who bounced drunkenly into view astride the back of a wooden and canvas stag. On her head, a stuffed seagull bobbed threaten-ingly from a wire, spreading its wings over her glistening shoulders.

'Do you know what a Doris is?' said Malcolm, stepping up and planting a kiss on the girl's thigh as she passed. 'A Doris is a shell-less mollusc with gills on her back.'

From between the legs of a papier mâché boar, the male midget grimaced at David Sinclair and piped, 'Beware the sins of the flesh,' in a thin, trembling voice. Malcolm Leslie laughed and pushed the midget so hard that he fell reeling back in a series of somersaults to end up standing on his head.

'Our little friend, whose sins may be hired from a circus at twenty pounds a night, may have a point,' he said, 'but personally I subscribe to the opinion of Fraenger, who interprets this particular work of the master as an indication of the positive path to attaining full harmony between nature and the human soul.' He winked at David Sinclair. 'I see you know nothing of the Adamites, yet behave in the manner of a convinced Brother of the Free Spirit.' Climbing on to the edge of the bandstand, Malcolm waited till the stag came into view and with one swift movement, swept the girl from its back and deposited her on the floor before his companion. 'Mr David Sinclair, Officer of the Mercantile Marine. One time school friend.' Doris inclined her head and seagull feathers brushed the fool's cap. 'Doris is a shell-less mollusc, my part-time model and full-time muse.'

David surveyed the plump girl, whose legs were encased in orange tights and whose breasts were barely kept in check by a sort of bolero of wide string mesh. 'Delighted to have the pleasure of meeting you,' he said gravely.

Dancers, driven to greater and greater excesses of frenzy by the music, were pressing in on them from every side. Malcolm removed his spectacles and cast a jaundiced eye over the heaving throng. 'My studio is upstairs,' he said. 'The atmosphere is quieter and besides, I have something there which I know will be of greater interest to you than this sham affair.'

They turned to go when suddenly the midget, who had crept up unnoticed, leapt forward and with both hands, grabbed one of Doris's spangled nipples which projected through the net and pulled on it with all his weight till the girl bent double, squealing with pain. David spun round and caught the midget in a vice-like grip. The Chinese clown raised the struggling little man above his head, and bellowing 'Beware the sins of the flesh,' hurled him headlong over the circle of animals into the middle of the band, where he crashed down in a tangle of upset amplifiers and twisted cymbals. Ignoring the confusion thus caused, Malcolm took his two companions by the arm and ushered them away from the fountain of youth to where a dimly lit stair-way led to the upper floors of the college. On each step of the stairway, figures lay in drunken sleep or necking with the abandon only alcohol can arouse. Like people moving through a casualty clearing station at the scene of some disaster, Malcolm, Doris and their nautical companion picked their way through the bodies to where, at the top of the stairway, a substantial barricade guarded by three uniformed porters prevented revellers from invading those areas of the establishment in which tuition normally took place. While Malcolm, by virtue of his position as guest lecturer, was prevailing upon the porters to have an opening temporarily cleared in the barricade, a casualty who had been crouching on the top step, comforting a drunken Chinese companion, beckoned to David Sinclair and hissed through a gryphon's beak, 'Take care, David. Do not enter by the gate of ivory, for you must come out by the gate of horn.'

What possible meaning could such a warning have conveyed to our nautical friend? He followed the artist without question down a lengthy corridor which ended at a quite unremarkable door of varnished wood. The studio was in darkness when they entered. While Malcolm fumbled for the light switch, Doris drew close to David and whispered, 'Perhaps you dealt too harshly with the midget. Even the smallest of us has the right to an opinion, and who are we to prevent him from demonstrating it?' Before he could protest his good intentions, the lights flickered to life and David found himself in a stark, lofty room, one wall of which consisted entirely of inward-sloping glass. Apart from a desk and a couple of decrepit couches, the furnishings of Malcolm Leslie's studio were restricted to plain, dusty drapes suspended from steel girders near the ceiling and several frames, stands and revolving platforms on which the three dimensional efforts of his post-diploma class were displayed in various stages of completion. The furthest corner of the room was sectioned off by two long curtains, on which the stains of paint and plaster formed a streaky pattern. As though oblivious to the presence of his guests, Malcolm bustled about, sorting through sheets of multi-coloured paper that littered every surface in the room and lay strewn in confusion on the floor. Selecting one or two to serve his needs, he unrolled them on the desk, swept the remainder to the floor and beckoned David to join him. The seaman stepped carefully across the carpet of drawings as though each footstep might destroy a masterpiece, and peered over the artist's shoulder.

On the well-thumbed sheet of cartridge, bold charcoal marks and subtle pencil strokes blended, diverged and intersected. At the top of the sheet, an antiquated, four-wheeled wagon was delineated in ink with almost technical accuracy. Partly superimposed on its frail outline, a bold, charcoal study of galloping horses leapt from the paper, nostrils flaring, blackened hooves losing themselves in a great smudge of dust which in turn merged into a ghostly, full-face study of a head. Despite the mastery of line, the portrait somehow seemed incomplete, as if at the last moment, it had been abandoned in favour of the hurriedly drawn group of fisher-folk that filled the bottom third of the paper. Without comment, Malcolm Leslie raised one chubby fist, let the sheet spring back into a roll to reveal beneath it a delicate still life in muted, sepia chalks. The artist's memory had served him well. Each knot mark was clearly shown on the wooden wall. The rusty bird cage did not deserve a highlight, but where the upper rim of the tin of curry powder met the background, a curved white line emphasised the embarrassingly vacant space between the two pictorial elements. A composition crying out with disharmony. Malcolm Leslie narrowed his eyes and looked up at David Sinclair.

'When I first began this project,' he said, 'I conceived it as a large mural, perhaps in bas-relief, but certainly in monochrome, for who can quite recall the colours that glistened beneath the flight of gulls? The sketches, as you see, were taken to an advanced stage. I even went so far as to instruct my carpenter to build a framework on which to commence the finished work. It is still lying in the yard, unused and warping out of shape through exposure to the weather. Something was lacking. Somehow the project demanded a unity beyond that of wood and plaster. I tried several possible solutions without success. Two years passed and I was close to giving up when, quite by chance, the solution presented itself to me in a most extraordinary way.' He rummaged in a drawer and held up two rumpled newspaper clippings. 'Through the words of a seven-year-old, I realised that full expression of my subject did not lie in recreating elements of the past, but in employing pure symbolism of the future. Cart wheels, wire cages, feathers, the chromium of a coffee machine, in which I intended framing my mural, suddenly seemed meaningless. By constant application, ceaseless mental endeavour, I reduced the motifs of my project to two major elements, two existing, organic units which symbolise my entire conception.'

He handed one of the scraps of newsprint to David and moved to the curtain behind which lay the only concealed part of the room.

> I like Doctor Millar because he helps me at the hospital. I like his clean white coat. He writes my name in a big book. I was in the hospital because I have sore ears and can't hear well. I have been in hospital six times with Doctor Millar.

'A letter in a children's newspaper competition,' said Malcolm. 'Touching, don't you think? I made contact with the worthy doctor at his clinic which specialises in ailments of the ear. When I first explained my project, he showed the reserve characteristic of the medical profession, but when I suggested that any profit resulting from the sale or exhibition of the piece be immediately given over to further research into cosmetic surgery of the ear, he soon came round to my way of thinking. I persuaded him to make anatomical charts and models available to me, and to assist me with specialised advice while I constructed the basis of my composition. I like to think that I proved to the good doctor how close the relationship between science and art can become, when united in a common cause. Within a month, the first part of my project was complete. Our collaboration came to an end. Dr Millar returned to his white coat and big book, having been party to what, I feel, is a unique creation in the history of art.' He swept back the curtain and there it was. Fifteen feet high from lobe to helix. Free-standing. Totally divorced from skin and hair, yet flesh-coloured, glistening, completely accurate in every detail. Malcolm Leslie stepped into the shadow of the giant ear and lovingly rubbed his hands over its surface. 'Fibre-glass on a wood and metal frame', he murmured. 'Each section was moulded separately, then assembled round a heavily weighted base. Despite its height, it is completely stable. Should it be exhibited outdoors, the strongest winds will not affect it.'

With moist, wide eyes, David approached the ear. His lips moved, but no words came. He stood transfixed before the monstrous, sculptural memory till Malcolm's voice once more broke the silence. 'Impressive, don't you agree? A purely organic form. A natural, physical cavity. A cornucopia which will provide a perfect setting for the second element of my composition. But you seem perplexed. Let me explain my intention.'

He took David's arm. 'Step, if you please, on to the lobule. It is quite strong enough to bear your weight. From there you can see how the helix, scapha and anti-helix naturally lead the eye to the centre of the structure. Now step between the tragus and anti-tragus, into the innermost cavity. You will see that here, beyond the intertragic-notch, I have diverged from the pattern of nature by constructing a small, horizontal platform. A base, if you like, for the second element.' He stooped, pressed a switch at the side of the sculpture, and at once David found himself illuminated by cunningly concealed lights. 'The second element,' said Malcolm, 'will be positioned exactly where you are standing. Nothing is more fitting than that you should first occupy its place, for in our reunion tonight, I have gained access to that which is the embodiment of water and chromium, gulls, flannel and dust.'

David looked from the cavity of the ear towards Doris, who was stretched out asleep on a couch. 'I should have thought your full-time muse could easily furnish you with inspiration. Or perhaps a visit to a saddler would supply a motif closer to your needs.'

The artist laughed. 'How little you can see, though you are looking from the very centre of the world. Can you dictate the actions of a muse? Even now, Doris is sawing wood; cutting down every tree that breaks the shadow of a red-brick chimney.' The small eyes narrowed. 'And words concerning leather are better left unsaid. My information comes from wood-pulp, not calf-skin.'

David stepped down from the fibre-glass cavern and took the second scrap of paper which Malcolm offered with a quivering, sweating hand.

SINCLAIR—CAMERON. On Friday 18th April at Stonehaven. David Henry, younger son of Mr and Mrs W Sinclair of Kirkcaldy, Fife, to Eva, only daughter of Mr and Mrs A L Cameron, Stonehaven, Kincardine.

The tiny strip of newsprint was marked and discoloured. It was all of five years since David's future in-laws had insisted on placing the announcement. Had Malcolm carried it with him all that time through sentiment, or had five simple lines of type been the goad that had driven him to create the object in whose shadow the seaman stood?

'The press is a medium from which few secrets are withheld. With application, one discovers so much more than the tongues of gossips can convey.' The artist's eyes were fixed on the ground. 'Five years ago I found that clue, and even then, the seed of an idea germinated in my mind. In black and white I possessed, if you like, the door behind which lay the second element of my composition. But I had no key. Throughout the years, my resolution grew, only to diminish when my efforts were disappointed. Countless other projects became my chief preoccupations, and indeed rewarded me with what, in our profession, passes for success; nevertheless, so long as that scrap of paper lay in my wallet, I knew I could never be free of the greatest challenge, the overwhelming desire to recreate the second element of my earliest inspiration.' His brow was wet. White blotches marked the knuckles of his fleshy fists. 'The north-east coast was part of the country that I neither knew nor liked, yet six times, at first by train, later in my car, I travelled to Stonehaven. I visited every café in that cold little town, walked down every street, made myself known in the bar of every hotel without success. Chance did not let me meet her in the street. The cold recalcitrance of the people to whom I spoke froze any likelihood of achieving my goal. Even today, it fills me with shame to think, as I so often do, of my naive, underhand behaviour. When the matter came to Doris's attention, believe me, she is a muse, she scoffed at my lack of confidence. With her assistance, I convinced myself that accurate visual memories were sufficient for my purpose. I set to work. The outcome stands behind you. Plans for the second element are already underway, but your appearance here tonight has rendered them unnecessary.'

With slow deliberation, the seaman in a fool's cap sat down on the lobule of the monstrous ear. 'You imagine I can help you. What in heaven's name do you want from me?'

'An address. Simply an address and some words to say to get me what I need.'

'If you think for one moment ... '

'Regard it, David, as the payment of a debt. Doesn't guilt like yours require atonement?'

On a shabby couch, the muse stirred and watched the artist and the seaman bend low over a writing desk. The scraping of a pen slid through the silence, then she rose and followed them out through the gate of horn. At the top of a wide flight of steps, a gryphon who was finishing a paper-backed book looked up just long enough to catch the reproach in David Sinclair's eyes, then lowered his beak and gently pecked the shoulder of a Chinese lady.

In the Footsteps of Marie Grosholtz

JOE O'ROURKE

Holding the stump of a candle out in front of him, Mr Da Silva crawled for the last time round the perimeter of the room and came to rest at my feet. Throughout the exercise, the candle flame had remained unwaveringly perpendicular. Da Silva looked up and a smile spread through the wrinkles on his swarthy face. 'No draught, Joe. Very good. Very good. This place will do.' Thank heavens for that. It was the fifth room in which he had performed his pyromantic display since Malcolm Leslie's studio at the College of Art had been pronounced too draughty for his purposes. We were now above Malcolm's gallery, in a second storey room which, until recently, had housed exhibits in need of renovation or awaiting display. Not giving Da Silva the chance to change his mind, I at once set about looking for power points and, having satisfied myself that the wiring would stand the load of his portable furnace, ushered him downstairs to where Malcolm waited in a considerable state of agitation.

It had all started the day before, when Malcolm pushed open the tastefully engraved glass door of the gallery which I have managed for him for several years, and introduced me to his companion with the words, 'Joe O'Rourke, meet Tony Da Silva, whose fingers create flesh from vacant air.'

Experience has taught me to dilute the more extravagant statements of my employer. I inclined my head slightly and surveyed the wrinkled, dark skinned little man with critical curiosity. Despite his well kept grey suit, Da Silva had a worn out, rumpled appearance, as if he had travelled many miles without the opportunity to change or shave. This theory was further strengthened by the heavy leather suitcase he held in each hand. For an instant, it seemed as if he expected me to relieve him of his burden, and like a hotel porter, escort him to a comfortable room. When, however, I made no move to assist him and glared at the highly polished linoleum on which he obviously intended to deposit the cases, Da Silva lowered his eyes and hurriedly struggled over to a carpet, on which he laid his baggage. At this juncture, a cab-driver appeared in the doorway and made it known in no uncertain terms that, while his meter was still running, he was double parked and not prepared to hang about much longer. Malcolm and Da Silva hurried out immediately. Out of curiosity, I followed them to the steps, at the foot of which the cabbie had dumped four large wooden boxes and a metal chest. While Malcolm settled with the driver, Da Silva struggled to lift the first box up the steps but its weight was clearly beyond his strength. With growing annoyance, I removed my jacket and, by the time Malcolm was once more on the pavement, had carried the four wooden boxes into the lobby of the gallery. The chest was less easily dealt with. It must have weighed upwards of two hundredweights, and was so awkward in shape and bulk that the combined efforts of Malcolm and myself were required to transport it indoors.

Ever since Malcolm and I became associates, we have observed separate and strictly defined functions within the organisation. While he concerns himself with creating works of art, lecturing and travelling both at home and abroad in his capacity as a celebrity of the fine arts, I accept a salary in excess of five thousand pounds per annum, superintend exhibitions at the Leslie Gallery, organise his periodic lecture tours and still have ample free time to pursue my private preoccupations in literature, ceramics and a girl called Naomi. Our interests seldom, if ever, clash and merge only on the balance sheet. My annoyance was therefore quite under-standable when, on that bright May afternoon, Da Silva and Malcolm invaded my customary tranquillity. Had the various chests and boxes contained exhibits for display in the gallery, I would have known long in advance. Before I asked, Malcolm understood that an explanation was in order.

'All our lives,' he said, 'we have believed that natural, three-dimensional realism finds its finest expression in the classical sculpture of the ancients. Last week, I was introduced to Tony and subsequently my eyes have been opened on a completely fresh field—not a new method of recreating nature, for what in the world is new, but a technique and expertise which can combine with modern creative vision to produce a new experience in classical realism.' My expression could scarcely have convinced him, for a hint of anger crossed his face. 'I know it's in your character to scoff,' he said, 'but don't judge too hastily. Tony. Open up a box and give Mr O'Rourke a lesson in appreciation.' A lid was lifted and reluctantly I gazed upon a tangle of severed limbs resting on a bed of straw.

'Waxworks,' I mumbled in surprise.

'Precisely. Waxworks. Tony Da Silva's craftsmanship is removed only in time from that of the young Marie Grosholtz. Till now, his talent has lain unnoticed, restricted by the dictates of finance to the creation of maudlin, wax flowers, or grotesques for travelling side shows. How fortunate that our paths should have crossed at this moment. While I can help him achieve the rewards which have so long eluded him, he can bestow on my second element a realism only excelled by nature itself. But don't concern yourself with the details of my plan. Because a certain part of Mr Da Silva's process requires a completely draught-free environment, we have found it impossible to undertake the project in my regular studio. A room here must be used instead.' Leaving me no time to object, he turned and grasped the little man by the hand. 'Unfortunately I must leave you now. I have a lecture scheduled for four, and this evening I must address some damned old women on the subject of modern art. Mr O'Rourke will see to everything you need and entertain you in my absence. Until tomorrow then, about ten.'

Which is why, later that evening, I sat opposite Tony Da Silva in a quiet but rather exclusive restaurant and totted up expenses in my head. Da Silva ate selfconsciously, as if unused to dining in such affluent surroundings. He had about him a strange air, a furtive, almost subservient humbleness which seemed more fitting to the character of a gypsy than an artist. Indeed, it is doubtful whether such a loose classification as 'artist' could ever convey an accurate impression of this remarkable little man. During the course of our afternoon together, I had made it my business to discover as much of Tony Da Silva's history as he was prepared to reveal.

He was, it seemed, of Portuguese origin, though he had come to London at a very early age when his father settled there as agent for a wine shipping concern. In his new surroundings, far from the friendly sun, the senior Mr Da Silva had dedicated himself to wine with somewhat more than professional zeal and had eventually expired in a tavern at Wapping, leaving his wife just enough to secure a steerage passage back to Oporto for herself and the three youngest children. By this time, Tony had become apprenticed to an Italian gentleman who specialised in stucco work. Electing to remain in London, he bade farewell to his family and busied himself with learning the art of moulding and casting statuettes in plaster. His skill and reputation grew, and had the Italian not become jealous and talked too often about the attitude of the authorities to unregistered aliens in time of war, he could easily have set up on his own account with great success. As it was, he left London and reappeared near Manchester, where he found employment repairing and redecorating a travelling fun-fair, which the exigencies of war had rendered temporarily inoperative. It was here, he maintained, that he first began making original plaster figures to decorate stalls, the fronts of booths and the mechanisms of steam organs that supplied music to the roundabouts. By chance, his work came to the notice of a showman called Glick who, at that time, was being treated particularly harshly by the caprices of the international situation. Only a letter from a rabbi and hurriedly completed amendments to Glick's obscure passport had prevented him from being interned. Glick owned a boxing booth which, in happier times, had toured the country in company with a 'Salon of Curiosities'. In market places and on village greens, he had offered country lads a chance to prove their manhood, while their girl friends enjoyed the horror of inspecting Siamese twins, a bearded lady, Waldo the Giant, and such other aberrations of nature as he had been able to assemble. Now, however, his boxers' fists were pummelling the mud of Passchendaele, his Siamese twins had split up and the bearded lady, succumbing to the call of King and country, had given up her padding and gone to work in a shipyard. Only Waldo the Giant remained, growing thinner and more sickly by the month and when at last Waldo was admitted to a hospital from which he was unlikely to return, Glick resolved that something must be done. His proposition had at first astounded Tony Da Silva, not because its demands on his skill were too great, but simply through the sheer effrontery of the idea. Having learned to his cost the fickle nature of even the most unusual forms of humanity, Glick had resolved to master his staffing problem once and for all. On the premise that savings on food and salaries would amply compensate his initial outlay, he requested Da Silva to create for him a complete range of life-sized plaster grotesques which could be painted in natural colours and displayed to the public in glass tanks and jars as if they had been preserved in formaldehyde after death. The prospect of much needed cash had soon overcome Da Silva's moral scruples and he set to work, constructing in the space of a year Alvin, the Three-Legged Child, The Three-Eyed Head of the Burmese Wild Man, Rufus—Half Man Half Dog, and a twelve-fingered hand. Glick was happy enough with the uncanny objects which Da Silva unveiled to him, one by one, in the dimly-lit boxing booth; but the artist was conscious from the start that plaster was not enough to simulate exactly the subtle tones and textures of dead flesh. He prevailed on Glick to postpone the date of delivery and at once set about experimenting with paints, varnishes and waxes which would finish off the figures to his satisfaction. His efforts were rewarded with partial success. Despite his total ignorance of chemistry, he came up with a waxen jelly which, when hardened, bore a passing resemblance to skin. He coloured it with oil paint and handed over the completed works to a delighted Glick.

This bizarre commission marked the turning point in Tony Da Silva's career. Whereas he had previously regarded himself simply as a maker of moulds and plaster casts, from this time on he became more and more preoccupied with the creation of waxworks. As soon as the war ended, he bought a ticket to London and, taking his courage in both hands, presented himself at the world-renowned establishment founded by Madame Tussaud. It must not be imagined that Tony, at this juncture, considered himself an accomplished worker in wax. He presented himself in all humility as an experienced plaster moulder and was taken on as a trainee in the casting department.

Until Tony Da Silva stepped through the door of the Leslie Gallery, my knowledge of waxworks was minimal. In common with most people, I had always supposed the life-sized replicas of monarchs, murderers and politicians to consist solely of wax, perhaps supported by a wire frame. Tony dispersed my illusions. While faces, heads and hands are indeed hollow wax castings, he explained that it is normal for those parts of the body which are covered by clothing to be constructed in plaster of Paris to afford greater strength to the structure. Assisting in the production of such bodies was his chief concern though, as is only natural, he soon picked up the techniques required to cast the waxen sections of a sculpture with complete accuracy. He worked hard, was well liked and showed such deep interest in every process of construction that soon his skill could have been in use in every department. The method of producing waxworks at Madame Tussaud's was a far superior process to the simple one he had evolved in Manchester. Before embarking on the master sculpture, which was done in clay, Tussaud's experts furnished themselves with hundreds of exact measurements of their subject, took count-less photographs from every angle and meticulously collected information on colour and texture of hair, skin colour, complexion, and the like. The sculpture was then completed. Such portions as were to be represented in wax were moulded and carefully cast, then passed to the cosmetic department for colouring, the addition of eyes and the insertion of hairs, one by one, into the waxen scalp. A superior process, Tony Da Silva thought, but not so very different in end result from his own, till one day near closing time, when a colleague and he were moving Dr Crippen on to a trolley in preparation for his biannual clean up, Glick burst through the last, straggling party of visitors and seized Da Silva by the throat. The struggle that ensued put several well-known waxen figures in jeopardy. The enquiry that resulted filled the traditional home of waxworks with acute embarrassment and brought Tony Da Silva instant dismissal.

Glick, it transpired, had been plying his trade at New-market, where advantage could be taken of the considerable crowds that had assembled for the races. Things had been going well. His booth had been full and a sizeable queue was waiting for admission to the Chamber of Death, as he had renamed his show, when, owing to deterioration of the wax, the chin had suddenly detached itself from The Three-Eyed Head of the Burmese Wild Man and floated to the top of the tank, revealing unmistakably white plaster beneath. Incensed at having been duped, and delighted at having discovered a fraud, the crowd had at once burst open the remaining jars and bottles to satisfy themselves of the true origins of their grisly contents. When Glick had attempted to save what he could of his collection, they had set on him, dragged him outside and tossed him in a horse-blanket until two burly constables intervened and escorted him from the scene with a warning never to show his face in the locality again. Like all who practise an itinerant profession, showmen have an uncanny knack of transmitting information concerning the whereabouts of others. Thus Glick knew exactly where to find Da Silva and, having gained the satisfaction of seeing the cause of his misfortune lose his job before his very eyes, went on to demand that Da Silva make good the dreadful loss he had sustained. Without finance, or employment, Da Silva per-suaded Glick to buy him such materials as he would need and then constructed a completely fresh collection of horrors for the showman, making use this time of the secrets he had learned at his recent place of work. The results exceeded Da Silva's wildest hopes and so impressed Glick that he forgot the quarrel, set his enmity aside, and suggested that they form a partnership. The Magnificent Parade of Terror was born and met with immediate success. Together, they toured to every part of Britain, with the understandable exception of New-market. Audiences were spellbound. They bought first one motor van, then another, and soon were able to give up living in their caravan and instead take rooms in a hotel in whatever town their show was on display. Da Silva persuaded Glick to give up any pretence that the exhibits on display were real. The showman feared that people would lose interest when all they had before them was a show of wax, but he was proved wrong. Takings reached a record.

In return, Glick insisted that they take the show abroad and arrangements were made to tour the Continent. On a fine spring morning they sailed from Folkestone with two motor vans full of waxworks carefully stowed on deck. Their route took them from Boulogne to Paris, then south through every town and village from Orléans to Limoges. Da Silva frequently visited convents along the way where after praying with true Catholic fervour and making a suitable donation to the holy charity of the establishment, he purchased from the Mother Superior quantities of hair shorn from the heads of initiates before taking their vows. They spent a fortnight at Toulouse, were presented to the mayor, then, to Da Silva's secret regret, decided against passing through Spain, where the bloody Civil War was drawing to a close. By way of Narbonne and Marseilles, they reached the Riviera where they put on five gala shows. They crossed Italy in September and wintered in Vienna. How Tony Da Silva's face lit up at the memory of those days. Coffee in the Wienerwald. Dancing through the night at the Prater. It was he who had suggested they move north through Czechoslovakia. His motive was simple. Glass eyes. No finer specimens were available than those produced in Silesia. Centuries of traditional craftsmanship showed in every life-like facet. At the gallery, he had laid out for my inspection a hundred examples of the glassmakers' art. Fifty pairs, fifty different shades.

In Czechoslovakia he had bought his eyes, while in Prague and Brno, their exhibition was greeted with rapturous applause. In Krakow, they were given permission to set up their display in a theatre, and Glick, who understood something of the language, was invited to give a talk on the local radio station. But time was running short. Da Silva wanted to be back in England in time to prepare for the coming summer season. He was full of ideas for new, more ambitious displays and besides, through so much travelling, many existing items were sadly in need of repair. They made Warsaw the last stop in their itinerary and from there travelled to the Baltic coast, where arrangements had been made to sail home.

In the free port of Danzig, which had suddenly decided not to be so free, Da Silva went aboard the ship to supervise the loading of the waxworks. They had decided, in the interests of economy, to sell off the two motor vans and replace them with two new ones when they reached England. Glick was late. The ship was about to sail and Da Silva feared he had been unable to sell the vans. If only Glick had not chosen to run the last few hundred yards down the quay, he might not have attracted the attention of the two men in brown uniforms who decided to check his passports and were fascinated by their discovery of a letter from a rabbi in a wallet full of multi-national currency. They kicked poor Glick back up the quay to await the Third Reich and Da Silva sailed to England alone, accompanied only by personal baggage, a number of shabby waxworks, one hundred glass eyes and a sizeable quantity of multi-coloured hair which had been denied ordainment in holy orders.

At home and penniless, Da Silva had attempted to raise a loan and re-establish The Magnificent Parade of Terror, but he found the market for travelling side-shows even more depressed than it had been when he had first encountered the profession. There was no demand for waxen terror when real terror was mounting daily. Taking a hint from his late father, he became a connoisseur of wine. When supplies of wine ran dry even before the last of his money, he took a job making wax flowers, which were just going out of fashion on the hats of elderly ladies and here he remained until demand finally ran out, his employer went bankrupt and a midget appeared at the door of his lodgings with a proposition. Show people never forget. The midget's father, who proved to be equally dim-inutive in stature, had worked with Glick in the early days. He remembered Da Silva and offered to put in a good word for him with the owner of the circus with which they travelled. Despite the fact that he was now over seventy, Da Silva had been taken on as a handy man. When Malcolm Leslie visited the circus in search of accomplices to complete his charade for the Arts Ball, he had been introduced to the old handy man who insisted on carrying among his luggage the remains of his creative past. The examples which Da Silva modestly displayed in his little caravan had, so he said, immediately fired Malcolm Leslie with enthusiasm. A bargain had been struck. In return for Da Silva's advice and expertise, Malcolm had agreed to use the remnants of the Magnificent Parade of Terror to create a permanent work of art.

Tony Da Silva and I went downstairs to tell Malcolm that a suitable room had been found, in which the waxwork could be cast without exposure to draughts which cause uneven shrinkage and distortion. Delighted at the news, Malcolm slapped the table with his hand and stretched his arm round Tony's frail shoulders. 'Then everything is ready. You have no idea, old friend, how deeply I regret that you cannot witness the initial stages of our project, but an agreement has been made which I am unable to break. Such is life. I must rely on the skills you have taught me to bring back all the information you require. While I am gone, prepare the makeshift studio as you think fit. Joe will assist you in every possible way.'

We went out with Malcolm to where his car was standing in the street. Saturday morning shoppers were already strolling along the pavements, pausing from time to time to peer through the windows of the exclusive, expensive antique shops that occupied the basements of adjoining buildings. As Malcolm drove off into the traffic, I detected a single tear between the furrows of Da Silva's cheeks. He turned, and slowly I followed him back into the gallery, where I hung the 'Closed for Business' notice on the door. Later that day, after four labourers had carried the portable furnace upstairs and set it up beside Malcolm's heap of wire and clay, I smoked too many cigarettes and watched while Tony opened his dusty wooden boxes and spread their contents on the floor. Heads, arms, hands, a leather bag of Silesian glass eyes, coil upon coil of shining, tissue-wrapped hair. I took the hammer which he offered me, and together we smashed up the head of The Burmese Wild Man, shattered the limbs of Alvin and Rufus— Half Man Half Dog and dropped the pieces, one by one, into the stone cold cauldron on the stove.

Slug Road

MALCOLM LESLIE

Slug Road. There is such a place. The address stood out bold on the folded sheet of paper on my dashboard. Dave's letter had been typically, perhaps deliberately vague. He had simply mentioned that, from a certain date in May, he was leaving on a prolonged voyage to the Far East. His letter gave no hint of whether he had secured his wife's co-operation in my project, or indeed if he had broached the subject with her at all. As I drove, I speculated on my reception and turned over in my mind a selection of excuses or, to be precise, justifications which I could present to Eva if the necessity arose. My uncertainty led me to adopt what, in retrospect, can only be regarded as comical extremes of subterfuge. Beside my attaché case, which contained the equipment I would need, there lay a canvas bag filled with rock samples and two geological hammers that I had borrowed from a friend with an amateur interest in the subject. If my arrival proved completely unexpected, I intended to use some story about being in the locality in search of semi-precious stones and having, quite by chance, discovered her address from a fellow geologist who had known her at college. Semi-precious stones indeed. Would time have so drastically frayed our relationship that I would be forced to fall back on pathetic, schoolboy excuses for my conduct? Granted, the years had rubbed the corners off my memories, but rather than detract from their value, this natural erosion of detail by the passage of time seemed to have ground them to a lens through which I could focus even more closely on the highlights of our time together. I was too much of a realist, however, to delude myself that Eva would necessarily share this rosy but, I maintain, accurate in-terpretation of the past. What for me was inextricably associated with the flight of gulls over sweet-smelling pine cones, might for her only mean dust and red-lead. I neither expected nor hoped that, on this occasion, our relationship could be anything other than that of artist and model or, at best, of old friends combining to create something of permanent value from the past. Although my thoughts were naturally centred on the object of my journey, I could not ignore the nagging possibility that Dave had indeed made a full confession to her, and that she had agreed to the undertaking only to please him. No matter how I tried to put the dreadful likelihood from my mind, I found myself becoming more and more preoccupied with this interpretation. Suddenly, I was afraid that Dave and Eva had agreed on the matter between themselves, making light of my project and thus robbing me of its value at the very moment when success was within my grasp. Overcome by depression and doubt, I stopped the car and fought with the temptation to turn back. Was it purely chance that I chose a lay-by above the cliffs of St Cyrus for the scene of my disquieting mental struggle? I had put the car in gear, ready to make a U-turn, when my eye caught something moving at the edge of the land, where the cliffs dropped down to the beach. A tiny figure, then another. Three in all, creeping sideways along the rim of the world like crabs. Their capes and anoraks billowed in the wind, but they paid no heed to the elements trying to pluck them into the air. Their eyes were on the rock, from which, with little hammers, they struck lumps of stone to fill the canvas satchels at their waists. Amateur geologists. Cancelling my indicator, I steered straight ahead and accelerated up the road to Stonehaven.

Slug Road. There is such a place. Granite houses built to shield granite Victorian souls, revealing the character of their present owners only in the colours of paint on doors and window frames and the choice of flowers and shrubs in their little gardens. Houses on both sides of the road, then only on one. With difficulty, I read the numbers, to which several proprietors had added names. *Greenbank, Tralee, The Lodge, Pomona, Fairview*. The house whose number lay on my dashboard was larger than most. A detached cottage, to which attics, several extensions, a garage and a fresh coat of whitewash had been added to endow it with an air of middle-class respectability. The name on the door was Cameron. A moment's pause and Eva, wearing slacks and a baggy pullover, opened it in person. Her hair had grown. In fact all of her had grown except her height, which seemed shorter than I recalled, though she was standing on a step. She looked at me as though I were a tradesman whom she could not remember having asked to call. I hurriedly removed my spectacles and said, 'Good afternoon, Eva.' Three words. 'Good afternoon, Eva', and recognition dawned. As if triggered by a spring, her hands fluttered to smooth down the pullover, then swept unconsciously upwards to her hair.

'Sorry, Malcolm, so sorry. Please come in. Dave said you might drop by.'

I followed her into the house. A spacious lobby, airy, clean, but furnished in a manner that suggested she and Dave were not the sole occupants of the house. She hurried down the corridor before me, drawing closed a door on the left, lest my eyes should light on some domestic disarray.

'I hope you don't mind the kitchen; Dave and I have our own sitting room through there, but it's an awful mess. And Maggie's in the back garden. I must keep an eye on her.'

Of course, Maggie, their child. I sat at the table in their spotless, modern kitchen while she leaned over the sink and made noises through the window at the invisible Maggie. The black material of her trousers stretched tightly over her rump, revealing the outline of a girdle beneath. Yes, she had grown all right.

'What a pity you couldn't have come a couple of days ago. Dave has just left on a voyage and my parents are in Aberdeen for the weekend, visiting relatives.' She turned and smiled in a manner that owed more to suburban politeness than to friendship. The barriers were not down yet, but there was time. Plenty of time.

'What a pity,' I echoed dutifully. 'But he did mention why I particularly wanted to see you after so many years?'

'Not really. He said you might ask me to help you with remembering things for a picture or something.'

'Not a picture. A sculpture.'

She was surprised. 'How can you forget things in a

sculpture? What can't you remember?'

I looked straight into her eyes, which tiny wrinkles had not made less appealing, and said, 'You.' Inwardly I chuckled, for a slight widening of the dark eyes betrayed that she could not decide whether I had spoken in jest, or whether my single word held a deeply significant meaning which had escaped her. Unwilling to relinquish my position while I held the advantage, I was about to come straight out and tell her my intentions when an urgent squeal from the garden thwarted my plans. I followed her outside and watched as she lifted the child from its pram and rocked it rhythmically in her arms. Suddenly, I became aware of the words she was murmuring to the little red-faced figure.

'Come on, now, Maggie. You mustn't cry. Come on, now. Uncle Malcolm has come to see you.'

Uncle Malcolm. Jesus Christ! I peered at the tiny bundle, waved a finger and made what I hoped were suitable noises of introduction.

'Come on, then. Uncle Malcolm would like to hold you. That's a good girl.'

She didn't even ask Uncle Malcolm. She presented the child with a bare-faced statement, and held it out in my direction, so that its arms and legs waggled about for support. Having, with some difficulty, manoeuvred the baby into the crook of my arm, I cast Eva a reproachful glance, only to find her shaking with silent laughter. My annoyance at having had the tables so neatly turned on me gave way to amusement. For the first time since my arrival, my attention focused on the front of her pullover. Why hadn't I noticed earlier? Perhaps through having recently had a child, or merely as a result of the weight she had gained, the physical attributes for which she was particularly noted had expanded far beyond the limits of my recollection. Regardless of the pullover's heavy camouflage, the sudden burst of humour had injected them with a life of their own. They swung, trembled, jumped for joy till Eva, blushing slightly, checked their movement with folded arms. I was forced, there and then, to make a concentrated effort to control my emotions and remind myself of the detached, cynical relationship I had determined to establish, without which I was convinced my task would prove impossible. I returned the child to her and pretended to admire the garden while she settled it once more into the pram, then pushed pram and contents indoors. Once again in the kitchen, I watched her moving about, going through all the little domestic motions of preparing the child for bed. The world in which I had found her could not possibly have been so different from what I had imagined. Nevertheless, it intrigued me almost to the point of obsession. Where did the baby sleep? Why were the flour and biscuit tins painted blue? Who had chosen that particular make of washing machine? Although I scarcely felt at ease in that environment, I wanted more and more to be accepted, to be made to feel at home and therefore to be freed from my responsibility. What was to prevent me from spending a quiet, simple evening in my capacity of 'old friend'; indulging, should the occasion present itself, in a mild, harmless flirtation and taking my leave after supper with a promise to call again when Dave was at home? My own weakness of character horrified me. It was the feeling of my own indecision that took me by surprise, but what unsettled me even more was that I accepted it with what almost amounted to pleasure. Before she took the baby from the room, Eva turned.

'Would you like . . .?'

Not the traditional refuge. Not a cup of tea.

'. . . a can of beer? You'll find some in the fridge.'

I had hoped she would offer tea, and give me some foundation at least on which to rebuild my resolve. Nevertheless, I took the beer and, showing not the slightest respect for propriety, wandered in and out of the rooms on the ground floor. Eva was gone quite a while. I could hear her moving about upstairs, talking continually to the child, though it was clearly incapable of understanding her. A blue and white door led me into what she had described as their 'sitting room'. Here, she and Dave had evidently been allowed complete freedom of choice with regard to furnishings and decoration, and had done up the room in what they considered a modern, contemporary style. Taken individually, there was nothing at all objectionable in the various items of furniture, but some indefinable lack of subtlety in their arrangement, however, had endowed the room, when viewed as a whole, with a jarring, cluttered quality which I found immensely amusing. Displayed in cabinets and on shelves were trophies and souvenirs from every part of the world. Carved wooden elephants followed each other across the bookcase, the replica of a Red Indian peace-pipe hung on the wall next to a framed brass-rubbing from a Bangkok temple. Little coloured banners, embroidered with Chinese characters, served as table mats and the wide, white-washed cavity that had once formed the hearth held a splendid model junk in lacquered ebony. Approaching to study more closely the inlaid woodwork of its hull, my attention was caught suddenly by a framed photograph on the mantelpiece. At once, I was overcome by annoyance and embarrassment. Who had taken it? What right had these people to display such a picture? He was no relation of theirs. I was seized by a sudden desire to break the frame and destroy the coloured en print it contained, to push the deckhouse into Auckland harbour, and, at a stroke, get rid of the suntanned arms and short-stemmed pipe that seemed so at home behind glass on a stranger's mantelpiece. The framed print was in my hands, mere seconds away from ending its life against the tiles of the fireplace, when I heard footsteps and turned to find Eva standing in the doorway behind me. For some reason, she had changed into a red dress and brushed her hair in a manner that gave it more body, and was vaguely reminiscent, I told myself, of the style in which she had worn it just after leaving school. The effrontery of the photograph dispelled any misgivings I might have had about proceeding with my task. All I wanted now was to get it over with, collect the details, take the measurements and leave; however, it was clear that anger could achieve nothing. I would never reach my goal without considerable tact and diplomacy. To that end, I rose, replaced the photograph and complimented Eva on her appearance, taking care to mention the word 'elegant', which I remembered having been a favourite of hers in the past. She pushed aside the books and magazines littering the sofa opposite me, and sat down.

'I told you the room was in a mess.'

'Nonsense', I replied, 'it has a warm, lived-in atmosphere that I find quite charming. Did Dave bring back all of these splendid ornaments?'

'Most of them,' she said, 'but, of course, I chose some of them myself when I was in Japan.'

The voyage she had made with her husband to the Far East had deeply impressed her. For almost an hour, she talked happily about her experiences ashore and on board ship, affording me the perfect opportunity to probe gently beneath the surface and, through chance remarks and indirect, light-hearted questions, discover something of the true relationship between Dave Sinclair and herself. Once the initial bashful-ness of discussing her husband in the presence of another man had been dispelled, she started to speak with complete freedom about their life together, letting herself be carried away by memories while I listened appreciatively, secretly watching out for any sign of weakness or disharmony, any chink in the armour, through which I could press home my advantage and win her co-operation. With disarming frank-ness, she explained that she was very fond of Dave and, now that they had a family, found plenty with which to occupy herself when he was away.

'It's difficult at times.' she said, 'living with relations, but, of course, when Dave gets a command, we'll buy a house of our own.'

'Up here?'

'Oh dear, I hope not. It's so quiet. I'd rather like to move down to Edinburgh. There are some lovely houses in places like Barnton and Cramond. Do you stay in Edinburgh these days?'

When I explained that I owned a Georgian house in the New Town, she went into raptures, and insisted that I describe to her every detail of the furnishings and colour scheme. Thus, I discovered that in her attitude to housing, Eva had, in fourteen years, adopted a status-consciousness that bordered closely on snobbery. Similarly, and I pride myself that, in this respect, I could still detect a trace of my early influence, her attitude to aesthetics and the arts fell into a closely defined pattern with which she clearly hoped I would agree. When, for any reason, I disagreed, she hastily modified her argument to include my point of view, thus emphasising that, as far as art was concerned, she trusted my judgment implicitly. This in itself was a great step forward. While she prepared a light meal, I excused myself, fetched my attaché case from the car and laid out on the table before her a series of photographic enlargements depicting my major sculptures. As I put down each picture, I listed the name of the work, its size, the material of which it was constructed and its date of completion. Finally, with a theatrical flourish, I threw down the last picture. Not a photograph this time, but a sketch I had drawn when planning the uncompleted mural. A sketch done from memory, helped only by the tiny photograph of a hockey player in an old school magazine. A bold sketch in flesh-coloured chalks of a nude, in curved, swelling lines. A sketch, in fact, of Eva Sinclair, née Cameron, as naked as the day she was born. Eva's cheeks were flushed, perhaps through embarrassment but, more likely I thought, through excitement which caught the words in her throat and would not let her tear her eyes from the little sheet of cartridge paper. Leaning over her shoulder, I said softly, '*The Second Element*; Life-sized; Waxwork: to be completed approximately six months hence.'

In showing her my previous work, I had hoped, to some extent, to convince her of the authenticity of my efforts. To prove, if you like, that I was an artist of some standing, for whom it should be considered an honour to sit. Now, I was obliged to fall back on less substantial reasons, play up to her emotions, appeal to her vanity. Words like 'intrinsic innocence of art', 'purity of form', 'simplicity of line' tumbled from my lips. I sought out her deepest self-deceptions, shaped my argument around them and then, with the aid of far from logical rhetoric, refuted each objection she raised to the scheme.

'But how did you do this? You've never seen me completely undressed.'

'That's why it's so bad.'

'No. It's not bad.'

'But with the subject so close at hand, a hundred

ridiculous flaws stand out clearly. It makes me want to do so much better.'

'A waxwork,' she murmured. 'Surely you can't do that here. How long would it take you?'

'A couple of hours at most to get all the information I need.' I patted the attaché case. 'After that, I won't have to trouble you again.'

'What will Dave say? What if he finds out?'

'He already knows,' I whispered. 'Before I even considered coming here, I made a point of gaining his consent.'

Eva's principles were, like most people's, based rather on irrational suggestion than clear, logical thought. Though still apprehensive and shy, the opportunity to appear as a real work of art undoubtedly attracted her. I did not find it at all difficult, under such circumstances, to combine with the idea of 'purity of purpose' and 'artistic zeal', behaviour which, seen through less star-clouded eyes than Eva's, could easily have been interpreted as debased, immoral and well-nigh adulterous. Quite unintentionally, she made me play my trump card and, from that moment, I knew she could not back down.

'Why are you calling it *The Second Element?*'

I had not omitted to pack a stick of crayon in the attaché case. With long, fluid lines, I sketched round the imaginary, nude Eva, lines which were far from imaginary in conception. I put the little figure in perspective, framed it in a natural cradle between tragus and anti-helix, thrust it like a stopper into the centre of *The First Element*, and in so doing, thrust Eva into the past, where seagulls combined with cement dust and shooting sparks vied with red-lead. My purpose had been achieved. Without acting in any way like a bully, I had channelled Eva's actions exactly to suit my requirements, though she, at all times, had been motivated solely by the desire to act in accordance with her own deep-seated self-deceptions. I watched as Eva closed the curtains on a bright evening sky.

Measurements

MALCOLM LESLIE

Eva Sinclair, née Cameron, undressed with her back towards me, facing the orange velvet curtains at the end of the room. She performed the function neither more nor less awkwardly than countless others who, in my fourteen years as an artist, have presented their bodies before me to have them transmuted by chalk, charcoal, paint or clay into what people are pleased to call a work of art. Eva Sinclair, née Cameron, removed from her body in the following order, a red dress with black braid round the hem, a size forty, C-cup brassière, a stretch nylon pantie-girdle, two size five high-heeled mauve suede shoes, a pair of honey coloured tights with a small ladder in one toe and a twenty-one jewel ladies' Omega wrist watch. Eva Sinclair, née Cameron, placed the above items one by one on a chair, then turned to face me. It is generally supposed that artists, like doctors, have the capacity to examine a body in a remote, professional light, completely detached from the dictates of feelings or emotions. This is only true, I maintain, if the object under scrutiny also adopts a completely passive and disinterested role. The moment either of the parties gives way, admits the humanity of the other, there is an immediate breakdown in the code and the rapport necessary for an efficient working relationship is jeopardised. I therefore made a great mental effort to sever emotion from intellectual skill, and to approach my subject strictly from the latter viewpoint. With clinical control, I extracted calipers, tape measure and Polaroid camera from my case, opened my loose-leaf notebook at a fresh page and twisted down the lead in my propelling pencil.

'Subject: Sinclair, Eva, née Cameron. Sex: Female. Age: approximately thirty-two years. Weight: one hundred and forty-eight pounds.'

I saw a female body, white, smooth and somewhat deteriorated through age and having borne a child. I raised the camera, pressed the button and framed my subject in a rectangle. But Eva wanted more. She wanted to smile at the camera, to examine the instant photograph when I peeled it from its backing paper. She wanted to look, to giggle, to move about and thereby transform herself from Subject: Sinclair, Eva, née Cameron, into a pin-up model, a cheesecake whore. My eyes had seen a female body, but the camera, lying, true-to-life machine, had thrown up in my face an image of unbridled sensuality, a glowing, proud Hippolyta, too ripe and overblown for fashionable beauty.

'Once again, Eva. Turn around, Eva.' Where she had previously bounced, she wobbled, laughing at the shivers that trembled through her vast protuberances of flesh. I spun the dial, punctuated the silence with silent, blue flashes, rotated her through three-hundred and sixty degrees, charted her contours, committed the bend of her legs, the curve of her belly and breasts to four inch by five inch rectangles of sensitised paper. And as, section by section, Eva's body was dismantled and stored for safe keeping in my notebook, she became less and less inhibited till I almost despaired of completing the task. 'Stand up straight, Eva. I must take accurate measurements.'

I walked round Subject: Sinclair, Eva, née Cameron, trying, with my eyes, to transubstantiate her into a blend of beeswax and carnauba wax.

'Crown of head to ground: sixty-four and three quarter inches.'

Obligingly, she held the end of the tape while I stooped down and, for a moment, smelled the slightest scent of almonds near my face.

'Crown of head to chin: eleven and three-quarter inches. Crown of head to top of breast bone: eighteen and a half inches.'

Under the scrutiny of calipers and tape measure, Eva decided to lay bare her soul to match her body, and fell to raising spectres from the past.

'Fourteen years. What a pity it has taken so long. And who

would have imagined our reunion to be like this? We should have corresponded in the early days. Do you remember how we promised ... but somehow, with Dave and everything, it didn't seem worth while ... '

'Crown of head to navel: thirty inches.'

'... and when we moved up here, we simply lost touch. Not only with you, but with everyone we had known at school. You probably imagine that the affair with the tree made me leave you for Dave. I know it must have seemed so at the time, but surely our paths were already diverging ...'

'Crown of head to crotch: forty and a half inches.'

'... and no one can be held to blame for that. It seems to me the teacher was at fault. He should have spoken out and claimed responsibility before it was too late.'

My fingers prodded her pliant flesh, seeking out points of reference.

'Distance between left and right acromion processes: twelve inches. Let's not talk about it. What's past is past. Let sleeping dogs lie.' And for her benefit, I conjured up Rufus—Half Man Half Dog, whose shattered limbs were to supply the waxen likeness of her features. I filled the space between orange carpet and orange ceiling with a verbal procession of The Magnificent Parade of Terror, took her on a journey which began at Manchester, detoured round Newmarket and ended up aboard a steamer on the Baltic Coast. I drew comparisons between her hair and that of novices about to take their vows in holy orders.

'Left acromion process to left nipple: ten and five eighths inches. Right acromion process to right nipple: ten and a half inches.'

With sharp, jagged pencil marks on virgin paper, I found my way out of the sanctified pine wood. By presenting to her the colourful history of the materials which were to take the form of *The Second Element*, I sought to emphasise the drab existence of my subject and bring her once more under my control.

'The triangle between nipples and navel: eight and a half inches, ten and three quarter inches, ten and a half inches.'

Stepping back, I strove to visualise the figure mounted in

its proper place, illuminated by lights concealed in the crevasses of a fibre-glass ear. Alas, the background of mundane reality impinged on my vision, driving me close to distraction.

'Distance between iliac crests: nineteen inches.'

Images of domesticity, bizarre reminders of her husband leapt at me from the background, shattering the sterile, clinical conception in my brain. Chinese banners and an ebony junk could not be ignored. Sun-tanned arms and a short stemmed pipe watched me from above the fireplace. I saw a female body, but found myself imagining another presence in the cosy room in place of my own. I saw Sinclair, Eva, née Cameron, playing with Sinclair-child on the carpet, starching regulation shirts, sewing golden rings to dark blue doeskin and opening Eva-legs during protracted periods of well-earned leave.

'Left iliac crest to greater trochanter: six and a half inches. Right iliac crest to greater trochanter: six and a half inches.'

Sensing my distraction, she followed my glance to the mantelpiece.

'Dave met your grandfather in New Zealand. Such a nice old man. We're going to send him a picture of Maggie when she's a little older.' She spoke these words in complete innocence, without the slightest shadow of atonement. How could she possibly be free from complicity in the guilt? With stabbing pencil, I attacked the paper.

'Distance between the anterior superior spine of the ilium and the centre of the patella: eighteen inches.'

With jagged pencil lines, I bisected the sheet and between the certainties of anatomical measurement, I conducted an inquisition upon the uncertainties of the past.

'How old were you when you joined the swimming club? How many gulls swooped over the tidal basin when ... What colour were the bathing caps? When was there cement dust between your toes? Was it Jimmy Barrie or Sandy Syme who first called you by the nickname? Were there three or four performances of *A Midsummer Night's Dream*? And later, behind the swimming hut, was I the only one? Remember! Centre of the patella to medial malleolus at the instep: thirteen and three quarter inches. What were the names of the ships in harbour that night? Why did flames pick out the word "ΠΕΙΡΑΙΕΥΣ" on a rusty metal hull? How many sparks lost their lives in the tidal basin? And how did you clean the red-lead from your fingers before breakfast? The malleolar angle measures thirty-three degrees.'

Between anatomical certainties, to the right of a pencil line drawn in anger, I noted the indictment, amassed the total of her guilt. But throughout it all, Subject: Sinclair, Eva, née Cameron, could see no further than her nose, or, at best, the trembling tips of her gigantic breasts. When I had committed the last measurement to paper, she obediently stretched and pirouetted in front of me, allowing me to pinpoint every blemish on her skin.

'Small mole on the back, just below the left scapula. Shaves her armpits once a week. Six transverse stretch marks on the belly. A scar two inches long on the inside of the right ankle.'

And then the eyes. No tears, despite the recent memories. Only a slight dilation of the pupils, indicative perhaps, of her mounting excitement as I placed my hand over her forehead and turned her face towards the light.

'Eyes medium brown with a narrow, green halation round the iris. Whites clear, marked only slightly with traces of red in the corners.'

Perhaps because of the pressure of my cool hand against her forehead, perhaps through having stood so long under the cold penetration of my stare, Eva suddenly threw her arms round me, longing for my frank, clinical appraisal to be supplemented by warm caresses. The sudden onslaught quite took me aback. To steady myself, I clasped my arms round her waist and found myself supporting the entire bulk of her body while, regardless of my protests, she kissed me with a moist mouth and sensually impatient tongue. Thus intertwined, we stumbled across the room till something caught me behind the knees and sent me sprawling on the couch with Eva firmly locked above me. My mind was in turmoil. From the outset I had feared something of this nature, but had naively assumed that I would more likely succumb to the temptation than she. Of course I was playing a dangerous game. Had I not wanted to steal from Dave Sinclair, coldly, calculatingly like a thief, the very essence of his domestic existence? Had I not wanted to make public every angle, every facet, every secret blemish of his wife's body? But now that she lay over me, thrusting her breasts in my face and murmuring, 'Malcolm, Malcolm, Malcolm, do you still love me?' I recoiled in horror at the very enormity of the situation. To conclude a perfectly conceived exercise in revenge, the result of years of planning, in a welter of commonplace adultery was unforgivable. Yes. I wanted to steal Dave Sinclair's most treasured possession, to ransack his thirteenth bower, but all the satisfaction lay in picking the lock, not in blowing the door from its hinges with gelignite.

Grasping Eva's shoulders, I pushed her away from me. 'Not now, Cans. Not now. I'm not finished.' Why, for the first time in my life, did I use the nickname, the common, four-lettered name that had so incensed me fourteen years before? If it had arisen from some unconscious attempt to humiliate her, it was unsuccessful. Eva sat back on her heels and watched me picking up my scattered notes from the floor. My fingers trembled as I stuffed the notebook and camera into my attaché case. I wished for nothing but that the ensuing moments should pass as quickly as possible, that I should be released and free to drive off into my own life without a backward glance at the wreckage I had caused. I didn't want to touch Eva's body again, not even to look at her face, flushed and apprehensive on the couch. I wanted to forget the real Eva and get to grips with her waxen image, which would be truer than life, much more predictable and in no way given to unbridled outbursts of adulterous passion. Only one thing remained to be done. One detail to complete the dossier. 'Have you a pair of scissors in the house?' My question seemed to surprise her, to bring her back, perhaps, to the reality that she was sitting naked, cross-legged on a sofa in her own house before a man who was not her husband, and who, for fourteen years, had claimed no more than a fleeting moment in her thoughts.

'Scissors?'

'Yes. I need some samples of your hair.'

Slowly, Subject: Sinclair, Eva, née Cameron, rose from

the couch, massaging the red weals where I had gripped her shoulders. She padded out of the room, stubby toes deep in the pile of the orange carpet, and I packed up the remainder of my belongings ready to leave. When she returned, a familiar Chinese dressing gown concealed her body. The realisation that I was about to leave, that, after all, I had merely wanted her as a subject on which to practise my professional skills, had sobered her. Thankfully, she made no attempt to catch my eye. In each hand, she held a little bundle of hair and, as she offered them to me, asked, 'Will I be able to see it when it's finished?'

More to myself than to Eva, I said, 'I'll send you an invitation to the unveiling . . .' and took the bundles, one soft and glistening dark brown, the other reddish and slightly redolent of toasted almonds.

Part Two
THE THIRD OFFICER'S STORY

KG5

King's Cross Station, 5.45 am. I edged my two suitcases as far forward as the crowd round the trolley would permit and shouted over the head of a grubby little man for a cup of coffee. The white plastic buttons on the fat negress's off-white overall strained against the mass of winter coats and sweaters it was their duty to contain. She rolled her eyes and applied herself to the glass-covered box of congealing pies on her right. At the third attempt, I caught her undivided attention and, perilously close to the ear of the grubby little man, exchanged a pound note for a plastic cup of scalding amber liquid. A good inch of this liquid had found its way, via my sleeve, to the concrete floor of the station before I realised that all was not well. The negress was holding up my note between two greasy fingers, peering at it as if it were something obscene, and rolling her eyes till all I could see were their whites, floating in a smudge of startlingly blue make-up.

'You only got Scotch ones? Don't like Scotch ones. Ain't ya got somethin' smaller?'

At the risk of causing permanent burn damage to the neck of the grubby little man, I might have attempted to extricate an acceptable Bank of England note from my wallet. At the risk of incurring the negress's eternal displeasure and vocative abuse, I might have suggested that King's Cross was a singularly unfortunate choice of venue for someone with an aversion to Scottish currency. As it was, I cursed and juggled desperately with the scalding cup, raising my eyes only when a nearby voice boomed out,

'Here, take it off this and gie the wee laddie his money back.'

The big man in the long black coat pushed forward, dextrously swept aside all opposition with his elbow and

completed the transaction, thrusting the unacceptable bank-
note into my top pocket.

'Gospel! Didn't expect to see you here,' I exclaimed.

'Aye. The *Skaith* is it? I'm joining her as well. And that's a
coffee you owe me, mind.'

He picked up one of my cases and I struggled after him
with the other to where his luggage was piled in a grimy British
Rail barrow. Jock Spence, nicknamed 'Gospel', from Aberdeen, sixty-one years old and eighteen stone. I had sailed with
him several times before, but only aboard the *Blairhall*, for on
the *Hall* Gospel had been as much a fixture as the derricks and
deckhouses. A radio officer for forty years, he had spent well
nigh twenty of them on that ship and, through time, had
become something of a legend in the company, though there
were conflicting opinions on whether the legend was good or
evil. We dumped my luggage on top of his and looked
dejectedly towards the open end of the station, through which
the wind drove gusting sheets of fine rain.

'We sold the *Hall* in Taiwan last trip,' he said, as if
anticipating my question. 'They flew everybody home. Chartered a bloody plane, they did.'

There was no sugar in my coffee and despite the burn
marks on my fingers, it was already growing cold. I put down
the cup at the bottom of a pillar and thrust my hands into my
trouser pockets. Gospel stared pensively into the drizzle.

'You have to go anywhere before joining?'

'No. I'm heading straight for the ship. I hardly slept at all
on the way down. What a bloody journey.'

'You should have come from Aberdeen.'

He took the drawbar of the barrow and I pushed it from
behind to where the last few passengers were queueing for
taxis. The driver slid down his window and shook his head.

'Can't take all that gear, mate.'

'Aye, you can,' said Gospel, heaving the first suitcase into
the taxi so that the vehicle rocked on its springs. 'King George
the Fifth Dock, Number Four shed.'

Outside the station, the rain seemed thicker, wetter.
Gospel adjusted his vast bulk on the seat, delved into the
folds of his famous black coat and produced a slip of paper

which he handed to me.

'A crew list. How the hell did you get a crew list?'

Shrugging his shoulders, Gospel smiled knowingly. Twenty years in the company give one certain privileges. I held the paper steady and let my eyes run down the typed list of ranks and names.

SS BLAIRSKAITH — LONDON
List of European Crew

Master: D H Sinclair *Stonehaven*
1st Officer: A Brown *Musselburgh*
2nd Officer: I P Gow *Lossiemouth*
3rd Officer: A K Dewar *Perth*
Senior Cadet: R R Hislop *Edinburgh*
2nd Cadet: G O St John-Browne *Sevenoaks, Kent*
3rd Cadet: T Walker *Bristol*
Radio Officer: J T Spence *Aberdeen*
Trainee Radio Officer: W Muir *Leith*
Chief Engineer: P A Stenhouse *Dundee*
2nd Engineer: J Mackintosh *Glasgow*
3rd Engineer: W R Graham *Greenock*
4th Engineer: A Sutherland *Clydebank*
5th Engineer: R E Walls *Liverpool*
6th Engineer: N A MacLeod *Barra*
7th Engineer: W T Wood *Birkenhead*
1st Electrician: B McAvoy *Glasgow*
2nd Electrician: G A Kirk *Oban*

'D H Sinclair. Wasn't he mate on the *Blair Drummond?* This must be his first command.'

'His first voyage, anyway. He did a relief coast as Old Man on the *Hall* just before we took her out east for the last time.'

A young master. That was a change. Quite by chance, the last four captains under whom I had sailed had all been well over fifty and, though I appreciated that junior officers were liable to be posted throughout the fleet more or less at random, I could not help regarding myself as having recently been somewhat overexposed to traditionalism and entrenched attitudes of command. Similarly, the names of the senior and third cadet served, to some degree, to brighten the gloom that had descended on me since leaving home. My most vivid recollection of Roddy Hislop was of a dishevelled figure trying, with the aid of a streetsweeper's broom, to fish his shoe from the Water of Leith before it disappeared into the slime. Roddy had been in no way to blame when the head of the broom chose to part company with its shaft and submerge along with the shoe; but the streetsweeper had not seen matters in the same light. Had a policeman not been immediately to hand, Roddy might well have been spared the unfortunate incident in the cells when, in attempting to signal to his anxious friends outside the station, his remaining shoe had flown from his grasp and projected itself through a window which happened to be closed at the time. Little wonder that such an unnerving experience had taken its toll during the oral examinations next day. Though Roddy modestly laid the blame on the stammer, with which he had been afflicted since birth, I am convinced that, had it not been for the shoes, he too would certainly have been in possession of a Certificate of Competency, Second Mate (Foreign Going) and no longer heading the list of cadets.

Tom Walker, named as third cadet on Gospel's crumpled list, had a quite different reputation in the company. Although he had been at sea barely two years, his fame as a fanatical teetotaller had spread before him and, like most stories based on hearsay rather than accurate information, given rise to countless ludicrous anecdotes concerning the lengths to which he would go to prevent alcohol touching his lips. In fact, his reason for strict abstention was quite simply that any form of alcohol made him violently ill. On Tom Walker's first voyage, I had been senior cadet aboard the *Blairholm*, and well remembered the incident when we finally succeeded in spiking his orange juice with gin. He had been confined to his bunk for three days, while the remaining cadet and I were obliged to work overtime to complete his duties.

Attempting to make conversation, I mentioned the incident to Gospel, whose only reaction was a muffled snort. It was no time for joking. The rain swept across Commercial Road in great, grey sheets, driven by a wind that came from every direction at once. The taxi rattled through the spray like a ship, almost alone between the drab, grey buildings. On Silvertown Way, a huge lorry pulled out in front of us without warning. The taxi slithered to a halt and our driver stalled his engine. We were still sitting there ten minutes later. At 7.05 am, we arrived at the ship. Gospel reached the top of the gangway with a great wheeze and crashed his cases down on deck.

'All that and he wanted a tip! Tip him in the bloody dock.'

Joining ship. Two words that between them suggest bustle, activity, excitement, the anticipation of far horizons or, if one is closer to the realities of life at sea, merely introductions, evaluations, work, the end of a leave. As is usual with our company, *Blairskaith*'s complement was made up of European officers and a Chinese crew. The system worked well. Since they first began trading with the Far East early last century, Blair Lines had gone to great pains to build up a cordial and mutually advantageous relationship with the people of Hong Kong. Through the years, the company had developed what the Chairman, in his annual report, was pleased to call a 'dual nationality', in that the Head Office and European Crew Department were in the United Kingdom and a large subsidiary office with the Chinese Crew Department was in the Crown Colony. Though this state of affairs was frequently more reminiscent of a split personality, there nevertheless existed between the two races aboard each vessel a code of respect and proper conduct which, if adhered to, made for a happy ship and a high standard of efficiency.

At the door of my cabin, a steward was stacking suitcases in the alleyway. Clearly, the Third Officer whom I was relieving had not yet gone ashore. I struggled past and set about arranging my belongings. Presently, the Chinaman's head appeared in the doorway. He grinned, disclosing five enamelled teeth, two red, three blue, each set with a yellow-gold centre.

'I your steward, Leung Wing Pa,' he said importantly. 'Other Sam-fo in smokeroom. I fix your things. I fix.'

And so it all began. Joining ship and everything these two words entail. Fundamentally, the sea has much in common with every other profession. I was quite simply starting a new job, and behaved in exactly the same pattern as anyone in a similar position ashore. I introduced myself to my colleagues, discussed particular aspects of the ship with my predecessor, made new acquaintances and renewed old ones, inspected equipment, found my way about. In every respect, SS *Blairskaith*, berthed opposite Number Four Shed, King George the Fifth Dock, was a perfectly average 14 650 ton general cargo vessel. She was manned by characters neither more nor less interesting than any others with whom I had sailed, and who combined to form a perfectly average crew. Every indication suggested that we could expect a perfectly average voyage.

Just before lunch, Roddy Hislop stuck his head round the door of the smokeroom. 'Here Andrew, have a look at this.'

I followed him into the alleyway and the Second Mate stubbed out his cigarette and ambled after us. The rain had stopped and the dockers were working again at the forward hatches. On the quay, a white Mercedes sports car was edging its way between the lorries and trailers towards the bottom of the gangway. From the deck of the ship, it was impossible to see who was at the wheel of the little car, but the whistles and gestures of the dockers suggested that the opulent vehicle conveyed something of considerable interest. The Mercedes pulled up directly below us and from the driver's door there emerged first one, then another long white boot, an astonishing expanse of thigh and a short fur coat, topped by a mop of shoulder-length blonde hair. No one paid much attention to the thin young man who stepped out of the passenger seat, for the blonde was bending over the boot, removing boxes and cases and consequently exposing a further stretch of thigh to the dockers, a dozen of whom had gravitated to the end of the gangway.

'Any wives or passengers this trip?' Roddy Hislop glanced hopefully at the Second Mate.

'No. Not that I know of.'

Between them, the blonde and the thin young man hauled a vast cabin trunk from the little car and struggled with it to the bottom of the steps. Urged on by his mates, one of the dockers doffed his cap and offered to carry the trunk aboard.

He was more than half way up the gangway before he realised that the blonde had no intention of following him. She remained on the quay, exchanged a few words with the thin young man, hugged him swiftly and ran back to the car. As she drove off, she blew a kiss through the open window. When the docker met the thin young man on deck, he made a remark that was far from complimentary and left the newcomer standing before us in a state of considerable embarrassment. The Second Mate took his hands from his pockets.

'Crew?'

'Giles St John-Browne, second cadet.'

The Second Mate said, 'Show him his cabin, Mister Hislop, and let's go to lunch.'

Going down the starboard alleyway, the cabin trunk piled high with suitcases between them, Roddy Hislop said, 'Your girl looks quite a cracker. A real bit of class.'

The colour rose slightly in the second cadet's pallid face. 'Oh, yes. Yes, of course.'

'Known her long, then? She can't be short of loot to afford a wagon like that, or is it her father's?' They stopped outside the cabin St John-Browne was to share with the third cadet.

'It's hers, all right. She's a fashion model, actually. We met up West. There's a great deal of money to be made in modelling these days, so Shirley does quite comfortably.'

'I'll bet she does.'

Arthur Brown, the First Mate, dabbed his mouth with a napkin and stroked his beard. It was a particularly well kept beard, full and trimmed to a point in the style of Edward the Seventh, who was in Arthur Brown's opinion, the most splendid monarch who had ever ruled Britain and a fitting character on which an officer and gentleman could model himself. Arthur and I had been at Nautical College together and, although he was studying for his master's ticket while I was merely up for second mate's, he had invited me to his home on several occasions for a meal. His wife was a fat, jolly girl with a passion for antiques and a flair for exotic cooking. Every room in their little house in Musselburgh was festooned with pictures in old frames, gilt mirrors and heavy mahogany furniture which went well with the substantial air of their owners. It occurred to me that Arthur could not be much younger than D H Sinclair, our new master. Perhaps he was even a few months older. I wondered how long it would be before he too was given a command.

'The Old Man's due aboard at seven tonight', Arthur said, 'and we sail at eleven tomorrow morning.'

I worked until six o'clock, then changed and went up the road with Roddy Hislop, John Mackintosh the Second Engineer, and the trainee radio officer, who had never sailed with our company before. The latter spent all evening talking about the North Atlantic run, which he considered vastly preferable to the Far East. We didn't argue with him. He would learn through time. The pub in Wapping was an old dockside inn which had recently been modernised by a large brewery. It was suffering from a revival, and we had to pick our way between MGs and Jaguars to reach the door. Inside, we found a corner as far as possible from the juke box, but which offered an unrestricted view of the middle-class talent lining the bar. The sparky brought up the pints.

'Plenty of skirt in here tonight, eh?' said the engineer. 'Better than what you get in New York.'

The sparky cast a jaundiced eye over the giggling crowd by the bar.

'All fur coats and no knickers, that lot,' he said. 'The States beats London hands down.'

'You want to go to Dennistoun Palais,' Mackintosh replied, and concentrated on his pint.

'What's wrong with British birds, then?' Roddy Hislop said, looking at the girls. 'Bet you wouldn't say no to a leg over Nigel's fancy woman.'

'Giles,' I corrected him. 'His name's Giles St John-Browne. According to the crew list, he comes from Kent.'

'Bloody English,' muttered the engineer.

'B b bloody nice bit of crumpet, though. I never thought she'd get all that leg into her wee car. And all that gear he had too. Cameras, binoculars, stereo record player, he's like a walking department store.'

'Who is?'

'St George-Dragon.'

'Must have friends in the company.'

'You never know.'

When we left, before closing time, the rain had started again. It took twenty minutes to find a taxi.

At 07.45 next morning, I knocked and entered Captain David H Sinclair's dayroom to fill in the master's draught book. The Old Man was sitting at the writing desk, the sheaf of papers before him gleamed in the yellow light of his desk lamp. He rose when I came in. I stepped across to the book and introduced myself.

'Andrew Dewar, Third Officer, sir.'

He was even younger than I had expected, perhaps thirty or thirty-two at the most and extremely powerfully built. I noticed the four new gold rings on the sleeves of the jacket hanging on the back of his chair. The Old Man intercepted my glance and the trace of a smile lingered for a moment on his face.

'Eighteen feet six inches forward, twenty-two feet aft.'

He looked over my shoulder as I entered the figures in the book.

'You're from Perth, Mister Dewar?'

'Yes, sir.'

'I came down from Stonehaven today. The weather's just as bad there. Still, we'll soon be away from it all. How long have you been with the company?'

'Seven years, sir. I joined as a cadet.'

'Ever sailed on the *Skaith* before?'

'No, but I've done five voyages on her sister ship the *Blairlogie*.'

'Then you should know your way around this one. Both ships are identical and all the navigational equipment is the same.' He took a packet of cigarettes from his shirt pocket and offered me one. When I declined, explaining that I had given up smoking, he nodded and resumed his seat at the desk. 'Wise man. I'm trying to cut down myself.' I turned to go, but as I reached the door, he said, 'One moment, Mister Dewar.' He held his cigarette lighter out in front of him between thumb and forefinger, so that the flame licked round the casing and high into the air. 'Do you know what this is, Mister Dewar?'

'I'm afraid I don't quite ... '

'Fire, Mister Dewar. Fire. Whether aboard ship or on shore, its danger can't be overemphasised. I have seen what fire can do. I have watched flames eating boards and tarred paper. I have seen a man fighting them with an empty extinguisher and, believe me, Mister Dewar, it's damned well not going to happen aboard my ship.'

'I checked the fire-fighting gear yesterday, sir.'

'But not, it seems, in the passengers' saloon.'

'Yes, sir. The extinguisher's brand new. I read the label.'

The Old Man stared for a moment at the flame, then flicked his lighter closed with a snap. 'The label said it was brand new, but not that it was empty. Next time, take the lid off. See that it's replaced and you'd better check the rest of the gear again. That's all.'

I stood by the engine-room telegraph in the wheelhouse and watched the rain cascading down the bridge windows as the little grey tug nudged us into the river. It was all grey, the tug, the wharfs, the warehouses, the river and the vast foredeck of the *Blairskaith*. My gaze travelled from Li Sau, the Chinese quartermaster, past the pilot standing at his shoulder and rested on the Old Man, close up to the windows, peering through the clear-view screen. His coat was wet from the rain on the wing of the bridge.

'Everything all right, Mister?'

'All right, sir.'

A perfectly average ship. Quite simply starting a new job.

London–Dakar

Hail, bright abode, where song the heart rejoices,
May lays of peace in thee never fail,
Long may we cry with loyal voices,
Prince of Thuringia, Landgraf Hermann, Hail!

The chorus of the Metropolitan Opera hurled their voices against the three-inch oak door of the junior cadets' cabin and fought a losing battle with the low hum of machinery in the starboard alleyway. Leung Wing Pa lurched down the white painted passage on his way to the laundry with an armful of dirty linen. He stood aside to let me pass, and as I drew level, twisted his features into a grimace and poked one finger of his free hand into his ear.

'Singin' music no good,' he said, grinning broadly.

'That's grand opera, Wing. You should listen to it. Get some culture into your life.'

'Culture no good. Sound like cats.'

A wind had come up and the ship rolled lazily as she nosed into the swell. I went up to the next deck, past the dark, empty passenger accommodation, and climbed the companion way that led to the wheelhouse. At the top of the steps, Arthur Brown was shaking water from his oilskins.

'Looks like we're in for a blow.'

I took the oilskin coat from the First Mate, pulled it on over my uniform jacket and went out on to the starboard wing of the bridge. It was very dark, pitch black and overcast with no stars. Arthur joined me and we stood listening to the rushing of the black water and the wind whipping over the dodgers and humming in the aerials overhead. We were well into the Bay of Biscay and making a steady fifteen knots.

'Who's in the fun palace tonight, then?'

'It's pretty quiet. Roddy and the second sparky were there, and the leckies are playing the plumbers at Scrabble. If the excitement gets too much for you, St John-Browne's giving a grand opera in the cadets' cabin.'

'Jesus Christ! Not again,' exclaimed Tom Walker, the junior cadet, who emerged from the chartroom. 'He played that bloody thing all the way down the Channel. I'll wrap his record player round his bloody neck.'

The First Mate looked up from the radar and raised his eyebrows. 'Come, come, Mister. We don't often have the chance to sail with an intellectual.'

'I'll have one orange juice in the bar,' the cadet muttered darkly, 'and if he doesn't turn it off after that, I'll turn him off for good! My exams are more important than his damned opera.'

The watch was changed. Li Sau took his place at the wheel and the quartermaster whom he had relieved reported and left the bridge. Roddy Hislop appeared, buttoning up his jacket. As he passed Tom Walker on the companion way, he said, 'I hear Giles has organised a special wee concert, just for you.' The First Mate's laughter faded into the distance, leaving the wheelhouse in silence, save for the muffled, monotonous rushing of wind and sea.

About half an hour later, the radio officer came into the chartroom and, with great solemnity, placed a slip of paper bearing a radio message on the table before me. His face had the serene, tranquil expression of a man who, assured of his own salvation, views the quirks and foibles of less grace-favoured mortals with benign tolerance. I read the message.

'TTT Storm Warning = Biscay-Finisterre SW Storm force 11 increasing force 12 imminent.'

Gospel fixed his eyes on the white deckhead of the chartroom and said, 'I doubt He's not very pleased with us this trip, boys. But I dare say it's all we deserve for spending our leaves in the sensuality of the tavern and bawdy-house instead of in His kirk.'

Solemnly, I filed the weather report and noted with amusement the amazed face of the senior cadet, who had overheard Gospel's remarks from the doorway. Jock Spence was, indeed, an amazing radio officer. Perhaps through a genuine, deep-seated conviction, or more likely to relieve the boredom of lonely watches in the radio shack, it was his custom to attribute all messages of a portentous nature to an authority considerably greater than the meteorological transmitter at Portishead. Gospel had been the *Blairhall*'s self-appointed link with the Almighty. And now that the immaculate crew department in the sky had ordained a change of ship, Gospel was clearly resolved to bestow on the *Blairskaith* all the benefits of his unique liaison. Granted, there was always a twinkle in his eye which suggested that his inspiration was as likely to stem from a bizarre sense of humour as from divine pre-destination, but to my knowledge no one had ever dared to question him closely on the subject. Several masters who had encountered him suspected that in matters of extreme urgency Gospel took instructions directly from above, by-passing the meteorological transmitter altogether, and they organised elaborate spot checks to catch him out. On each occasion, Gospel's information proved completely sound and the masters retired in confusion to await the next grace-filled message. Furthermore, Gospel's unique rapport with the Almighty naturally gave him access to all manner of information not usually divulged to ordinary radio officers in the merchant service. Out of the blue, he could predict ship movements, destinations, cargoes and even leave arrangements with deadly accuracy, and while certain sceptics maintained that his years of experience had simply enabled him to break the private code used between the master and the company, the majority of the crew was happy to accept Gospel's own explanation and believed implicitly the titbits he let drop, as if by accident, in the bar.

'See what you can do about it, Gospel.' He shrugged his shoulders and turned to leave the chartroom.

'I'll try, Third, but it'll not be easy.'

Roddy Hislop waited till the sliding door had rolled shut. 'He's clean off his head.'

'Sparkies are all like that. It's sitting on your own listening to other people talking that does it. They all go off eventually.'

'You don't say.'

'Call the engine room and check how many revs we're doing. I'll let the Old Man know we're in for a force twelve.'

There was nothing to it. There seldom is. The wind, as predicted, increased to gale force twelve, and with it, the sea rose till silver spray pitched high over the bows to spread in a regular, glistening sheet across the darkness of the foredecks. The *Blairskaith* shuddered from the impact of the waves, but her rolling was scarcely sufficient to disturb my mug of cocoa on the edge of the chartroom table. At 21.45 the Old Man came into the wheelhouse, made certain that we were in danger neither from the weather nor from traffic in our vicinity, then stationed himself close against the wheelhouse windows, beckoning me to join him. The wind had brought with it a fine, dampening rain that coursed obliquely down the heavy glass panes in dark, shimmering rivulets. Captain David H Sinclair gazed through the watery screen to the smudge of white where our bows met the sea and said, more to himself than to me, 'Nothing. Nothing at all. We took the *129* through worse than this in the mouth of the Forth.'

'The *129*, sir?'

'A motor fishing vessel. All of fifty tons, she was, but one of the handiest wee boats I ever sailed in. Were you ever in the Sea Cadet Corps, Third?'

'No, sir. Our school had an army cadet unit, so I didn't get the chance.' For the first time in years, I recalled endless drilling on the playing fields, monotonous weekend camps near Pitlochry and the handful of teachers-cum-officers who saw in the cadet force an opportunity to vent all the pent up anger and frustration so peculiar to their profession. To my mind, the only positive skill I had acquired during three years in the midget army was an embarrassingly obscure one. Nevertheless, I mentioned it self-consciously.

'They taught me to play the bagpipes.'

I had been expecting an outburst of laughter on the Old Man's part, but surprisingly his expression grew more grave. For a long while he directed his attention to the sea, and when at last he turned to face me, he spoke with great earnestness, as if I had touched off a spark within him.

'The finest seaman I know fought behind the bagpipes. In

the cold of Murmansk, caught between the ice-floes at Pechenga, they took a piper with them when they crossed the snow on sledges to fight the Bolsheviks for food and supplies. Imagine, Mister Dewar, the overwhelming whiteness of snow and sky, thirty sailormen and ten marines as helpless as ants save for the piper, countering the wind with his music, leading them towards the black dome of a monastery which held the only hope of food and shelter. Not that he was a real piper. The column was led across the ice by a stoker, second class, from Greenock, who had won the pipes in a card game at Gibraltar and taught himself to play. But that piper, who wore a seaman's cap, three greatcoats and rags over his boots; that piper, who lost two fingers through the cold, was to save my friend's life. Our sailors were unaware that the monastery was occupied by Finns who mistook the slowly advancing column for marauding Bolsheviks. Their bullets took the sailors completely by surprise. Just as the marines withdrew to bring up a heavy machine gun, my friend fell shot through the arm and he would certainly have died of cold and loss of blood had not the piper wrapped him in one of his own coats and continued to play, standing in full view of the Finnish snipers, until they realised that the foraging party was British and stopped firing.' Captain Sinclair's eyes were distant, his thoughts miles from the dimly-lit wheelhouse of the *Blairskaith*. 'If it hadn't been for that piper,' he said, 'I would not be where I am today. He saved the man who made me go to sea. He matched the *Atholl Highlanders* against the Arctic wind and left open the door to my whole existence. You are the piper on this ship, Mr Dewar. Live up to it.'

'You're both missing the point,' said Giles St John-Browne, drawing his knees up to his chin and clasping the can of beer more closely against his legs. 'Elizabeth's death lifts the curse from Tannhäuser. In the end, pure, sanctified love triumphs over the sensual attractions of Venus.'

Through the open scuttle, the disc of brilliant blue sky framed his head like a halo. The second electrician had not the slightest interest in grand opera, but as the smokeroom was deserted, he had followed the music to the cadets' cabin. Lazily, he narrowed his eyes and tossed his cigarette end over the table to land dead in the centre of the waste bucket.

'Then if Elizabeth wins,' he said with the deliberation of someone who has performed a considerable feat of deduction, 'why does she get killed at the end of it?'

Rather than find a reply to this extremely pertinent question, our host changed position on top of his bunk just sufficiently to lean over and extract another can from the case which lay on the edge of the day bed. Devoid of a head to support it, the blue patch took the shape of a perfect circle diagonally dissected by the lattice-work jib of a crane. Now and then, a puff of white smoke would join the jib and cut across the circular patch of sky from left to right, forming for an instant a white saltire on a blue field, before drifting away behind the green edge of the porthole curtain. The slightest change of position would have enabled me to trace the course of the smoke across the docks and over the roofs of the buildings beyond, but the view from Dakar Bunkering Berth Number Two scarcely merited the most modest expenditure of energy. I thought better of it and contented myself by saying to Giles, 'I bet Shirley's dead keen on the pure sanctified love bit.'

The second electrician spluttered into his beer.

'Do you play these records to her as well?'

Ever since her brief but memorable appearance in London, St John-Browne's girl friend had been a favourite topic of conversation aboard ship. Not that there had been anything particularly remarkable about her. In fact, Giles scarcely mentioned her himself and whenever her name cropped up, exhibited symptoms of such acute embarrassment that people were sure to bring it up once or twice a day simply to delight in his discomfiture. Maybe owing to his reticence, we found it difficult to imagine what a London fashion model could possibly see in a mere cadet in the merchant service, who seemed too thin, pale and stooping to have much success with the pushers on Commercial Road, far less with the ladies of fashionable Chelsea society. All manner of fictitious stories arose, circulated, were modified and embellished only to reappear again in a different form. Giles took it all in good part. He had little option, for human nature being what it is, the more vehemently he objected, the more ruthless would have been his persecution.

'Here's to Shirley,' the second electrician said. 'Long may her bum bounce.'

St John-Browne's face reddened, but rather than saying 'Cut it out lads,' or, 'Who wants a cig?', or trying in some other way to change the subject, he looked the lecky straight in the eye and said, 'Do you want to see it?'

'See what?'

'Her bum.'

The second electrician's jaw dropped. St John-Browne opened a drawer beneath his bunk, took out a glossy magazine and, after selecting the appropriate page, folded the remaining pages back on each other and threw it across the room to land on the electrician's lap. George Kirk pursed his lips.

'This isna' her. You're having me on. It says here that she's called Candice.'

'That would be the editors. They just say anything. Make up names to suit themselves.' He turned to me. 'Ask Andrew. He's seen her before. He'll tell you if it's her or not.'

The lecky passed me the folded magazine. On the front cover, the publication described itself as 'The best in sophisticated adult entertainment for men'. Sure enough, the young lady who disported herself in full colour over pages 28 to 32 bore considerable resemblance to the blonde-haired driver of the sports car in which Giles had arrived at the ship. This lady, however, had cast off fur coat and boots in favour of eight gentleman's watches, four on each sinuous arm, and a slim gold chain round her waist, from which hung a pocket knife, a gold-plated fountain pen, two cigarette lighters and several other unlikely articles of apparel intended to bestow on the unashamedly sexy photographs, the redeeming appearance of an advertising feature. Few readers, I imagine, could have paid much attention to the merchandise, for the girl's gleaming, naked body, contorted into a variety of poses loosely inspired by the classical ballet, demanded complete concentration. The caption read, 'Lovely Candice has done her

Christmas shopping early this year. But who needs Santa Claus when gifts come in a package like this?' Almost apologetically, the editors had added the prices of the various items at the foot of the page. I was reluctant to commit myself.

'It could be the same girl. Roddy got a closer look, though. Why not ask him?'

Giles snorted in exasperation.

'Just a moment.'

He rummaged in the drawer and came up with a little cardboard box full of thirty-five millimetre slides. One by one, he withdrew them and passed them round so that we could squint at them against the patch of light from the porthole. They had been taken on a lawn, where everyone was dressed in their finest clothes and grouped round a long table set with an expensive buffet meal. The men, with the exception of Giles who was in his uniform, wore morning coats with grey top hats. A society occasion, no less. Although most of the slides contained large groups of no interest to us, at least two showed the lady in question. They contrasted so ludicrously with her appearance in the magazine that neither the electrician nor myself could help laughing out loud. Standing daintily beside Giles the girl in the huge hat and demure pink dress looked as if butter would scarcely have melted in her mouth. I passed the slides to Giles, who packed them once more into the box.

'Now are you satisfied?'

The second electrician let a low whistle escape between his teeth. No matter how impossible it was to imagine Giles and Miss Shirley/Candice together, or how difficult it was to imagine Giles in any sexual context whatsoever, the evidence was undisputably there. The second electrician winked and picked up the magazine from the floor.

'Ye'll no be needin' this, then,' he said. 'It's like money in the bank. Ye don't need to see it to know it's there.'

More quickly than I had ever seen him move before, Giles leapt up and snatched wildly at the waving, glossy pages.

'Give it here! Come on, Kirk, it's mine.' Colour rushed to his cheeks. His face contorted till his nose stood out white in a blotch of red. Giles was almost six inches taller than Kirk, but whereas the cadet immediately adopted a traditional boxing stance, jabbing from right and left, the electrician was content to juggle to and fro like a fan dancer holding the offending publication above his head until a particularly well-placed punch landed on his face. In one movement, Kirk seized Giles round the waist and kicked out viciously at his legs. They lurched across the cabin, knocking books, glasses, empty beer cans to the floor. Giles puffed and wheezed and cursed and when, at last, helpless with laughter, the electrician released his hold on the tattered magazine, Giles grabbed the remnants of crumpled paper and hurled them through the open scuttle where the pages fluttered, one by one, into the murky, stinking water of Dakar harbour.

'Get out!' said Giles St John-Browne. 'Go away. Leave me alone.'

In the alleyway, the second electrician rubbed a swelling on his lower lip and said, 'I'll do that wee bastard one day.'

'No you won't,' I said, and walked down the oppressive, white-painted passage towards my cabin. Behind me, the sound of a record player at full volume reverberated against the sheet metal plates.

> To mortal combat I defy thee!
> Shameless blasphemer, draw thy sword.
> As brothers henceforth we deny thee,
> Thy words profane too long we've heard!
> If I of divine love have spoken,
> Strength'ning valour, sword and heart,
> Its glorious spell shall be unbroken
> Although from life this hour I part.

Dakar–Durban

Second Steward Li Yiu Mun was the Old Man's Tiger. It was his duty to attend the master in his cabin, to organise his laundry and wardrobe and serve at table when the captain chose to eat alone in his dayroom. Thus, Li Yiu Mun was of considerable consequence in the *Blairskaith*'s Chinese hierarchy, and was only happy if he knew every item of the captain's routine, every facet of his behaviour and the purpose and function of every one of his personal possessions. The Tiger went over to the scuttle, drew back the green sailcloth curtains and opened the porthole sufficiently wide to allow a dry, warm draught of air to dispel the stale tobacco smoke in the master's dayroom. For a moment, he looked down on the light grey bow of the ship cutting its way through the azure water of the South Atlantic, on the masts and deckhouses, on the group of sailors on the foredeck, busily splicing wire ropes under the watchful eye of Ho Man Tin, the bo'sun; then he turned and drew the curtains over the open scuttle so that their edges flapped listlessly in the breeze. Li Yiu Mun was not happy. Every aspect of Captain David H Sinclair's dayroom created an impression of orderliness, comfort and complete normality, yet the Tiger's expression was one of distinct uneasiness, as if somewhere in that scene of nautical domesticity there existed a threat to his own wellbeing. He flexed his knees ever so slightly in sympathy with the motion of the ship and stared fixedly at the top of the dresser. He had felt like this two years before when he was an ordinary steward aboard the *Blairholm*. On that voyage, the second mate had been to blame. Li Yiu Mun remembered the bad joss, remembered smelling the devils in the second mate's cabin. And when, crossing the equator, the second mate had removed a casket from his suitcase and, before the assembled ship's company, spread the ashes of his grandfather into the ship's shining wake, Li Yiu Mun remembered the fear. They had said it was a burial; the last request of an old seaman who had plied these waters under sail and steam for sixty years, but the bad joss was there. Despite the firecrackers and joss-sticks which the second mate allowed the Chinese to light in his cabin and the fireworks they set off regularly for two days, the devils had followed the *Blairholm* like a black, invisible streamer. For a whole week, no ship crossed their wake to sever the fatal link and on the eighth day, the number one painter had fallen to his death from the engine room catwalk. Li Yiu Mun remembered and peered towards the dresser with increased suspicion.

'Fix us a couple of gins, Yiu!'

In one movement, the Tiger whipped a white duster from under his left arm and ran it along the edge of the writing desk. His face once more became an expressionless mask. Crossing to the cabinet, he poured some gin into two glasses, added tonic and placed them before the master and the Chief Engineer, who sat down at the table. Captain Sinclair said,

'That'll be fine, Chief. It will help in making out the abstracts.' He sniffed his gin and raised his glass to the Chief Engineer. 'Now, how about a hand of cards, Peter?'

This was the Tiger's cue to leave them. He ran his duster a last time along the back of a chair, stepped out into the alleyway and closed the cabin door silently behind him. In the pantry at the end of the port passage he found Leung Wing Pa squatting with his back against the bulkhead, rolling himself a conical cigarette out of grey paper and thick, black tobacco. The Tiger crouched beside him, accepted a cigarette, and together they inhaled deeply through cupped hands. Humming gently, the ventilator muffled their excited voices and drew the two grey wisps of smoke through the metal grille overhead.

It was 13.25 on the seventh day out of Dakar. Beneath the ceiling of the officers' dining saloon, the large, white-enamel fan blades revolved languidly with insufficient force to disturb the heavy, oppressive atmosphere. Lunch was almost over. White-coated stewards were moving about between the tables, picking up dessert plates and empty coffee cups. Already several engineers had lit cigarettes and wandered through to the bar in the smokeroom. I watched the level of coffee in my half-empty cup rise first on one side then on the other at each gentle heave of the ship, leaving a tiny, irregular tidemark on the glossy china, and felt pleasantly drowsy. Diagonally opposite me across the table, Arthur Brown contemplated his last spoonful of pudding and said to no one in particular, or so it seemed to me:

'The best lobster thermidor I ever had was in the Philippines. A little restaurant in Manila, up at the back of town. Blessed if I can remember its name. There were only four tables, and you could see that the owner wasn't accustomed to serving Europeans, but what a spread he laid out for me. I wanted the recipe to take home to Pat. She's mad on sea food. The waiter didn't understand and brought us the bill instead. Christ! What a price! He really took us to the cleaners. I had to tap the Chief Engineer for my taxi fare back to the ship, but it was worth it just for those lobsters.'

'Port View Hotel, Port Swettenham,' said the Old Man, shaking his head. 'That's where you find the best sea food in the East.'

'I know the place,' said Gospel. 'Run by a Malay called Laurence, of all things.'

The Old Man grinned. 'That's right. I took the wife there one trip. He organised a special table for us, four waiters, chilled wine, liqueurs, the lot. Eva was really impressed. There's not much to attract a woman in Swettenham.'

'I've applied to take Pat along next voyage,' the First Mate said. 'The trouble is she can't stand too much heat. Even in Italy she went bright red and blistered all over. Something to do with her skin. However, I finally persuaded her, though I expect I'll spend the whole trip rubbing her with calamine lotion.'

'That should be fun,' said the Chief Engineer, rising to leave the table. 'If you get tired, I'm sure the boys will lend a hand.'

We all laughed and I pondered with amusement the prospect of Arthur Brown and his wife promenading under the awnings like King Edward the Seventh and Queen Alexandra aboard some long forgotten royal yacht. My own association with women was, at that time, divided fairly equally between two young Edinburgh ladies in the nursing profession and a girl from my home town, whom I had known from school days and had come to regard, without really having given the matter much thought, as my unofficial fiancée. One after the other, I pictured these girls in the role of wife aboard ship and speculated on their different reactions to such an alien, totally unfeminine environment. Surprisingly, the young lady who showed up least satisfactorily when subjected to this hypothetical comparison was the very one to whom I considered myself most permanently attached. Though the discovery neither pleased nor saddened me, I was sufficiently preoccupied by the subject of shipboard wives to mention it to Roddy Hislop when I joined him in the bar.

'When I was second cadet on the *Blair Drummond*,' Roddy said, carefully pouring beer from a can into a glass, 'we had David Sinclair's wife aboard for one trip.'

'The Old Man's wife?'

'He was first mate then. Must be about two years ago, maybe even more.'

'Her name's Eva, isn't it? He mentioned it at lunch.'

'So it is,' said Roddy, taking a long swig from the glass and wiping the foam from his upper lip with the back of his hand.

'She'd be quite young, too. It must have been okay having a young bird aboard. How did she look?'

Roddy wrinkled his brow and waved one hand in the air, as if caressing the side of a Grecian urn. 'Short, dark and busty,' he said. 'The kind that you can't keep your eyes off, and she knew it too. Used to do her bronzing on the monkey island in a white bikini that would hardly keep her tits in. But Mister Sinclair put a stop to that because the duty cadets were always finding excuses to go up there.'

'And I always thought you were a leg man.'

'There was nothing wrong with her legs either,' Roddy murmured, closing his eyes to assist his mental picture. 'In

Singapore, he bought her a cheong-sam with a high neck and slits right up the side. She used to wear it when they had drinks in the passenger saloon. Yes, sir. There was nothing wrong with her legs.'

For some reason that I cannot quite explain, the thought of Captain David Sinclair possessing an attractive, even sexy young wife rather astonished me. Of course, there was absolutely no reason for this not being the case. The Old Man was remarkably young for his position and quite handsome in a rough, monolithic way. However, in the two weeks that I had known him, his attention had seemed to focus so exclusively on the correct, efficient running of the ship that I had taken him for a rather dull, introspective person, completely expert at his job, but in no way liable to set the world on fire in either his official or private life. On the occasions when he had spoken to me on other than nautical matters, his conversation had consisted of an unusual blend of comic anecdotes and obscure, inward reflections that embarrassed us both. The story of the piper was typical. It was almost as if he needed an anchor, a solid point of reference round which to construct any informal dialogue. During the eight to twelve watches, when we found ourselves on the bridge together, he frequently returned to the same subject, mentioned old pipe tunes, asked my opinion of various Scottish melodies and, in general, left it to me to broaden the conversation and steer it along whichever path I chose. In short, he was a quiet, shy man whose authority over officers and crew was based on exceptional professional skill rather than a domineering personality. That evening, in view of what Roddy Hislop had told me, my curiosity was aroused. When I joined the Old Man on the wing of the bridge I spoke casually, keeping my eyes on the blue-black horizon.

'Your wife must be looking forward to another trip out East.'

By his tone, I could tell that I had surprised but not offended him.

'Not now,' he said. 'Not since the kiddie arrived. It's thirteen months old now.'

'Then she'll have plenty to keep her occupied when you're away.'

'What do you mean by that?'

'I only thought . . .'. But he was gone. Into the wheelhouse and down the companion way, looking neither to right nor left as he went. My cheeks burned hotter than the humid night air and I stayed alone for a long time before rejoining the cadet in the wheelhouse.

Before I opened my eyes, I sensed Leung Wing Pa moving about in my cabin and heard the teacup rattle on his tray. He pulled back the curtain on the forward porthole, flooding the narrow room with pale, penetrating, unescapable daylight. From beneath the sheet I mumbled, 'Morning, Wing', and reached out to turn on the radio beside my bunk. Music crackled from the set, and for a moment I lay listening to the music, the faint rushing of the water and the perpetual, vital throbbing of the ship at sea. Mornings were good. I enjoyed waking to these sensations, the sounds, the smells, the quiet, rolling vibrations of our engines at full speed in a calm sea. Lazily, I stretched out my hand to the exact spot where the steward had placed the cup and propped myself up on one elbow. The tea was against regulations. It was the result of a private arrangement between myself and the steward, whereby I exchanged a portion of my tobacco ration, somewhat superfluous to a non-smoker, for the regular beverage which I found essential since having given up the more noxious habit of indulging in an early morning cigarette. Leung Wing Pa was still there, standing in the middle of the cabin doing nothing in particular, peering at me with a peculiarly bashful expression. Taking a quick sip of the warm, tasteless liquid, I said, 'I gave you my laundry last night.' The steward nodded, but made no move to leave. Like a schoolboy caught out in a prank, he shifted awkwardly from one foot to the other and pulled at the lapels of his white jacket with thin, bony fingers. 'All right, Wing. What is it?' Wing stared at the floor, as if scrutinising the pattern on the straw matting, then with sudden resolve, spoke out in his high, sing-song voice.

'What for funny box in cap'in's cabin, Sam-fo?' He made a gesture with his hands to indicate a small rectangle.

'Box? Where about is it?'

'Cap'in's cabin, Sam-fo. Box on dresser.' I looked at the Chinaman with amusement and replaced my cup in its saucer.

'Hell, I don't know, Wing. Maybe it's for binoculars or a sextant.' The steward rolled his eyes, as if he were conversing with a simple-minded person.

'No binocular. No sextan',' he said. 'Small-piece box, Sam-fo. What for?'

'A watch, then, or jewellery. Cuff-links perhaps.' The unprecedented interrogation was becoming tiresome.

'No cuff-lin's,' said Wing, shaking his hand in the vicinity of his ear. 'Tiger no hear watch or cuff-lin's.'

'If the Tiger's so damned inquisitive, why doesn't he open the bloody box himself?'

The steward grinned, displaying his remarkable teeth with the gold enamel insets.

'Box got lock. No can open box. You look-see, Sam-fo.'

'Oh, piss off, Wing. And shut the door!'

Durban–Djakarta

A beam of light emanating from the left of the First Electrician's black silhouette cut through the blue darkness and cast the technicolour leaves of an elm tree against the canvas screen on the after end of the accommodation. Beneath the elm, an avant garde Edinburgh schoolmistress, Miss Jean Brodie, held her class of little girls enthralled by the magnificence of her prime, while beneath the screen, sixteen Chinese seamen and eight European officers sprawled on coamings and hatch covers and followed her progress with varying degrees of boredom or amusement. Far away on our port beam, the lights of a tanker moved slowly along the indistinct blue margin between sea and sky. It was time for me to go on duty. As the film was not a recent one, almost every one had already seen it ashore, but it relieved the inevitable monotony of nine days at sea in the Indian Ocean, and I was annoyed at missing its conclusion. Picking my way between the spectators, I climbed the ladder to the accommodation and went to my cabin before reporting on the bridge. The handful of Christmas cards I had bought in Durban lay untouched on the dresser. Untouched, undedicated, unaddressed. A rapid mental calculation showed that, unless they were posted in Djakarta, my seasonal felicitations were in danger of arriving sometime late in January. Something had to be done. I collected the bundle of cards and envelopes and thrust it determinedly into the breast pocket of my shirt.

The First Mate, it so happened, had not seen the film before and demanded a summary of the story so far while we hurriedly performed the formality of changing watch.

'It's not your type of flick at all,' said Roddy Hislop. 'Not a bit of flesh in it up to now.'

Arthur Brown winked. 'It had an X Certificate in the UK.

The flesh must come later.'

Although Tom Walker, the third cadet, was now off duty, he seemed in no hurry to leave the wheelhouse. I noticed the pile of text books under his arm.

'How's your studying going? Still having problems with St Giles Cathedral?'

'Not any longer. Something seems to have shaken him up a bit. In fact for the last week or so, he's been quite bearable. He thinks someone has it in for him.'

'The second lecky?'

'Don't know. He didn't say.'

'Nonsense,' said Roddy. 'The lecky wouldn't risk getting DR'd over an idiot like Giles.'

Later, alone in the chartroom, I spread out the Christmas cards on the table before me. Eight cards, each in its own way conveying the smug, self-satisfied, blessed cosiness of the season of goodwill. Snow scenes from South Africa. Stage coaches and merry, old world inns from the Transvaal. Robins and holly leaves from Capetown. Delighted by the incongruity of the situation, I began to read the verses.

> May the robin's merry song
> Bring you happiness all year long.

> The bells ring out their Christmas cheer,
> To echo through the coming year.

> Far from warm and friendly hearth,
> Our children often roam,
> But at this joyful, holy time,
> They think of the folks at home.

The last was definitely the one for my parents. The remaining five verses proved to be in Afrikaans, a possibility that I had overlooked when buying the cards. Eventually I selected three of them for the young ladies in my life, judging even the most mundane observations on robins and bells to be considerably more impressive when delivered in an obscure foreign language.

Robins and bells did not concern Li Yiu Mun. Seasonal greetings had no place in the letter he was carefully composing at a table in the almost deserted crew accommodation. He wrote quickly, fluently, in long vertical lines of Chinese characters, holding his gold-plated ball point pen in a manner derived from the traditional brush writing of his ancestors. When he reached the bottom of each line, he paused, narrowing his eyes to aid concentration and block out the strident voice of a demented Scottish woman being betrayed by a scholarly protégé on the far side of the bulkhead. Had the Tiger confided the contents of his letter to any European, he would have found them a bewildering combination of hypotheses and speculation, the gist of which was almost unintelligible to a western interpretation of logic. To an oriental, however, this blend of metaphysics and innuendo would have been perfectly understandable and, indeed, given rise to considerable concern. Which is exactly what Li Yiu Mun intended.

The Tiger wanted to be transferred to another ship. His family was an old and honourable one, with a long tradition of service to Blair Lines. Accordingly, he addressed his discreet enquiry not to the Crew Superintendent, but to his own brother, who was employed as a clerk in the company's Chinese Crew Department in Hong Kong. It must not be imagined that, because he desired a change of ships, the Tiger called to his assistance all the spirits, the bad joss, the latent devils which he described with candid thoroughness in his letter. He did not conjure fear from the dark corners and passageways of the *Blairskaith* to suit his own purpose. It was there already. Not desperate, immediate fear, but rather a permanent lack of wellbeing, a perpetual sensation of uneasiness that showed itself in countless indefinable ways. Leung Wing Pa knew it, so did Huen Yiu and Li Sau, the quartermaster; but only the Tiger let it prey on his mind. He saw bad joss following the ship like a great black flag, and wrote this in his letter.

With a muted burst of music, the film came to an end, leaving Li Yiu Mun in silence, save for the periodic exclamations of the bo'sun and the chief laundryman playing fan-tan at the end of the saloon. Rapidly he re-read what he had written, sealed the airmail letter and sat back with a quiet smile. In merely looking at the flimsy, folded sheet of blue paper, he was experiencing a peculiar sense of release as if by the timely application of a medicinal remedy he had escaped infection. Down the alleyway came the sound of people returning from the film show. They would tell him about the woman with red hair, who taught little girls under an elm tree. Slipping the letter into his pocket, he rolled three cigarettes and took them across to the card players. The bo'sun and the chief laundryman looked up in surprise. It was many days since they had seen a smile on the face of the Tiger.

Captain David H Sinclair navigated his ship through the Sunda Strait, which separates the Indonesian islands of Java and Sumatra, with a skill and confidence rarely shown by masters with twenty years' experience of these waters. He gave his orders with quiet, precise determination, and when the grey, morning silhouette of the Sumatra coast slipped away on our port quarter and we nosed slowly between the numerous dusky islands of Djakarta Bay, every deck officer experienced a sense of admiration not entirely devoid of envy, which quite clearly showed the company's wisdom in David Sinclair's recent promotion. We docked at the old harbour district of Tandjung Priok in steady, warm rain that endowed the sprawling, ugly city with a transient, indistinct beauty. Later, after breakfast, when the rain had faded to a fine shroud of steaming mist, I stood under an awning and watched the dockers arriving to discharge the machinery we had shipped from Rotterdam. Our consignment for Djakarta was a small one of no more than a hundred tons. Replacement parts for a shoe factory, and as we were not scheduled to load any cargo, our stay would be restricted to eighteen hours. The brevity of our visit did not concern me, as Djakarta is by no means my favourite port. Nevertheless, the people moving about on the quayside, the fishing boats that dotted the pale, still water of the bay, the smell of the humid air assured me that I was in the East once more and I felt the pleasant sense of delight and excitement which, ever since my first voyage, I have experienced on arriving in this part of the world. My reverie was brought to an abrupt conclusion when the trainee radio officer emerged from the accommodation, leaned out over the rail nearby and leapt swiftly back as a cascade of moisture fell from the edge of the awning down the neck of his denim shirt. He shook the water from his collar with an expression of abject misery.

'So this is the Mystic East,' he said and spat between the side of the ship and the quay.

'Okay. It doesn't hold a candle to New York. But you haven't seen it all yet.'

'You going ashore?' the sparky grunted.

'Only to post some mail and have a few beers.'

'Mind if I come along? At least you know your way about town.'

I sat with the third cadet and the trainee radio officer in a bar diagonally opposite the main post office and drank Tiger beer from chilled bottles. The sliding doors separating the bar from the pavement were drawn back and jangling music from the antiquated juke box competed against the roar of traffic in the street. Several Indonesians in jeans and baseball boots were standing at the bar and the barmaid chatted to them in what sounded like a mixture of Dutch and Chinese. Another girl picked her way between the tables, collecting glasses and, when necessary, serving drinks to the only other customers, who were also Chinese. I considered her to be rather pretty, but when she smiled in our direction she had no front teeth.

'Don't fancy that one much,' said the sparky. 'Though you could say she suits this joint.'

Roddy Hislop said, 'Isn't that the Tiger coming out of the post office?'

'Who knows?' said the sparky. 'Tiddlies all look the same to me.'

File Cards

Mr Archibald Tulloch stood at the window of the Blair Line's office in Hong Kong and indulged in that particular brand of self-pity peculiar to those whose most cherished ambition has, at the last moment, been cruelly and irrevocably thwarted. Beyond the sheet of plate glass, the roofs of Whitfield Barracks stretched southwestwards as far as Canton Road. Beyond Canton Road, the cranes, masts and funnels of Ocean Terminal marked the perimeter of Kowloon Peninsula, the boundary of Mr Archibald Tulloch's professional sphere of influence. Lethargically, he moved to the single pane of glass which the designers of the office block had made capable of being opened, folded it carefully inwards and leaned out over the stainless steel sill. A warm draught of asphalt and petrol fumes rose from Nathan Road, four floors below. Mr Archibald Tulloch coughed sharply and closed the window. Beneath his breath, he cursed the British Crown Colony of Hong Kong, cursed the neo-colonial clannishness of its white residents, cursed Marine Superintendent Hector Elliot, his aloof, urbane superior; and inwardly, most vehemently of all, cursed the cruel caprice of nature that had arrested his growth at five feet three inches while permitting that of Miss Catherine Blair to progress unabated to the totally unladylike stature of six feet exactly. To this reason alone, Mr Archibald Tulloch attributed the fact that Dougal Elliot and not he was, at this very moment, waiting in the lobby of the Peninsula Hotel to escort the sole heiress of the Blair Line fortune on a guided tour of the colony.

Dougal Elliot, the Marine Superintendent's son who held a junior post with the Hongkong and Shanghai Banking Corporation, was the product of an educational system whose characteristic mark was immense social arrogance matched only by utter professional incompetence. The knowledge that Mr Elliot senior was fully aware of his son's shortcomings, and extended him only the minimum of fatherly courtesy necessary for both of them to exist tolerably within the confines of the Crown Colony, should have brought some measure of consolation to Tulloch. In his present mood of melancholy, however, it merely emphasised the only conceivable reason for the Marine Superintendent's decision to delegate the task to his son. Involuntarily, Archibald Tulloch stepped back to measure the height of his reflection in the window.

It would be churlish to suggest that Tulloch's keenness to establish a liaison with Miss Blair was based solely on the possibility of professional or pecuniary advancement. He had joined the firm three years previously at Elliot's invitation when it had become evident to them both that his talent as a linguist was being wasted on the routine translation of trading documents for his previous employers. Elliot had offered something unusual, the chance to converse and deal with the Chinese community on a personal level, normally encountered only by officials of the police or Colonial Administration. And indeed the promise had come true. Tulloch was now completely responsible for recruitment, negotiation and administration within the Chinese Crew Department of Blair Line and he had ample opportunity to practise his quite exceptional skill in the Cantonese and Mandarin dialects for which he was rewarded with a comfortable salary. Despite his professional advancement, however, he was immensely perturbed by his social status. Since his arrival in Hong Kong five years previously, he had remained firmly at the bottom of the social ladder. He had joined the proper clubs; from time to time he had been invited to gatherings of prominent and influential people at the home of the Elliots or his former employer, but in the main, without having been obviously ostracised, he found himself outside the accepted circle of fashionable society and obliged to seek friendship among the more junior military officers and their families and among such portions of the Chinese community as would accept him. Archibald Tulloch had seen the much-publicised visit by the chairman's daughter as his last chance to turn the tables on the Elliots of this world and bulldoze his way into the inner circle. It was common knowledge that Sir Gilbert Blair, the chairman and sole shareholder, was now well advanced into his seventies and that his entire holdings were destined to devolve on Catherine, his only daughter. Tulloch had researched further. Within the last two months, he had discovered that Catherine Blair was forty-two years old. Photographs had shown her to be far from attractive, which perhaps accounted for the fact that, apart from a brief engagement to a guards officer which terminated when he was killed in Aden, she had never married or, indeed, had any permanent male companions. Extensive postal communication with the archivist of a well-known London society journal revealed that Miss Blair had been educated at Roedean, lived in an adequate, but not pretentious London mansion, usually confined her vacations to touring the mountain regions of Europe, where she could indulge her interest in rare alpine flowers, and was active in supporting a charity devoted to rescuing distressed work horses, pit ponies and the like. The local librarian had remarked on Tulloch's recent choice of books, but neither Elliot nor his wife had been able to disguise their amazement when Tulloch had modestly shown himself to be an authority on every topic listed under 'Particular Interests' on the confidential briefing which the company's publicity department had thoughtfully forwarded to the Marine Superintendent two days before Miss Blair's arrival. The choice of escort had been obvious. If only, thought Tulloch, the company had not seen fit to append in a discreet footnote the information that Miss Blair stood six feet tall. Neither the magazine nor the photocopied newspaper pictures had given any indication of Miss Blair's exceptional height. Tulloch shuddered as he recalled the way the Superintendent had drained a glass of gin and, with awful finality, pronounced the words, 'It'll have to be Dougal.'

Tearing himself from the damning reflection in the window, Archibald Tulloch considered the possibility of absenting himself from work and spending a couple of hours in one of the noisy little bars that crowded the side streets to the east of Nathan Road. Of late, he had been repairing more and more frequently to such establishments, where everyone was accepted at exactly the value of the dollars in their pocket-book, and where he could quietly withdraw into himself and ponder his insurmountable misfortune. The memory of the foul draught of air that had greeted him on opening the window made him think better of the idea. He thought for a moment of taking the car and driving through the new tunnel to Victoria. Instead, he decided to walk to Star Ferry Pier and cross over to Hong Kong Island in the traditional way. The sea breeze would probably prove beneficial and, besides, the girlie bars of Wanchai, whose dubious character normally repulsed him, seemed particularly attractive in his present frame of mind. He slipped on his light, tropical jacket, straightened his tie and was in the process of drafting a brief excuse for his absence when the door opened and Hector Elliot lumbered into the room with an armful of freshly typed files.

'These are for the Crew Department. Be a good chap and drop them in there. Or were you going somewhere?'

Archibald Tulloch straightened out the piece of buff coloured paper on the shiny surface of his desk, folded it carefully and dropped it into the wastepaper basket. 'Only to the Crew Department,' he said.

Marine Superintendent Hector Elliot was a huge fat man with an air of worldly well-being that at once attracted Tulloch and repelled him. He approached and deposited his burden on the desk with the characteristic wheeze of a man unaccustomed to even the slightest physical exertion. The pink flesh of his neck, which always smelled vaguely of talcum powder, bulged over his stiff white collar.

'Something wrong, old boy? Worried about how Dougal will treat her ladyship?' Elliot helped himself to a cigarette from the box on Tulloch's desk and occupied the space the other man had recently vacated by the window. 'Don't blame you. But that damned school taught him manners, if nothing else. He won't muff things, oh dear me, no. Which reminds me, you must come up to the house on Christmas Eve. We're holding a little dinner party. You can talk to her ladyship about fetlocks and Leontopodium alpinum.' He laughed hoarsely. 'Didn't know you had it in you. Still waters, eh?'

'Of course, sir.' Tulloch flicked through the files and rose to leave. Hector Elliot watched him go with benign amusement. The little man always reminded him of something out of a pack of cards. A king perhaps, or a jack. Yes, that was it, a little jack of clubs that should be printed on cardboard instead of wandering about an office. He shook his head and when Tulloch closed the door, stooped to the wastepaper basket and read what was written on the folded sheet of paper.

Tulloch ran downstairs to the next floor and stepped through the glass doors of the Crew Department. Now he could be cool, businesslike, impressively in command. He handed the files to a secretary and went over to a board on which were pinned lists of Chinese seamen at present employed by Blair Line. Several minutes elapsed before Tulloch realised that Li Ho Mun, his chief ledger clerk, was standing beside him for no apparent reason. He looked enquiringly at the Chinaman, who lowered his head deferentially and indicated that they should withdraw to a more secluded part of the office. Intrigued by his clerk's unorthodox behaviour and not a little relieved to find something other than Miss Blair with which to occupy his attention, Tulloch followed Li Ho Mun into the glass walled cubicle normally used for interviewing prospective crew members and listened with controlled excitement as the clerk explained, in vivid Cantonese symbolism, the absolute necessity to transfer his brother, Li Yiu Mun, to another ship immediately he docked in Hong Kong. Under other circumstances, Tulloch might have dismissed the matter out of hand or, perhaps, acceded to the Chinaman's request in the belief that some pressing family matter was the underlying reason for such an unusual demand. In this instance, however, Li Ho Mun had provided him with a perfect subject on which to focus his somewhat distraught faculties and he found himself treating the case with deeper and more thorough concern than even the Chinaman had hoped. While the clerk read and re-read relevant passages from his brother's letter, Tulloch took copious notes. Then, promising to do everything within his power to resolve the situation, he dismissed the clerk and sat back pensively in the black leather chair. The problem was a ticklish one. Matters of nautical administration were the concern of the Shipping Department in London and fell entirely outwith his field of jurisdiction. He had no pretensions to being an authority on seafaring. Granted, he was occasionally required to visit one or other of the Blair Line's ships when it docked in Ocean Terminal, but his knowledge was strictly limited to matters of pay, work contracts and leave conditions for the Chinese crews and secretly he was always glad to return to the relaxed atmosphere of files and reports in which he felt more at home. Similarly, the names of the European officers, which were scribbled on his note pad, meant little or nothing to him. Recruited and controlled by the European Crew Department in Edinburgh, they seldom had cause to visit his particular preserve, though he had inevitably encountered several of them at periodic official functions held in the Hong Kong office. He most definitely regarded Blair Line's sea-going personnel as a race apart. Rather apprehensively, he lifted the telephone and asked to be put through to the Marine Superintendent's office. The secretary who answered was fortunately on good terms with him so he encountered less difficulty than expected in persuading her to furnish details of the *Blairskaith*'s master and first mate. Flushed with success, he left the glass box and strode over to a wall map on which the current positions of the company's fleet were marked with coloured pins. SS *Blairskaith*, at present in Manila, was due to sail for Hong Kong in twenty-four hours. Consulting the calendar, he discovered that she would dock in Ocean Terminal early on Christmas Eve for a stay of four days. Carefully, he added this information to his notes and when he returned to the glass cubicle, found two slim, green folders on the desk.

'Sinclair, David Henry. Age 32 years. Home address ...'

The personal details contained within the file were not new. Smudged amendments in Biro, the result of the Marine Superintendent's periodic attempts to keep information up-to-date, served only to emphasise the chaotic lack of communication between the head office of the company and its branches. Tulloch viewed the document with interest. Neither the name nor the home address of the master of the *Blairskaith*

held any significance, but as he read further, he became
conscious of a most disconcerting suggestion of familiarity
between the subject of the slim dossier and himself. The last
four typewritten lines clinched the matter. They jolted his
memory into action, sent his thoughts reeling back three years
to an evening so overwhelming that he had virtually forgotten
its less significant details.

'Married April 18th, 19.... Accompanied on voyage by
wife, Spring 19....'

And beneath these typewritten dates, someone had added
in longhand: 'Due one more accompanied trip before expiry of
present contract.'

Three years. The links which were eventually to lead
Archibald Tulloch's reluctant memory to an ink-filled jam jar
in the back of a newsagent's shop in Kirkcaldy started with a
tall, bronzed, thirsty specimen of Australian womanhood
called Inez, a former girlfriend of Dougal Elliot's. Inez, a
stewardess with QANTAS, had been on stopover in Hong
Kong and Tulloch had agreed to meet her in the Fanling Golf
Club as a favour to his employer's son, who had found himself unavoidably detained that evening with embonpoint of a
more appealing hue. Tulloch had made a poor stand in for the
man-about-town. The first ten minutes had completely
exhausted any common topics of conversation between the
aerial goddess and himself, and thereafter, Inez had applied
herself to demolishing a fair percentage of the club's stock of
gin and vermouth, which she mixed herself and drank from a
long, tapered glass, with such intense dedication that the mere
recollection brought beads of sweat to Tulloch's brow. For
three years he had sought to draw a mental veil over the
subsequent course of that evening. He had trained himself to
forget dancing the conga on a crowded table top, the frowning
restaurant manager, the expression on the face of a Chinese
police sergeant when he tried to explain his presence at dawn
on the beach of Repulse Bay, barefoot and wearing a pink
dress round his head like a turban. The final indignity of three
cracked ribs sustained in the parting embrace as the dripping
owner of the dress was conducted to a waiting Landrover had
been almost blotted from his mind. Yet four lines of type had

thrown these ten disastrous hours into such vivid relief that they might well have happened yesterday.

Tulloch found himself confronting skeletons from the past, for early that fateful night, he remembered noticing an unusual entry in the visitors' book of the Fanling Golf Club. The detail was such a minor one that it had lain neglected. But someone who has a file-card for a memory can never rid himself of facts set down in black and white. The Christian name had been stroked out and the nickname lettered carefully above it. Four letters. Three consonants, one vowel. Surely he should have guessed then, but at the time he couldn't imagine any possible reason for her being in Hong Kong. He had seen no connection between the crudely altered signature and a blue school blazer, whose contents once had borne the same description.

Tulloch laid aside the file, and on a fresh sheet of Blair Line notepaper set down a list that had nothing whatever to do with affairs of the mercantile marine. It began with the words, 'His bicycle was black.'

Manila

'Fourteen quid!' Roddy Hislop picked up the guitar and struck a couple of chords. 'You paid fourteen pounds for this?'

'That's all,' said Giles St John-Browne. 'The man asked for nearer twenty, but I beat him down. Just listen to that tone. Don't you think it's a really good buy?'

'Goodbye to fourteen quid,' replied Roddy, who knew something about guitars. Giles would doubtless have countered this remark, had not the First Mate at that moment stuck his head round the door of the smokeroom and told the second cadet to collect the ship's mail which the Filipino Agent had just deposited in a sack at the bottom of the gangway.

On deck, a gang of seamen under the supervision of Tom Walker and the bosun, were closing the hatch covers, while the last group of dockers straggled towards the dock gates under yellow harbour floodlights. Arthur Brown emerged from the port alleyway closely followed by the Old Man. They both wore light tropical suits, and from the fresh parting in the First Mate's hair, I gathered they were about to go ashore for a night on the town. The Old Man spread out a brightly-coloured tourist map of Manila on a hatch coaming. He lit a cigarette and looked on while Arthur Brown tried to remember the exact location of the restaurant in which he had previously eaten such exquisite sea food.

'Spices,' said the Old Man. 'Spanish spices. He probably cooks Spanish style!'

'But he's Chinese, not Filipino.'

'Chinese are all over the place.'

'Quezon Boulevard, near the university,' said the First Mate, refolding the map. 'It's somewhere up there. In any case, the cab driver will probably know it.'

At the top of the gangway they encountered Giles St John-Browne with a half-filled bag of mail over his left shoulder. The task of sorting the ship's mail was, as a rule, undertaken by Captain Sinclair in person; but with a night in Manila before him and a taxi sounding its horn impatiently from the direction of the dock gates, he delegated the responsibility to me and went ashore with a good-natured wave of the hand. Giles disappeared on some private errand of his own and I went into the ship's office and, at a leisurely pace, began sorting the mail, which was larger than usual owing to the proximity of Christmas. The official company mail, fastened into convenient batches by heavy rubber bands, was easily identifiable, as also were the airmail letters for the Chinese crew which invariably bore Hong Kong postmarks and were often addressed in an amusingly obscure form of English, which must have taxed the ingenuity of the Filipino postal service to the utmost. The remainder of the mail consisted of personal letters for the officers of the *Blairskaith*. Pocketing the three which bore my name, I was about to head for the smokeroom to distribute the others when I noticed a large, flat envelope wedged at the bottom of the bag. Numerous stickers proclaimed that it contained printed matter which should not be bent, and on the front was a yellow label headed:

'Artworld. An International Journal of the Fine Arts.'

Giles St John-Browne seemed the only conceivable recipient of such an unseamanlike publication, but on closer inspection the name neatly typed on the yellow label proved to be that of Captain David H Sinclair. Hidden depths, I thought and was immediately reminded of an engineer who, for years, had received under the cover of *Ladies Home Journal* a publication which would have brought a blush to any lady's cheek. However, the engineer's happy arrangement came to a sudden and sorry end when a cadet carelessly directed the plain envelope to the captain's wife, who happened to be present on the voyage, rather than to its intended recipient. My curiosity was short-lived. Under no circumstances could I imagine Captain Sinclair indulging in this particular form of visual stimulation. I added the envelope to his batch of private mail and left the office, locking the cabin door behind me.

Besides, I was soon to find myself preoccupied with a communication of much greater importance.

My personal mail contained the predictable letter from
my parents, a rather risqué greetings card from the nurses in
Edinburgh and an insipid, traditional one from the young lady
in Perth, to which was appended the brief message that she
had become engaged to the son of a publican and intended to
marry early in the new year. Perhaps I had been half
expecting it. At any rate, the message hardly produced the
bombshell effect which its sender no doubt intended. Quite
contrary to the rules, I experienced neither the anger, jealousy
nor resentment generally associated with any sudden with-
drawal of affection. My mood, if anything, brightened, and
before going into the smokeroom, I collected one unwritten
Afrikaans Christmas card from my cabin. I handed out the
remainder of the mail, drank four gins and declined Gospel's
offer of a fifth. Leaning on the damp Formica bar top, above
the gentle vibration of the generator, I wrote out the address of
the prettier Edinburgh nurse and added beneath the unintelligible verse the words: 'Will you marry me?'

Eight hours out of Manila, Arthur Brown entered the
captain's dayroom in search of duty rosters from which he
intended calculating the amount of overtime due to the crew.
He found the rosters without difficulty and on the day bed he
also found a scattered pile of magazines which he leafed
through in the hope of discovering some reading material with
which to while away his off-duty hours. On board ship,
magazines and paper-backed books were regarded as common
property, so the first mate was not surprised to find that he had
read all but one of the magazines earlier in the voyage. The
one exception was sufficiently unusual to attract his attention,
and in the hope that it might contain some information on
antiques with which he could later impress his wife, he made a
mental note to tell the Old Man he had borrowed the
publication and took it with him when he left.

Four hours later, Arthur Brown reclined on his own day
bed with the winter edition of the quarterly magazine

Artworld. It naturally fell open at the page someone had marked with a paper clip, though in time Arthur would surely have found the article himself.

Vital Resurgence of Surrealism in Scotland
by Rudolf Ablemann

Edinburgh, the solid, grey capital of Scotland, that subtly Calvinist bastion of classicism tinted by the neo-gothic, where one always feels more firmly drawn to the earth than in any other European city, seems an unlikely birthplace for a dynamic sculptural movement to counter the pervading 'pop culture' of our times. My use of the word 'movement' is a deliberate one because, though this vitality of approach has manifested itself in a single work by Mr Malcolm Leslie (see Vol VII, No 2, p 16), *Angels on the Prairie*, I am confident that it must necessarily give rise to a wave of direct and immediate surrealism in a vein more uniquely refreshing than I have previously believed possible.

It is typically indicative of the intrinsic novelty expressed in his newfound artform that Leslie firmly denies his recent creation even the general, albeit outdated classification of 'surrealist'. He steadfastly maintains that his *Elements* is a deliberate, conscious attempt to recreate an existing truth, and by its restatement to provide a medium through which may be achieved the expiation of a nameless guilt. He is quixotically evasive when asked whether his 'truth' is a sculptural or philosophical one, preferring to describe it as 'social' and 'of a very personal nature'. However Leslie may interpret his own motives, the accompanying photographs must surely evince that he has created something unique in the annals of what we, at least, can only describe as supreme surrealism.

Elements was unveiled in the Leslie Gallery in the presence of Mr Malcolm Leslie, its creator, Mr Tony Da Silva, who supervised the construction of the waxwork portion, and the young lady who posed for the impressive figure study that forms the focal point of the work. The critical acclaim which has attended the sculpture since its unveiling, is doubly justified not only on an aesthetic basis, but on the interesting technical one that Mr Leslie has introduced, through Tony Da Silva, the almost forgotten art of creative waxworks. *Elements* is undoubtedly the long-awaited pebble, whose ripples of influence will do much to alter the surface on the stagnant pool of contemporary sculpture. I mentioned this to the artist when he consented to an exclusive interview for *Artworld*.

MALCOLM LESLIE   Ripples? You may be right, but I will be content if the ripples are those of memory on an oil- and cork-filled tidal basin.

RUDOLF ABLEMANN   I take it you refer to your private motive for commencing the construction. Do you find your creativity always requires a deep personal stimulus?

ML   No. It requires courage—to assemble the elements and to delve into the past, where gulls floated above the fumes of linseed oil.

RA   To turn, for a moment, to the first element. How did you come upon this statement of bizarre reality, the symbolism of the ear?

ML   By an accident.

RA   Purely by chance?

ML   By an accident involving eight steel-shod hoofs, four iron-hooped wheels, two legs, two arms and two ears. Forgive me for being obscure. The outcome of the accident to which I refer was perpetuated by a work of art, functional yet with its own beauty that far exceeded my modest offering and which, had it still existed, would have rendered my *Elements* utterly superfluous.

RA   What happened to this earlier element?

MODEL (with no other name but 'Cans')   It perished in a fire when the Greeks set Hook's howff alight.

ML   But no small silver buckle ...

RA   And so you settled for fibre-glass and clinical accuracy to form the memory of this early element which must be secret?

ML   Exactly. And with it, I have recaptured the sky, but not the gulls, the tidal basin, but not one white bathing cap, a red-brick chimney, but not a single grey particle of crematory dust.

MODEL   Dust and chimneys. He's boring you. Please,

Malcolm, keep to the point. The topic under discussion is a sculpture, not a schoolboy fantasy.

RA   On the contrary, dear lady. Our subject is Malcolm Leslie, the reality whose fingers hold a brush, whose pen signs cheques. The schoolboy imagery is important. Our readers want to know the machinations of a mind which will not credit itself with the creation of true surrealism.

ML   Your zeal for accuracy is frightening, but I shall do my best to answer in terms you will find possible to comprehend. Many years ago, I encountered my old art teacher, my first mentor in matters three-dimensional, who chose to put upon a simple application of basic physical laws involving blocks, tackles and a consecrated pine tree, the interpretation of surrealism. Since then I have paid scant respect to the field of artistic expression that goes under that name. Instead, I have sought to practise this art in reverse by creating a structure which, though pleasing to the eye of the connoisseur simply on grounds of its novelty and harmony of composition, confronts that smaller portion of humanity at which it is really levelled with an unavoidable symbol of the past, a direct, unescapable challenge to make atonement for their sins. If gulls, bathing caps and crematory dust are absent from the first element, they are fully encompassed by the second. Observe the few scattered feathers that lie at the figure's feet. The dust that encrusts those waxen soles and ankles originated in a crematory oven, I assure you, and those eight dark stains between the waxen fingers are not a botched representation of human blood. They are carefully applied from a gallon tin of marine red-lead, prepared to Admiralty standards.

RA   And red-lead has the power to expiate guilt?

ML   Only the power of suggestion. True atonement inevitably follows from within, as Cans will readily acknowledge, and as the seaman all too surely knows.

RA   What was the nature of this guilt?

ML   You border too closely on what is not your concern.

MODEL   A denial.

ML   Enough! Consider, if you please, the quality of workmanship in wax. Is it not entirely fitting that consecrated dust should mingle with human hair that has been denied ordainment in holy orders? What better mirror could seagull feathers wish than glazed Silesian eyes that have never looked upon the sea? And all that wax, the very substance of the body. Is it not appropriate that its origin was the fragmented, unharmonious grotesques of a travelling showman?

RA   Critics have suggested in the past that your own activities owe much to the art of showmanship. (I call to mind your airborne and inflatable gulls.) How do you counter this criticism, particularly with regard to your latest creation, which is bound to profit from the veil of mystery you weave around its inspiration?

ML   Let me tell you a little story from the past. Towards noon, when the sun was up and the air was free of sea haar, the playground (schoolyard) I frequented as a boy was diagonally bisected by the shadow of a chimney. Neither the rectangular chimney, which was barely forty feet high, nor its shadow, nor even its periodic ejections of grey smoke and pulverised ash provoked the slightest reaction from the countless children who sported in its vicinity. But mention the word 'ghost' here and there. Come between skipping-ropes and hop-scotch with a whitened face, muttering half audibly about figures who rise from the dust, chains that rattle and shadowy spectres whose cinder-dry throats echo their last shriek when flame met flesh and you spark off a legend. Childish wisdom, childish fear.

Run, run the shadow will come!

If you look at the smoke
and it starts to rain,
Your eyes will never
see again.

The bogey-man lives in the trees.
He'll bite your legs off
at the knees.

Childish wisdom, childish fear. Not one miner's son, not one son of a farmer, or builder or driver or labourer; not one lawyer's son, not even the policeman's son, strong as an ox at eleven, would dare put a foot into that pencil of shadow. The girls, taller and more stupid, were no braver. When the bell summoned them to their classrooms, they took a wide detour round the offending patch of darkness. And as the shadow worked its way from left to right across the playground, it pushed before it games of hop-scotch and rounders, grey-clad boys and blue-clad girls who would never completely forget its power and would merely pretend to laugh when age and advancement removed them to the more distant safety of the playground for second year pupils.

My chimney was a rarity. My chimney had a story and was therefore more real than a thousand other red-brick devices for the dissemination of gaseous waste. The incorporation of a legend in a work of art relieves the artist from responsibility, removes him from his position of high priest by neatly transferring the consequences of his work to that shady region of fantasy, myth and suspicion over which the legend holds sway. One need only think of *The Birth of Venus*, *The Creation of the Milky Way* or *The Garden of Earthly Delights*. Consider, then, the impact of another form of reality, wax and fibre-glass, when the legend that gives rise to their conception is identifiable only to three people in the world.

RA   Though the example of the chimney seems scarcely relevant, you have drawn for us an interesting verbal tableau. The inspiration, perhaps, for your next work?

ML   What an astute suggestion. Some day I may take it up, but at present, provided *Elements* achieves its desired effect, I propose to concentrate my future efforts on the more mundane and inestimably more satisfying subject of seagulls.

RA   I detect a hint of doubt. If *Elements* should not provoke the intimate and very personal reaction which only you can judge, will you regard the work as a failure?

ML   Other than financially, yes.

RA   Have you anticipated such an eventuality?

ML   I have recently read of a new flame-proof material,

capable of being moulded into any shape or form. Perhaps tar-paper roof and creosoted boards could be successfully simulated. Bottled gas would provide an eternal fire. ...

RA   Mr Leslie, we can undoubtedly look forward to a sustained outpouring of unique creativity. Thank you for allowing us this glimpse behind the scenes and for answering our questions so frankly. One final point. Are we likely to see *Elements* on exhibition in the States?

ML   The pleasure has been mine. As you know, a percentage of the proceeds are destined for medical research, and to this end, *Elements* will be exhibited in Edinburgh for three months. Mr Da Silva and I shall then commence a European tour, exhibiting in every major town in France between Boulogne and the Mediterranean, passing by way of Italy to Vienna and on through Austria, Czechoslovakia and Poland before concluding our journey on the Baltic Coast. After that, who knows?

Hong Kong

Tathong Channel, 08.45, Christmas Eve. Silent, save for the regular, soothing throb of her turbines, SS *Blairskaith* steamed towards the British Crown Colony of Hong Kong. Lamtung Island fell away on the starboard quarter, now barely visible through a microscopically fine mist that hung low over the choppy, green water and silvered the stays and radio aerials overhead. Somewhere in the watery mist a pale yellow smudge hinted at the presence of sun, but the air was still cool and the seamen on watch wore woollen jerseys over their tropical shirts. To port, the steep, hilly slopes of Hong Kong Island formed a jagged, blue-grey horizon, dropping sharply to meet the water in a margin of white foam. And as we altered course towards the distant mouth of Lei U Mun Channel, I picked out through the binoculars the radio masts high above Hak Kok Tau. The surface of Junk Bay stretched to starboard, flat as ink, ending in a grey haze through which Lei U Mun Point loomed suddenly as we approached the harbour boundary. As SS *Blairskaith* steamed slow ahead between Kung Am and Sin Chau Wan, the morning mist dispersed, the watery sun glinted on the surface of the sea and threw our surroundings into sharp relief. While to starboard, the hills continued to rise showing little sign of life, the ground to port fell away to reveal a straggling built-up area bounded by the masts and cranes of Taikoo shipyard.

'The Pearl of the Orient,' said Gospel, sweeping his arm expansively towards Hong Kong Island. 'A Chinese jewel in the British Crown. After this, ye'll never want to see New York again, laddie.'

The trainee radio officer cupped the mug of cocoa more tightly in his hand and peered across the shining expanse of water, dotted inshore by the ungainly black silhouettes of junks at anchor. To starboard Kowloon Bay, huge and silent, two nondescript grey vessels in the quarantine anchorage, and behind them, picked out by a string of lights, the runway of Kai Tak Airport projecting like a giant black finger across the water. Victoria gradually emerged to port. Block upon block of shining sky-scrapers thrusting upwards from a tangled mass of smaller brown buildings that jostled for place on the waterfront, engulfed the lower slopes and advanced in irregular ranks up the higher hills beyond.

'Nothing can touch this place, man.' Gospel continued his reverie. 'See over yonder. Wanchai. Some wonderful bars, wonderful places. Full of refugees, you see, so the prices are dirt cheap. I remember once going up the Wanch with a couple of Blair Line blokes and three RN fellows we met in a bar. You'd never believe ...'

'You're living in the past,' said the fifth engineer, who had joined them on the boat deck beneath the port bridge ladder. 'If Muir, here, likes Americans, Hong Kong should suit him down to the ground. You can't move for Yanks ashore. And if you've got no Yankee dollars, you might as well forget it. They all come up from Vietnam on R and R with money to burn.'

'And the Chinese let them burn it,' said Gospel, 'but they still prefer the British. It's all to do with tolerance and tradition.' The fifth engineer grunted and tossed his cigarette end overboard, but did not prevent Gospel from continuing. 'I was once in a bar standing next to a couple of Yankee marines. Full of bullshit, they were, and after three or four whiskies they noticed they were being charged eight dollars more for a drink than I was. Hong Kong dollars, mind you. When they complained to the mama-san, she threw them out. Threw them out! And they went away meek as little lambs, marines or no marines.'

'So we're still likely to make it with the birds?' asked the trainee sparky hopefully. The fifth engineer, who considered himself an expert on such matters, shook his head.

'If you go to Wanchai or Tsim Sha Tsui on the Kowloon side, you'll get pretty well what you deserve, and probably a dose into the bargain. Apart from that, Honkers is dead, you take my word. All this "Sin City of the East" nonsense is so much hot air invented to attract tourists. If you wanted the real thing, you should have gone ashore in Manila, up Dewey Boulevard.'

'Ah widna be so sure,' Gospel murmured to himself. 'After all, it's Christmas.'

But the engineer didn't hear, and said, 'Manila, Bangkok and Taipei are streets ahead of this dump. If you can find a Suzie Wong in Honkers these days, you're a better man than I am.'

As he spoke, the ship swiftly altered course to starboard and came round Tsim Sha Tsui towards Kowloon Peninsula and the crowded wharves of Ocean Terminal. Before going below, William Muir pointed to an impressive building near Star Ferry Pier.

'What's that?'

'That,' said Gospel, 'is the Pen Hotel. Only for peers, queers and Chief Engineers and much too good for the likes of you.'

'Hong Kong on Christmas Eve,' said Arthur Brown with a hint of merriment, 'is much too dangerous a place for the likes of you. So to protect the fragile flowers who will be manning our ship during the festivities, I took the liberty of phoning the Commandant of the Military Hospital. This most gracious lady completely understood the situation, and readily undertook to dispatch a group of highly trained army nurses to minister to the needs of the poor little souls too delicate to go ashore.'

Those more favoured officers about to disembark lined the rails and looked on wistfully as a fifteen-hundredweight truck drew up on the quay and disgorged a dozen gaily clad members of QARANC, who waved up at us and teetered, giggling, towards the gangway on high, pointed heels.

'I need hardly remind you, gentlemen, that these nurses are ladies who have been invited to a party and expect to be treated as such. Mr Dewar, as senior officer aboard, I expect you to make yourself personally responsible for their comfort and wellbeing.' A ribald roar from the duty crew drowned out the voice of the first mate as, one by one, the girls emerged on deck and were escorted to the bar in the smokeroom. I remained at the head of the gangway to watch the off duty men going ashore towards the buses and taxis that waited on Salisbury Road. The Old Man had already left in a company car, driven by an official of the Chinese Crew Department. Arthur Brown was going to visit friends who lived somewhere in Victoria, and Gospel, Roddy Hislop, the trainee sparky and Tom Walker, had set off for a night on the town, dragging Giles St John-Browne reluctantly in their wake. Apart from two ABs and a greaser, the Chinese crew were all on shore leave, visiting relatives in Kowloon or on Hong Kong Island, and I felt suddenly very contented alone on the vast deck of the *Blairskaith*. The warm air carried dance music across the water from a Swedish freighter berthed at the next pier. Out in the bay, the glare of a thousand neon lights reflected in the blackness, mingling with the riding lights of junks and coasters at anchor, and somewhere in the hills above Victoria, the flickering glow of fireworks pierced the night sky. Very slowly, I walked round the ship, checking hatches and derricks, lights and moorings before changing in my cabin and making my way to the smokeroom to sample the charms of a profession in which, of late, I had shown more than average interest.

So I was not present when Captain David H Sinclair sat down opposite a former schoolboy and distant colleague at a specially reserved dinner table in one of Des Voeux Road's better Cantonese restaurants.

'Personally, I can see no grounds for complaint,' said Captain Sinclair, perusing the vast, bi-lingual menu that had a golden tassle which dangled perilously close to the water jug. 'None of the matters you have mentioned were brought to my notice, or to the attention of my officers, so frankly I should disregard them.' His companion summoned a waiter with a wave of the hand and ordered for them both in fluent Cantonese. Then, reverting to his native language, he placed his fingertips together and said, 'You're right, David, of course. Nothing but silly superstition based, more than likely, on some personal discord within the Chinese crew which is far beyond either of us to resolve.'

The Captain grunted agreement and rather self-consciously let his gaze travel round the spacious restaurant, in which every table was occupied by successful, well-fed Europeans enjoying the conviviality of a night out in tastefully festive surroundings. For the first time in many years, the Captain was aware of an annoying sense of embarrassment. Perhaps it was because they were the only two men alone at a double table. The manner in which Tulloch's carefully manicured nails met just across the table was partly responsible. Why the hell had he accepted an invitation to dinner with this ridiculous little man whom he didn't know from Adam, but who addressed him in disconcertingly familiar terms that owed little to the commercial coincidence of shared employers? The waiter brought the soup, which tasted of warm water. Tulloch's fingers parted.

'Nothing gives me greater pleasure than enjoying good food and good company in pleasant surroundings,' said the little man. 'In the field of cuisine, the Orient stands unsurpassed. No doubt your wife appreciates the best in Chinese food since her visit to the Colony, some three years ago?'

Caught once more on the wrong foot, found out by the unexpected, Captain Sinclair mumbled a few words about his wife's visit, sought in vain to recollect her culinary preferences and, finding he could not, retreated in confusion behind his soup spoon. From the way Tulloch spoke and the unusual references he made, it was clear that he had either met both the Captain and his wife before, or had gone to considerable pains to check up on their backgrounds. But whenever the Captain came near to demanding an explanation, the little man turned their conversation so adroitly that David Sinclair invariably found himself discussing a topic completely detached from his intentional line of inquiry. Crab and vegetables came, then pork dumplings with sweet sauce. Over the steaming dishes, the Captain watched Archibald Tulloch and thought his own private thoughts. Who the hell is this guy? He knows me, knows Eva, lists every ship I've sailed on, tabulates every week of leave since I was a cadet. And his clothes, too—white dinner jacket, chocolate bow tie, yellow crocodile skin shoes. He's probably a queer. Look at his fingernails! And the voice; it isn't Scottish, never has been, though he goes on the whole time about Kirkcaldy and the school; even describes the blazer badge. If only I could remember him! But he won't spill the beans. Wants to go on to a cabaret in a private club he belongs to. He's got the cash. And outside on the pavement, should I leave or punch him in the mouth? Tulloch, like a tourist, insisted on taking a rickshaw pulled by a bicycle instead of a taxi, and as they approached the ridiculous conveyance, his fingers indicated its lack of cross-bar and he said, 'A suitable mode of transport for one who was denied the privilege of proclaiming news from between his knees.'

The penny dropped. The Captain climbed in beside the snotty-nosed little bastard who was always too insignificant to merit attention, the perpetual linesman and holder of jackets, whose fingers never experimented with George Black's aero-engine. Behind the bent, straining back of a coolie, they discussed news bulletins, triangular cardboard and a jam jar full of black ink.

Barely two miles away, in an atmosphere thick with cigarette and cigar smoke, Gospel seized five beer bottles by the neck and, holding them high above his head, edged his way towards the table round which the remainder of his party were sprawled in a condition of incipient intoxication.

'There you are. Two Tigers and three San Migs.'

Tom Walker, wedged in a corner between Roddy Hislop and the trainee sparky, peered apprehensively at the three half-full glasses before him, to which the fresh bottle was just being added, and closed his eyes.

'Come on, laddie,' said Gospel. 'We'll wean you off orange juice if it's the last thing we do!'

On a small platform somewhere behind the heaving mass of humanity, two Filipino girls in abbreviated cowboy suits twanged lethal electric guitars and sang *Bonnie and Clyde* in high-pitched, amplified voices. Giles St John-Browne, who

had lost his glass, was drinking straight from the bottle.
'Where are the hostesses?' he said. 'Hostess! Get me a
hostess!'

'You're not on a fucking aeroplane,' said the trainee
sparky. 'All the skirts in this joint are over at the bar beside the
Yanks and Germans. Not that any of them are worth a couple
of bucks.'

'S-s-speak for yourself,' said Roddy Hislop. Extracting
himself from the protective arm Tom Walker had stretched
round his shoulder, he approached the nearest girl and
touched her elbow. 'Excuse me, miss. Would you like to sit at
our table?' When the girl turned, she had gold teeth and no
bosom.

'Me no like you,' she said. 'You no good.'

Simultaneously, a fat, blonde seaman pulled her aside,
shouted 'Geh' weg, scheiss Engländer! Geh' weg!' and hurled
Roddy back into the crowd. With an agility that belied his
years, Gospel was suddenly between them.

'Ah'll knock yer bliddy square heid off,' he yelled, but
instead hit the German low in the stomach, knocking him back
over a table. A glass shattered on Roddy Hislop's head. The
trainee sparky grabbed a chair, and brought it down on the
shoulders of another German about to throw a second glass.

'Get out!' yelled Gospel.

Giles St John-Browne, with remarkable presence of mind,
climbed on to the table and carefully hurled a bottle in the
direction of the band. There was a flash, a sharp crack and all
the lights went out. The four British seamen raced for the door
while Tom Walker, suddenly alone, opened his eyes and
determinedly drained each remaining glass on the table before
following them unsteadily into the street. As a precaution,
they crossed the road and quickly put a block between them
and the bar before pausing to consider the situation.

'It wasn't worth all that,' said the trainee sparky, out of
breath. 'Anyway, the dolly was a bloke in drag. I'll bet my
wages on it.'

They waited for Tom Walker to catch up. A police
Landrover drove past travelling very quickly, its headlamps
on in the dark.

'Surely you know somewhere better than that, Gospel? You've been putting in here for years.'

The radio officer straightened his tie and rolled his eyes heavenwards as he did when communing with the Almighty. 'Oh, well,' he said, 'you've asked for it.' They had to haggle with the driver before he'd take all five in his taxi.

The establishment to which Gospel directed the cab was situated between a shoemaker's and a laundry on a narrow road well above Wanchai, where, on the lower slopes of the hills, the shops and offices and low-grade hotels began to give way to better class Chinese housing. A faded, unlit sign read 'Bar Hot Girl'. Before being admitted, Gospel exchanged hushed words with a huge Chinaman at the door and the rustle of banknotes was heard. Inside, the bar was dark, smoky, but not nearly so crowded as the previous one. All the men sitting at tables in the long, narrow room had girls with them, but there were plenty more girls waiting at the bar, wearing cheong-sams split up the sides so you could see their legs to the hip. The mama-san greeted Gospel like a long lost brother and brought to their table four girls and a bottle of Japanese whisky, for which they each contributed twelve Hong Kong dollars. The girls did not drink from the same bottle; their drinks were more expensive. Neither did Gospel, who presently made arrangements with the mama-san for what he termed a 'special'. He followed her through a small door to the left of the bar, accompanied by nods and winks from his shipmates.

The girls were not beautiful, neither were they ugly. What one lacked in face she made up for in figure and in another instance, the situation was reversed. They were very jolly; and the seamen became jolly too, ordered another bottle of Japanese whisky, filled and refilled their glasses, and danced from time to time when someone changed the record on the gramophone. Tom Walker sang *Mad Dogs and Englishmen go out in the Midday Sun*. The man who put on most records was a little Indian gentleman who attempted, between records, to emulate the patter of an American disc-jockey.

When he said, 'And now, from Charlie Pride, we have *Does my ring hurt your finger?*' all the seamen laughed, except

Giles, who didn't understand the joke. In all probability, the girls didn't understand either, but they all laughed too. Roddy, who was in a convenient situation to investigate the terrain beneath the folds of a cheong-sam, was content with what he found there, or perhaps the lack of it, and chose to retain that position for the remainder of the evening. After the ninth record, the little Indian came over and sat on the edge of the table.

'Chrissmass great festival for British sailor,' he said. 'For you to celebrate, I put on special show.' The trainee sparky prevented him knocking over the glasses. 'Special show,' said the Indian. 'You see! Special exhibish! Very special!'

'Where?' said Tom Walker, whose seventh glass was almost empty.

'Two house up street, in cellar,' said the Indian. 'Five gil, two boy, one dog. Very special exhibish!'

'Okay,' said Tom Walker, lumbering towards the centre of the dance floor.

'Thirty dolla,' said the Indian.

'Get stuffed!' said Roddy Hislop and the trainee sparky together, but Giles, who always had more money than anyone else, struggled to his feet and followed the third cadet towards the exit.

'I'm ashamed of you, St Giles,' said Roddy. 'That lovely pin-up girl in London and you go to bum-shows.'

Tears came to St John-Browne's eyes. His fists clenched. 'She isn't my girl. I never said she was. You made all that up yourselves.'

'But the photos, the garden party.'

'She's my sister. My sister, don't you understand?'

While Roddy was thinking of something to say, Giles pushed his way out of the bar. Everyone at the table was very silent for a while. As Roddy and the trainee sparky were leaving with their respective young ladies, Gospel appeared through the little door beside the bar.

'Had your "special" then?' asked Roddy.

Gospel pointed into the tiny room where the mama-san was clearing dishes from a little table. 'Best chow-mein in Hong Kong,' said Gospel. 'That's my "special", laddie.'

The cabaret took place in what had once been the ballroom of a traditional, colonial club. As a concession to modern fashion, the ceiling was painted obligatory black and several oscillating, fluorescent lamps had been carefully arranged to show up the customers in the most flattering light and disguise the labels on the wine bottles. Forty tables were set in closely spaced tiers round a central, square floor, on which it was possible for the patrons to dance between items of the cabaret. And to ensure that every patron could find a dancing partner, each table was equipped with a telephone and a little painted chart denoting the number of every other table in the club. This was of particular benefit to the young professional ladies, who sat discreetly on the perimeter of the establishment and used it to offer their services to the customers by remote control. After the seventh such call, Archibald Tulloch took the receiver off the hook. For form's sake, Captain David H Sinclair danced with a young lady from the next table, who came from Ipswich and was touring the world for six months in company with her parents. He returned her to the bosom of her family, having failed to elicit whether the Ipswich in question was in England, Queensland or, indeed, the State of South Dakota, and sat down out of breath. Tulloch's face was also flushed, simply through the exhilaration of sifting the card-index of his memory. Beneath fluorescent lights, to the music of a dance band, he juggled with facts, conjured up memories from the dim and not so distant past, presented them to the Captain and watched the emotions cross his companion's face with the rapidity of the oscillating illumination.

'Outside Ballantine's, do you remember? We first met when I came to work as a paper boy. By far the youngest. It seems to have been perpetually winter; always six-thirty in the morning, always half-light. For more than three years we saw each other only in the half-light, and later, at school, I doubt if you even noticed me at all, although I tried to help you once when you were sick in the bicycle shed after inadvertently swallowing an Oxo cube. Do you remember? You chased me off. You didn't need my help. And later, you accused me of cheating with my newspaper money. Senseless retribution, but nevertheless a decisive and lasting experience of my child-hood. How easily you forget. What trivial significance such matters must have held in your early system of priorities. A joke, perhaps, in which I played the ingenuous victim; for in the world of schoolboys, three years' seniority bestows an almost regal isolation. You scarcely took the trouble to look up from your activities when, trembling from a dare, I stumbled through the municipal foliage of the Garden of Remembrance one day after school. Heaven knows what you were looking for in the long grass behind the daffodil beds. A pen knife? A button? Perhaps a snug little nest hollowed out amid the dusty grass an hour previously by artistic fingers and athletic thighs. In any case, I took you for a ghost and made off long before you could have thrown a handy stone in my direction.'

A spotlight, piercing the multi-coloured haze, focused on the gold lamé form of an Australian chanteuse, the jarring blondeness of a natural brunette, the bold cleavage of the not-so-young. Safe behind a screen of darkness, the Captain concentrated on his thoughts.

That bastard with a computer for a brain. That little worm, no higher than my elbow. Nothing will satisfy him. Nothing can deter him from shovelling shit, running the tape, pulling cards from his memory bank. Thinks he knows the score. Talks as if things happened yesterday. Yet, was he there at all? Seems to know the lot, though he was too small even to be considered for the rugby team. What is he after? He must have searched the records, cooked the books. An eternal onlooker, trying to lay bare my soul with a knowing smile. A recapitulator. A bearer of grudges. Should have joined the police, but he's too small.

From the centre of the stage, over-ripe Australian arms extended like a crucifix, then descended in stilted, mechanical rotation. The voice was that of a twelve-year-old.

... Easy as learnin' your A B C,
So come on, come on,
Dooo ... the Locomotion with me!

Tulloch was talking once more, too quietly to be ignored. 'A pleasant little melody, popularised, I believe, by a young lady who rejoiced in the name of "Little Eva". A significant name, you will agree. Even a tragic one. Leaving aside the mother of humanity, in which we find its origin, have not the more famous of its subsequent bearers been distinguished by an ominous capacity for misfortune? One need only think of the late Frau Hitler, née Braun, whose incinerated remains were never found, or more recently, of the charming Señora Perón, embalmed and perpetuated as a saint for those in the southern hemisphere. Was it perhaps with her namesakes in mind that another of that name recently chose to have herself exquisitely duplicated in wax? But I have offended you. Allow me to explain. Two weeks ago, totally unheralded, I found among my private mail, a magazine intended for connoisseurs of the fine arts. Naturally, I assumed there had been some mistake: that the publication had been addressed to me in error; but curiosity prompted me to examine the magazine, and what I found there led me to conclude that it had been sent by none other than the Scottish artist whose latest work was the subject of its main feature article. I refer, of course, to our former schoolfellow, Malcolm Leslie, whose acquaintance I renewed several years ago while acting as interpreter to a visiting group of Chinese artists in Edinburgh. Since then, we have maintained an infrequent correspondence. Malcolm is a man of few words. How typical that he should inform me of his latest triumph this way, and how doubly auspicious that I should have the honour of entertaining a guest so close to the delightful subject of his masterpiece. What a sense of pride, what overwhelming fulfilment there must be in knowing that a loved one has been immortalised in her own life time. Re-created. Raised above the ranks of ordinary women to act as a shining prototype, from which will doubtless stem a whole new concept in sculpture, a vital new school of artistic thought. But I'm boring you. You clearly know the sculpture so much better than I. Even at the earliest point in the artist's development, you totally committed your practical skill to helping him realise his visionary ambition. If only the tree had not been so large. If only the plank had not been so terrifyingly far from the ground. I assure you, David, it was with your own safety in mind that I ran off and summoned the head janitor when you crawled for the second time on to that insubstantial piece of wood. You probably did not notice. You seldom did.'

On this occasion, Captain David H Sinclair did notice. Beneath a yellow spotlight, to the tune of *Waltzing Matilda*, he leaned across the table, raised Archibald Tulloch to his full, inconspicuous height with one hand and with the other, delivered such a devastating blow to the face that the little man was propelled eight feet backwards, to land amidst the delicate cut glass of a nearby table. The Captain administered a similar blow to a waiter, ill-advised enough to intervene, straightened his jacket and strode unhindered from the premises. Mr Archibald Tulloch, aware of a disconcerting, but not unpleasantly damp sensation at the back of his neck, removed his head from an upturned ice-bucket and opened his eyes to gaze upon an exquisitely scented flower, nestling in a flaccid bosom. While the fragile, white hand fluttered a lace handkerchief in the region of his bleeding mouth, Archibald Tulloch ignored Dougal Elliot's muttered threats and enunciated as precisely as his shattered dentures would permit.

'Delighted to make your acquaintance, Miss Blair. What an exquisite alpine rose. It must have been specially imported by air.'

As no taxis were to hand outside the club, the Captain lit a cigarette and set off on foot, hoping to catch a streetcar in the direction of Star Ferry Pier. Although it was almost midnight, the pavements were still crowded. He realised that within a few minutes, it would be Christmas Day. Had not a sudden stream of traffic caused him to stop at the street corner, he would never have noticed the object in the window of the little pawn-shop with the red neon sign that read 'We never close', in four languages. Casually, he approached the dimly illuminated window and peered between the bars of the metal grille, designed to safeguard the contents on display. When the Captain left the pawn-shop, he carried a bulky, brown paper package under his left arm. There was a new spring in his step and he whistled a jaunty, though unrecognisable tune through clenched teeth. Just as he reached Edinburgh Place, a group of Americans began to cheer and slap one another on the back. Several ships in the roadstead sounded their sirens. It was Christmas Day.

The party aboard SS *Blairskaith* had been fine, up to a point. The nurses, according to plan, had eaten and drunk and danced a lot, and behaved in an increasingly friendly manner towards the British sailors far from home. My particular concern was a plump, red-headed sergeant called Teresa, who came from Belfast and, at a certain point of intoxication, fell into deep melancholy over the troubles in her homeland, tightened her vice-like grip on my arm and snivelled into her beer in a thoroughly unfestive manner. Aware that the situation was clearly beyond recovery, I excused myself on the grounds that some routine nautical matter demanded my attention, and escaped from the smokeroom in the direction of my cabin. I was surprised to meet the Old Man in the alleyway. He was not due back aboard until eight in the morning. I was even more surprised when he greeted me heartily and invited me to join him in his dayroom.

Captain Sinclair went over to the dresser and poured two gins. Standing with his back towards me, facing the open scuttle, he seemed ill at ease; as if somehow he doubted his own authority. His light grey civilian suit heightened this impression, and I found myself considering the possibility that he might be drunk. But when he turned to lift a large parcel from the day bed to the writing desk, there was nothing in his movements to substantiate my suspicion: I accepted the drink and sat down while he carefully removed the object from its wrappings. With the air of a magician about to produce a rabbit from a hat, the Old Man whisked away the last sheet of brown paper and held the ungainly article up to view. An expression of unadulterated pride came into his eyes.

'What do you think of that, Mr Dewar? Just what we need. Just what the ship needs, eh?'

I took the bagpipes from him, cradled the drones over my shoulder and examined the antiquated instrument with what I hoped was a sufficiently critical eye.

'These haven't been played for years, sir. Perhaps there's

no reed and the bag may be perished.'

'Nonsense, Mister. What do you take me for? They're in perfect working order. Come on. Give us a tune.'

Of course he was right. I had no alternative but to rise to my feet, inflate the faded, tartan-covered bag and, with eyes closed through embarrassment as much as concentration, transport my thoughts to the days when, on a windy playing field that doubled as a parade ground, I had wrestled with the intricacies of a similar instrument. The Old Man winced at the first low, moaning yelps that issued from the chanter. My fingers fumbled to adjust the drones. But as the pipes became more familiar to me, as the sound swelled out to fill the cabin with a rough approximation of *The Braes o' Balquhidder*, his brow cleared and he refilled our glasses till they overflowed and the gin ran in droplets on the surface of the desk.

My involuntary concert lasted almost an hour, the only hour in which I was alone with Captain David H Sinclair. Yet even this statement is not strictly true. At one point, the second engineer appeared, accompanied by two dishevelled young ladies, seeking the source of the music; but the Old Man sent them on their way. He preferred to listen alone. And while he listened, he paced to and fro, drank glass upon glass of gin and sifted in vain through the chaotic heap of magazines on the day bed. While he listened, he described the most modern commercial coffee dispenser and assured me of its superiority over the chromium plated machine that had ... While he listened, he tabulated the total area of burial ground in the United Kingdom, weighed it against that devoted to military use and rough shooting, and came out in favour of burial rather than incineration by municipal crematoria. While I played, he considered the viability of commercial waxworks, ranged the galleries of Madame Tussauds and likened its Chamber of Horrors to a badly executed school play. To the *Reel of the Fifty First Division*, he voyaged to the Baltic, navigated the Danziger Bucht, plumbed the Vistula's mouth and found safe harbour in the People's Republic of Poland. To the sound of *The Dark Island* and *The Flo'ers o' the Forest*, he removed his jacket and carefully eradicated an offending bloodstain from its right cuff. When, at last, he dismissed me, and took the pipes with a promise to keep them safe for future use, the sweat that beaded his brow owed little to the warm draught from an open scuttle. On leaving my eyes were drawn to the top of the dresser, on which he ceremoniously laid the traditional Scottish instrument. The little, leather covered box that nestled beside the pipes was clearly designed to contain drawing instruments.

> St John-Browne's body is a-lying in a ditch,
> St John-Browne's body is a-lying in a ditch. ...

Tom Walker sidestepped the last military lady to leave the ship and bowed low before beginning his perilous ascent of the steeply sloping gangway to the deck. Roddy Hislop and the trainee radio officer, whose nocturnal activities had concluded in time for them to breakfast aboard ship, went to the rail to observe his erratic progress.

'What happened to you, then?'

'Come on up here, you dirty old man. Where's your mate? Where's Giles, then?'

Tom Walker heaved himself up the last few steps and crossed the deck with the studied delicacy of an elephant walking on eggs. Though his face was ashen, his expression bore the celestial serenity of the very drunk.

'St Giles,' he said with great difficulty, 'fell into a monsoon ditch while pursuing a little flopsy-wopsy who stole his wallet after the show. He could have drowned, but the ditch was dry so he broke his collar bone instead.'

'Where is he now?' asked Gospel, who had joined the trio.

The third cadet waved an arm in the direction of Hong Kong Island.

'In a nice little hospital somewhere in Victoria, with lovely little nurses and a doctor with a big black beard.'

Gospel seized his arm.

'What did the doctor say? Is he all right?'

The cadet narrowed his eyes.

'The doctor said ... the doctor said ... Oh, Christ! I'm going to be sick!' And he plunged down the port alleyway, his hand clasped to his mouth.

'If this is Christmas,' said Roddy Hislop, 'I don't want to be here at New Year.'

'You won't be,' said Gospel, who always knew more about the movements of the ship than anyone else. 'In four days we sail for Nagasaki, so you should bring in the New Year on the open sea. The best place, if you ask me.'

Three Days Plus

Gospel was always right. But before his prognostications came true, before SS *Blairskaith* cast off to take course for Japan, there occurred a series of events which even he could scarcely have foreseen. Admittedly, the first was predictable enough. Bandaged, and with his right arm in a sling, Giles St John-Browne walked slowly down the pier at noon on Boxing Day. Purely by chance, his arrival coincided with the departure of Marine Superintendent Hector Elliot, who had spent most of the forenoon closeted in private consultation with the Old Man. When they came on deck, neither the master nor his superior betrayed the slightest emotion. They shook hands amicably and walked towards the rail as if nothing within their comprehension could possibly have shaken their mutual confidence in rank, authority or the Company, on which it was founded. If only Giles had been a few minutes later. If only the officer and the gentleman had not been confronted by such a lame duck, such a sorry scarecrow of plaster and bandages, Giles would surely have escaped to suffer little more than the ribald sympathy of his shipmates.

I could easily have created a diversion, dreamt up an urgent message, found a loophole through which he could have slipped unmolested towards his cabin. But who would have expected such a reaction from the Old Man? I stood silent beneath the awning as Captain David H Sinclair petrified the cadet with his eyes.

'You're late, Browne. Twenty-six hours late, to be precise.'

'Yes, sir. I had an accident. ....'

'An accident, was it? According to the Crown Colony Police, you were drunk and disorderly. Drunk, Browne! The Police wouldn't lie to me, would they, Browne?'

'Yes, sir. I mean no. But they didn't charge me, sir. I 'phoned from hospital, sir. I fell into a ditch and broke my collar bone.'

'A ditch, eh? Bad luck. I hope you don't expect to be relieved from duty. We can't do without an indispensable man like you.'

'But my arm, sir. I don't see how I can ...'

'Write? You've got two hands, Browne. Two hands. Or are you worried about taking sights? I think we'll manage without your valuable contribution.'

No more words came. The cadet, as if uprooted, lurched towards the port alleyway and disappeared. Marine Superintendent Elliot inserted two fingers between his white collar and pink neck. His eyes, which during the Old Man's tirade had been carefully diverted towards the more pleasant prospect of Victoria Harbour, rested on the deck. He was a large man and could not cope with embarrassment. Nevertheless, something in his over florid colouring, something in the deliberation of his step as he climbed heavily down the gangway suggested, even to the least astute spectator, that all was not well aboard SS *Blairskaith*.

Masters of ships are in no way exempt from the emotions common to other mortals. Their humours rise and fall, their tempers flame and subside. When Giles St John-Browne propelled himself so inopportunely up the gangway, he fell victim to the wrath of an angry superior, but not of a bad Old Man. Whether good or ill, nothing is more unalterable than reputation, and David Sinclair's reputation as a master mariner remains intact to this day. Perhaps, beneath the awnings, in the presence of the Marine Superintendent, his reputation as a man suffered a temporary setback; but within the hour, those of us familiar with the handling of cargo well understood the Old Man's bad temper and the reason for Mr Elliot's prolonged consultation.

Along with plastic goods and furniture, cut price clothes and electric novelties, we had taken aboard at Hong Kong one hundred and fifty tons of nondescript military equipment which came in a great number of nondescript metal boxes and was destined for the United Kingdom to be replaced, refurbished or, perhaps, simply scrapped. In any case, we stowed the boxes safe and sound in the tweendecks of number two hold. No sooner were they in place, protected from the rest of the cargo by rush matting, than the military powers of the Crown Colony decided that seven weeks was an excessive length of time for their boxes to be at sea, and insisted that arrangements be made for their arrival in London no later than five weeks hence. While no one respected Far Eastern Command, or valued its important transport contracts more than Blair Line, it was clearly out of the question to re-route our ship, for we were bound for Japan and Taiwan before heading home. As usual, a compromise was reached. The *Blairskaith* was to remain at Hong Kong a further three days and then trans-ship the military equipment to the *Blairholm*, which was steaming towards the Crown Colony on her homeward voyage. Similarly, a less urgent consignment of Korean tobacco was to be transferred to our ship and conveyed to the United Kingdom by the more devious route. And everyone was happy, except perhaps the Old Man and Giles St John-Browne. The army was sure of getting its boxes home in time and the company was sure of retaining the contract. The Chinese sailors stayed two extra days with their families, and the European officers went ashore to the shops and bars, though this time no one seemed very keen to get drunk. Throughout the three days' wait, the Old Man stayed aboard, never straying far from his cabin where he busied himself with the countless clerical tasks required of a master at sea. While he was scrupulously polite in dealing with his officers, his face betrayed the worry caused by our unexpected change of schedule. Giles likewise stayed well clear of company during this period. His routine duties were made more awkward and tiresome by his injuries, and after work he usually retired to drink beer and listen to records in his cabin; for though the crew were generally sympathetic to misfortune such as his, the story about his sister had got around and he found himself simultaneously a minor hero and a laughing stock, which was quite beyond his powers of comprehension.

On the first unscheduled day in Hong Kong, when Giles

retired to seek solace in Wagner, he was not alone. Tom Walker was still confined to the adjacent bunk, the victim of severe colic occasioned by his uncharacteristic lapse from abstention. On the second day, motivated rather by antipathy towards *Tannhäuser* than his fitness for work, the third cadet rose from his sickbed to resume duty. On the third day, SS *Blairholm* docked at Ocean Terminal and discharged her cargo. On the third day, the nondescript military boxes were divested of their rush matting and trans-shipped to the *Blairholm* under the supervision of the second mate and his temporarily handicapped assistant, St John-Browne. Henceforth, I must be objective.

There once was a perfectly ordinary ship called *Blairskaith* which was obliged to wait three days over schedule in Hong Kong in order that vitally important military boxes might more swiftly be transported to their vitally important military destination. There once was a consignment of Korean leaf tobacco, conveniently packed in hogsheads, which was transshipped because of the military boxes and stowed in their stead in the tweendecks of number two hold under the watchful eye of the second mate and his less watchful assistant, St John-Browne. There once was an inconvenient squall of rain which happened to coincide with a particularly interesting telephone call for the second mate, leaving the second cadet alone to check the cargo. There once was a second cadet who chose, because of his injuries, to inspect the recently stowed cargo from the deck rather than descend the ladder to the hold before the hatches were closed. Was Giles to blame for declining to put a foot on that vertical ladder? Was the Chinese crew to blame for immediately closing the hatches under the watchful eye of Ho Man Tin, the bosun? Watchful eyes see only what is expected.

There once was a perfectly ordinary cadet whose injuries precluded him from descending a vertical ladder to inspect an unexpected consignment of leaf tobacco in the tweendecks, but who noticed nevertheless that one of the foremost hogsheads had been broached. There once was a cadet whose humiliation had been so complete that he neglected to report the occurrence. He left the deck with his eyes to the ground, and though his eyes might have registered the brownness of tobacco juice on the polished floor of the senior officers' alleyway, they did not uncloud until the chromium deck of a gramophone lay polished before them.

There once was a nurse, who was so amused by a recent experience that she wrote a letter to her friend in the merchant navy. The letter arrived in Hong Kong on the third day over schedule.

> Ward Four
> Ear, Nose and Throat Dept
> North Edinburgh Clinic
> 20 December

Dear Andrew,

I'm writing this at 3.15 a.m. during my coffee break on night shift. Things have been so much quieter since my transfer from Casualty to the ENT Unit that it's almost like a holiday. Yesterday it snowed for the first time this winter, but as usual the traffic churned it into grey slush within an hour. How lucky you are to be able to escape to a warm climate every winter and get paid for it into the bargain! Still, I mustn't complain. A nurse's life isn't always as dull as many people imagine. When I first heard of my transfer, I was unhappy at the thought of losing my friends in Casualty and having to start all over again in a strange department. Dr Millar, who is in charge of the Unit, has a reputation for being abrupt and difficult to deal with, so I wasn't looking forward to the move at all. How wrong can people be? Only two days after I started work here, he complimented me on my efficiency. You can't imagine a nicer person, no matter what other people say about his temper.

Last week he invited three of us to an official reception in an art gallery! It was like something out of a film, all the men in dinner jackets and the women with furs and jewellery. We spent ages deciding what to wear and were all rather disappointed when Dr Millar sent a note asking us to appear in uniform. Still, our picture got into the newspapers and there was even a five-minute report about it on the television news, though I didn't see it because I was on duty. When the girls in our flat heard about it, they went out and bought ten copies of the newspaper, so I've cut out one of the pictures and enclosed it with this letter. Sorry I had to fold it so much to get it into the envelope.

As you can imagine, many of the guests at the reception were artists and critics, all very knowledgeable and intense and quite different from the sort of people I generally meet. Most of them seemed dreadful shams, so conceited and preoccupied with their own importance. But then again maybe they were behaving in the only way they understand. It must be so strange, producing paintings or sculptures for a living instead of dealing with hard facts, even if these only concern damaged human tissue. But I'm becoming morbid, and I shouldn't, because I'm really very happy. There was wine and cheese after the reception. We all got rather tipsy and I met this cuddly old Irishman, who showed me all over the gallery and even unlocked a room to let me see the moulds from which the sculpture in the photograph had been cast. At one point, he even suggested that I might model for him sometime, because he's an artist as well as a gallery curator. But I didn't take him seriously. He didn't expect me to. It was very late indeed when we left the reception and Dr Millar paid for the taxi to take us home. We all had hangovers the next day and had to miss the carol singing practice in the nurses' home.

Of course, when the news got round, some of the girls at the hospital were jealous that they hadn't been invited and went out of their way to avoid us. They led a half-hearted campaign against us, insinuating that we were Dr Millar's pets, and that there must have been very special reasons for his favouritism. What rubbish! Apart from being more than twice our age, the doctor is a quiet, happily married man. A non-smoker and non-drinker who thinks of nothing but his work at the hospital. The Unit is his whole life. You should have seen his face when he was presented with the cheque for new equipment. Personally, I suspect he chose Jane and I simply because we were the best looking girls on the ward, and Augusta because it's always nice to include an overseas nursing student.

Something still remains in the air, a seed of mistrust, a

germ of envy, but we ignore it. Besides, it's almost Christmas and at Christmas time in hospital, no one has time for jealousy or petty squabbles. What a lonely time this must be for you, miles away from friends and relatives. Sometimes I wish I could shut my eyes and open them to find myself out there beside you in the sun. But what's the point in dreaming? I know I must keep all my love till you return at the end of February. I hear Sister coming up the stairs now, Andrew, so I must finish off. First thing in the morning I'll post this letter, but even then, I doubt if it'll reach you before Christmas. Please write to me if ever you have a few free moments.

Love Olive

PS I still haven't had a card from you, but there are five days left.

O.

Caption to an eight-inch, three-column, halftone newspaper photograph:

'Ere — 'Ere!

Four lovely girls, sitting pretty in the biggest lug-hole you've ever seen. But Ooops! What's happened to the third one's clothes? It's OK, Grandad, wipe the steam off your glasses. The chilly young lady in the middle is only a waxwork model, part of a modern sculpture by the artist, Malcolm Leslie, that has been raising funds for the Northern Ear Research Unit in Edinburgh. And the other lovelies? They're three pretty nurses who came along to collect the cheque for £3700 which was presented to Dr Angus Millar by the artist at a reception in the Leslie Gallery last night. The nurses are, left to right: Staff Nurse Olive Simpson, Nurse Jane Boyd, Student Nurse Augusta Rock (from Barbados).

On the third day over schedule, I smoothed out the folded newspaper photograph and fixed it to the white painted wall of my cabin with four pieces of sticky tape. Outside, the ship's watchman was shambling down the alleyway, wedging a rolled up copy of the *South China Post* and the *Hong Kong*

Standard behind the polished brass door knob of every officer's cabin. He handed me mine as I passed.

'Big blow comin' soon, Sam-fo,' he said, grinning broadly. 'Big blow. You see!'

The draught from the smokeroom fan barely disturbed the even blanket of blue haze from Arthur Brown's cigar. The first mate laid his beer glass on the table and looked up quizzically as Roddy Hislop traced the lines of the *South China Post* weather report with a chipped finger nail and read out loud.

'. . . severe tropical depression has now developed to typhoon and is reported to be 500 miles east south east of Hong Kong. . . .'

'That, gentlemen, is "Wilma",' said Gospel from the far end of the bar. 'We've been keeping our eye on her all morning.'

Few, if any, of the officers sprawled on the none too comfortable seating accommodation of *Blairskaith*'s smoke-room immediately assumed that Captain David Sinclair made up the multiple of Gospel's casually used pronoun. When Gospel said 'We', one generally gathered that the other party possessed prescient gifts far superior to those of the master of any vessel afloat. Only this time, Arthur Brown let the cat out of the bag.

Through his deep, smoky camouflage, he said, 'The Old Man asked Gospel to keep an ear out for the Taiwan and Japanese forecasts this morning. Wilma's not likely to cause us any problems.'

Deflated, Gospel grunted and stared at his beer. 'That remains to be seen,' he said eventually. 'We had a few words about it earlier, but He's not giving anything away. Not this time.'

This time, no one at all believed that Gospel's accomplice had been Captain David H Sinclair of the SS *Blairskaith*.

'What's upsetting Him? Who's put His nose out of joint this time?'

Gospel gazed wearily at the fifth engineer.

'You know better than I do who hasn't paid the price of his sensuality in the sinful Orient.'

As the occupants of the smokeroom dissolved in laughter,

Gospel let the flicker of a smile cross his weatherbeaten features and lumbered towards the door.

'Giles!' said the fifth engineer gleefully. 'Giles hasn't paid for his nooky.'

Gospel paused, his expression fading from amusement to petulant serenity. 'That wee laddie,' he said, 'has paid for more than you ever will in your whole life.'

We all laughed, and Arthur Brown bought the next round of beers.

After dinner on the third day over schedule, a young man named Wong Ching from Kowloon reported to Ling Chau, the chief steward. Wong Ching's credentials were completely in order. His superior could not have wished for a more fitting replacement for Li Yui Mun, whose doctor had obliged him to remain ashore owing to a particularly severe bout of Asian 'flu'. When Ling Chau introduced the new 'Tiger' to Captain David H Sinclair he nodded politely, but did not open his mouth to utter words of welcome, warning or command. The Old Man was content to nod and usher the two Chinamen from his dayroom, for on the third day over schedule in Hong Kong, his teeth had something better to do than form vowels and consonants out of empty air. Who can waste time on words when, between his teeth, he holds a quid of brown, juicy tobacco? The Captain's door closed. The Captain's teeth ground slowly, regularly from left to right. Let there be no mistake. The moist, glutinous mass which passed, ten times a minute, between David H Sinclair's left and right molars bore no resemblance to a gritty Oxo cube. The juicy mouthful between the Captain's teeth owed nothing to canvas wrappings or carefully compressed rope. Rum and curry powder were not involved. The taste on David's tongue came straight from the leaf, straight from the moist, Korean bundle that lay beneath the papers in the right hand drawer of his desk. Before leaving his cabin, David filled his pockets. Before he went on deck, he spat a long stream of noxious, brown juice through the open porthole into the waters of Ocean Terminal, which were already greyer and more choppy than they had been on the previous day.

On the fourth day over schedule in Hong Kong, I stood on

the starboard wing of *Blairskaith*'s bridge in the mist of a grey dawn and watched three tugs tow a Swedish ship, stern first, away from the piers of Ocean Terminal. The Swede had engine trouble. She was refitting condensers and had no choice but to ride out whatever 'Wilma' had in store at the typhoon anchorage behind Stonecutters Island. I looked on pensively as her huge hull left the quay and edged awkwardly into the channel. For my money, typhoon anchorages rated second only to harbours as places to avoid when a revolving tropical lady raised her head in your vicinity. But then, the Swede had no choice. A brown jet arched over the dodger two feet to my right and I turned to find the Old Man huddled against the repeater compass housing.

'We'll beat her by miles,' he said. 'We'll outrun her right up the Taiwan Strait.'

I agreed, because under such circumstances, there are few safer places to be than aboard a fifteen-knot ship with plenty of ocean to manoeuvre in. The Old Man spat once more.

'Don't ever let winds worry you, Mister Dewar. There's no wind in the world that you can't dodge.'

Though scarcely subscribing to his generalisation, I nodded vague agreement.

'We should be well clear in this case anyway, sir. The last report I heard put the centre just off Babuyan.'

'Quite so,' the Captain replied.

And at 08.00 hours on the fourth day over schedule, the pilot came aboard and SS *Blairskaith* cast off and headed out at half-speed through Hong Kong Harbour for Japan.

Up in Nagasaki...

The waters of Hong Kong Harbour were grey and choppy and slopped up under *Blairskaith*'s bow as she nosed round Tsim Sha Tsui and headed for the turning buoy. Somewhere high above the mainland, a glimmer of watery sunlight tried vainly to make its presence felt in the damp, overcast sky, but soon gave in and like the mainland hills and the Peak above Victoria, receded in a dismal blanket of cloud. A light sea was running and inshore, the black shapes of junks and coasters and walla-walla boats rose and fell at their haphazard moorings. Ahead of us, an old, smoky Liberian buffeted up channel. Already, a big P & O job had left its pier and was swinging out to pass Kowloon point. All had the same idea. All were making for the open sea and all the space in the world. I slid open the wheelhouse door and stepped on to the starboard wing of the bridge. To port was Kai Tak runway, with a 707 taxiing like a silver beetle in my binoculars. To starboard, Quarry Bay and Taikoo Shipyard, grey and indistinct; dead ahead was the turning buoy with its light flashing once every two-and-a-half seconds and a cutter standing off to take the pilot ashore.

'Maximum revs on no notice, if you please, Chief.'

The Old Man replaced the engine-room telephone and the *Blairskaith* picked up speed on course 126° true as the pilot cutter headed away from us, the pilot now a tiny, waving figure on its deck. Once more it came back to me, the feeling of delightful anticipation, the exhilaration of being part of a ship at sea. It seemed to emanate from the very heart of the ship, from the great, pulsing turbines, from the engine-room, with four engineers standing by on 'no notice', ready for instant action, from the plates and rivets and boards beneath my feet till it filled my whole body and I found myself grinning like a dog with two tails. When I turned to the wheelhouse, the Old Man was laughing too. His eyes gleamed and his massive chest heaved with amusement beneath the white drill of his shirt. For once, his jaws had ceased their grinding motion.

'We'll outrun her, Mister,' he laughed between newly yellowed teeth.

'A piece of cake, Third. Nothing to it.'

And suddenly, as though I'd never known before, I realised that the Old Man was barely ten years older than myself. Less, in fact. Barely eight. With patience and a little luck would I not soon be in his position? What was my exhilaration at merely being afloat compared to his at being in command; at having within his trust six million pounds worth of ship and cargo, and forty-five lives besides?

We ran Hak Tau abeam. Ahead of us, the Liberian altered course, heading south for Bangkok or Singapore. On our port bow, Lamtung Island rose bleakly through the mist, its barren outline punctuated only by the lights on Ngai Ying and then on Tathong Point. As we rounded the Point, the swell increased. Its surface became broken and disturbed and with it came the wind which whipped the tops from the waves and tossed their foam on to the fo'c'sle where it ran in bubbling torrents between winches and cables. The Old Man stepped back from the radar screen.

'Give her full away, Mister Dewar.'

Automatically, I reached for the brass handles of the engine-room telegraph and pushed them forward. Two double rings ahead. The faintest tremor ran through the full length of the ship as her turbines answered and her sixty ton phosphor-bronze screw bit the water to thrust forward at fifteen-and-a-half knots. The Old Man made for the chartroom.

'Keep your eyes open, Mister. Let me know if "Wilma" does anything unusual, and remember to watch out for fishing junks. These bastards never give up. Not in any weather.'

'Yes, sir.'

He pulled the door half closed.

'Get the Second to give me a call when we sight Pedro Blanco.'

Then the birds came. They came from Tai Long and Lo Chau, from Po Toi and Sam Kong and Wang Lan. Sea birds, land birds, black and brown birds, but predominantly, overwhelmingly, gulls. They soared, slanted, spiralled, skimmed the waves and mixed their whiteness with the windswept foam. They rose like a whirlwind and cast their shadow over our glistening bow. But their course was not like ours. They shrieked their panic to the waves. They rose and threw themselves northwest. Northwest against the watery sun. Northwest towards Tolo and Tai Pang Wan. Northwest into the hinterland of Wang Tung. Who could ignore their shadow? Who could turn a deaf ear to the million seagull cries? The shadow reflected on the brow of the quartermaster. The noise stunned Roddy Hislop and myself to silence on the wing of the bridge. The gulls interrupted calculations, came between parallel rulers and dividers and drew Captain David H Sinclair from the chartroom to stand beside us beneath a million beating wings.

'Bloody amazing,' said the cadet at last. 'What set them up? What are they afraid of?'

'They may be migrating,' I ventured lamely. 'You never know. It could be the weather.'

'Surely not "Wilma". She's three hundred miles away.'

'Maybe they can sense things in the air that we can't,' I muttered. 'I've certainly never seen anything like it in my life.'

Roddy Hislop turned to the Old Man.

'What do you think, sir?'

Captain Sinclair stood stock still, save for his jaws, and stared after the raucously retreating cloud, now dark against the sky, now light against the misty mainland.

'I reckon you should keep your eyes on the sea, where they belong,' he said and stepped back into the chartroom.

Rather than intercept Roddy's surprised gaze, I chose to scan the horizon once more through my binoculars, following the last, straggling smudge of gulls northwest, then I walked through the wheelhouse into the chartroom. The Old Man's eyes rested on me for barely a second, then returned to British Admiralty Chart number 1263, on which the battered chartroom lamp cast a soft, yellow glow. I approached to look over his shoulder. Before him, along the upper edge of the chart, were spread the four latest weather reports written in thin Biro on cheap, red lined paper, almost like greetings telegrams. Where Gospel had completed the forms, the printing was direct and carefully spaced. It became slanted and more agitated when the trainee radio officer had taken the watch.

'T T T Storm Warning.

At 30,0600 GMT. Severe tropical storm "Wilma" is reported to be within thirty miles of 20.4°N 121.5°E. Forecast to be quasi/stationary for the next three hours and then to move northwest at about 7 kts for the following twelve hours.'

Over his hunched back, over the dark blue epaulettes with four new gold bars, I examined the pencilled courses of ship and typhoon. He was right. Apart from a fairly rough passage, we were in no danger. No matter how hard 'Wilma' chose to blow, she would always be blowing astern; and miles and miles away at that. But still I could not rid my mind of the birds, of the huge, discordant cloud whose protests still reverberated against the wind.

'Have you ever seen them behave like that, sir? Birds. All at once. Just like that?'

The swivel seat squeaked as it pivoted and the Old Man looked up at me.

'No, Mister, I have not. But where birds are concerned, you can be sure their motives lie either in safety or in food. When safety is at stake, they never make a wrong move. It's not impossible, these days, for a ship to pass directly through the eye of a typhoon. We have the power, the engines, the technical know-how to be able to get away with it. But the only man I've ever met who actually steamed into the eye did so aboard the *Argus*, a little, worked-out gunboat, whose boilers would scarcely have kept our kitchens running. She made it, Mister. Into the eye, through it, and out again. Only the pressure sprung her forward plates and she sank two days later off Valparaiso in a calm sea with no loss of life. That was in 'ninety eight, Mister Dewar, when men were better than they are today and vessels were worse. But birds were just the same. In the calm, placid eye of that typhoon, when the stokers came up on deck for a moment to escape the heat and sweat of the stoke-hold, the air above them was alive with feathered shapes, wheeling and diving in the calmness of the lady's eye. Birds know the score. They seek the centre or follow a typhoon rather than run helplessly before it.'

'Yes, sir.'

'They're after food, Mister Dewar. Following fish. So keep an eye out, as I said, for fishing junks. Don't let yourself be shaken by a few gulls' wings.'

His fingers pushed the weather reports aside.

'It's Hogmanay tomorrow. The pipes are still in tune. You must teach me to play a few bars before New Year, Mister Dewar.'

I muttered something noncommittal and went back into the wheelhouse. Neither Roddy nor I spoke about the birds. Everything was very quiet, save for the faint click of the gyro compass, the sporadic tapping of the cadet's finger nails against the hood of the radar console and the wind whipping over the dodgers outside the starboard door. At an almost imperceptible signal from Roddy, I crossed to the radar screen. Dead ahead, between the electric green smudge of coastline and the open sea, the screen was peppered with a dozen tiny points of light. They were already visible from the wing of the bridge. Nine, ten, twelve bluff little junks rolling dangerously in the swell as they crossed our bows perhaps two miles away. Through my binoculars I scanned the starboard bow for more black shapes, more rakish lugsails which were the only indication we were likely to get of the size of the fishing fleet. It was useless to hope for a light or a signal from these hardy, suicidal, all-weather fishermen. The last junk passed less than a mile ahead of us. Five tiny figures in black sharkskin work clothes stood solemnly on her deck. These were men who neither knew nor cared about international regulations, men to whom the 'Rule of the Road' was an amusing inconvenience, adhered to only by the foreigners who usurped their national waters. Between the fishermen I made out the lumpy shapes of ropes and nets, which showed that they were not trawling. So we did not alter course, but passed close by the junks and looked down at their expressionless crews. In the stern of the nearest vessel, a little black figure casually struck matches against the wind beside the only lantern and when the matches ran out, turned away un-hurried, unconcerned, supremely confident in his little ship's ability for survival. In thirty minutes they were gone, their sails only fragile shapes on the horizon, heading for Hong Hai Bay and all the little fishing ports right up the coast of Communist China.

At noon I went below and put in an appearance in the smokeroom for a pre-lunch beer. Steadying myself against the motion of the ship, I took a seat beside Arthur Brown, who was finishing a half-hearted game of rummy with the Chief Engineer.

'If you ask me, chewing tobacco will rot your guts quicker than all the cigs you could smoke in a lifetime.'

Arthur shrugged.

'You're probably right, Chief. Can't say I go for it much, but I thought I'd better accept some after that blow up about the magazine.'

'What blow up?' I asked, as if I wasn't really interested, only making conversation.

'Nothing serious. Just a wee altercation about something he accused me of pinching. Bloody childish. He could have had it back any time, just for the asking, if he's that damned interested in fine art.'

'So you reckon he got the tobacco out of the cargo,' said the Chief.

'Stands to reason, doesn't it?'

'I've been wondering . . .', I said. But Arthur was scarcely in the mood for small talk.

'You're not paid to wonder, Mister. You'd better get on to the bridge or we'll be up on the chuckies at Pedro Blanco.'

So I reported back early. The Second Mate, who should normally have gone down for lunch, stayed on till we sighted the barren strip of foam-fringed rock and altered course to 068° to take us close along the China coast.

Framed in the chartroom door, the Old Man raised his cap to smooth his thickly matted hair.

'Wilma's on the move again. Northwest at seven knots, just like they said. We should feel the swell quite soon.'

The Second Mate prepared to leave.

'How long before we alter course into the Taiwan Strait, sir?'

'Thirteen hours, Mr Gow. Thirteen hours of fairly comfortable steaming, I imagine, but keep an eye on the barometer, Mr Dewar, and let me know of any drastic change.'

They went below, and once again I was in charge of the bridge while the Second Mate had lunch. The swell increased just as predicted, surging in great, heaving, lumpy masses beneath our starboard bow and sending streamers of spray high against the freeboard, over the gunnels and in among the hatch covers while the wind, not to be outdone, blew more strongly from northwest, sang in the stays and halyards and whipped viciously at the red and blue house flag on the mainmast. Under the opposing forces of wind and water, the *Blairskaith* trembled slightly, then settled to a slow, heavy roll as her twelve-thousand horsepower turbines drove her ahead at a steady fifteen knots.

Lunchtime was unusually quiet. Although I knew next to nothing of what had happened between the First Mate and the Old Man, I sensed a certain tension in the air, a sort of mutual embarrassment which filtered to the more junior officers, stifling any vestige of high spirits and restricting conversation to banal platitudes. Rather than endure a similar atmosphere in the smokeroom, I suggested to Roddy Hislop that we break open a case of beer in my cabin. Although I had intended to mention seagulls and fishing boats, to bring up the subject of magazines and Korean chewing tobacco, I didn't get the chance, for no sooner had Roddy sat down with an open beer can than he leapt to his feet once more, staring at the wall beside my bunk.

'Jesus Christ! It's her!' he cried.

'Who?'

'The one in the middle. The nude. It's the Old Man's wife!'

'Get away. That's not a woman. It's just a dummy like they have in shop windows. It says so down below.'

Roddy hesitated for a moment, peering at the newsprint image.

'It was three years ago, I admit. But she was with us for eleven weeks, so I had a pretty good look at her.'

'But you never saw her like that.'

'Near as damn it.'

'Lucky you! Anyway, you're off the beam there. An artist made that little lady. Bloody lifelike, isn't she?'

'Bloody sight better looking than the other three at any rate.'

'Always knew you had no taste. I'm getting married to the one on the left.'

'Oh hell ... I mean sorry, Andrew. Maybe she's not too bad at that. ...'

'Shut up and drink your beer.'

Deflated, Roddy sat down on the day bed.

'Even if that is a dummy,' he said at last, 'the artist would have used someone for a model. He couldn't make up a thing like that out of his head.'

'Sure,' I said. 'A housewife from Stonehaven with a one-year-old kid. The perfect model.'

'I still say it looks bloody like her.'

'You know what I reckon, Mister Hislop? I reckon you've been thinking about nothing but models since you saw Giles' sister. Obsessed with sex, you are. If you don't watch out, you'll end up going soft in the head like old Gospel.'

'Or our glorious leader,' said Roddy, dissolving in laughter and at the same time grinding his lower jaw from left to right in exaggerated chewing movements. 'They say he got it out of the cargo. That's not exactly normal, is it?'

'Come on, now, Roddy. We all help ourselves to odds and ends from time to time. Damaged items. Stuff out of broken cases. You know that.'

'Yes, but not tobacco. Not stuff to chew.'

'Maybe he's only trying to give up smoking. I haven't seen him with a fag since he began the chewing lark.'

'Who knows?'

After Roddy had left, I lay for a while on my bunk. Despite the throbbing movement of the ship, the slow, ponderous rolling that tilted the horizon in my porthole, I could not sleep and at last set off down the alleyway to take a shower.

If thou de. . .sire an unapproached perfection,
Behold the stars,
A. . .dore . . . adore . . . ad. . . their bright reflection.
They were not made to be . . . to be . . . to . . . belov'd,
They ne'er by human pray. . .er were moved.

Unbalanced by the motion of the ship, the stylus on Giles
St John-Browne's record player skidded from groove to
groove. The music swelled, coughed, stammered, only to surge
forth once more through the steel-plate wall that separated the
cadets' accommodation from the washroom. I listened for a
moment, amused and yet annoyed that valuable equipment
should be abused in such a fashion, then turned the tap and let
the hiss of water drown *Tannhäuser's* protestations.

About the same time, Wong Ching, the new Tiger,
standing in the alleyway of the upper deck, raised his eyebrows
as Captain David H Sinclair emerged from the master's
dayroom and made off along the corridor with a set of
bagpipes under his arm. His eyebrows were not raised for long.
What possible concern was it of his? Wong Ching permitted
himself a faintly sardonic smile, leant back against the
bulkhead and from his jacket pocket extracted a packet of
exclusive American cigarettes. Wong Ching considered himself very lucky. Never before had he been presented overnight
with a splendid job and a fat bundle of notes into the bargain,
just to make him accept. Wong Ching savoured his cigarette
and thought to himself how delicious the tobacco tasted in
contrast to the primitive native blend he'd been forced to
smoke on his last ship. There were perhaps two good drags left
between the glowing tip and cork filter when the Old Man
suddenly reappeared, careering down the narrow passageway
with a face black as thunder. The inch-long butt flew from the
Tiger's lips with the impact of the collision. He gasped and
pressed himself against the wall, but Captain Sinclair was
gone without a word. Gone behind the shuddering door of the
master's dayroom. Wong Ching stared for a moment at the
tiny smoking cylinder on the floor, then ground it beneath his
heel as he wandered pensively towards the pantry.

The shower had done me good. Even Giles' music seemed
brighter and I whistled as I strode into my cabin. From a

drawer beneath my bunk I took freshly laundered underwear, a new shirt and shorts, and spread them on the surface of the bed. But something else lay on the dark grey blanket. Something glistened between the neatly folded regulation shorts and shirt. My paper knife, 'A Souvenir from Perth', but now scratched, battered, bent almost beyond recognition And then I noticed. Above my bunk, between smiling nurses faces, on greying newsprint that still bore the marks of many folds, someone had made a vicious assault. Between the white-capped head of my future wife and the similarly uniformed image of Nurse Janet Boyd, someone had attacked the picture. Stabbed, slashed, hacked, cut. With rapid, angry strokes, 'A Souvenir from Perth' had set about the artist's creation. It had defaced her, decapitated her, eradicated her image for all time and in a welter of fury, driven on through ink and wood pulp into the layers of paint beneath to send thin slivers of white enamel over the desk and matting and blanket on the day bed. The jagged, tattered hole meant more than a thousand waxen faces. Scarred paintwork spoke more eloquently than a thousand newspaper captions. Trembling slightly, as if somehow I had myself been the victim of a physical assault, I changed my clothes then peeled the flimsy evidence from the wall and cautiously made off towards the First Mate's cabin.

Tweendecks

And so it all came out; or at least as much of it as Arthur Brown
and I could piece together. In the shaded stuffiness of his
cabin, we compared notes, sifted the facts and drew uneasy
parallels. The First Mate pulled at his beard above the
damaged photograph. I kept the record straight.

'The first cadet swore blind that the nude dummy between
the nurses was a model of the Old Man's wife. You can hardly
tell now, but it was a short, busty figure with black hair. Very
lifelike, too. If the caption hadn't said it was a sculpture, I'd
easily have taken it for real.'

'I know. Frighteningly lifelike, I'd say. Like a live human
being growing out of that damned ear.'

'But how did you . . .?'

'I've already seen it in the magazine. The one he went off
the deep end about. The one I borrowed from his cabin for a
few days.'

'You're having me on. The same sculpture? The same
dummy?'

'Exactly, only bigger and in colour.'

At that point words began to roll out of my mouth.

'So it was his wife. Why else would he have wanted the
magazine? It came specially from America ... I saw the
stamps on the envelope. He must have wanted to see the
pictures himself, and became angry when you borrowed it in
case anyone else recognised her. And when he saw the other
picture on my cabin wall, he must have assumed I put it there
because ...'

'... but it doesn't make sense. Plenty of women are models
and their husbands don't go around ... take Giles' sister, for
example ... unless ...'

'... unless he didn't like the idea. He's probably the

jealous type. Let's face it, how would you feel with your old lady plastered up all over the place stark naked?'

'But he was bound to know.'

'Maybe not. There was an article in the magazine, an interview with the artist who made the sculpture. He seemed a real queer fish. Talked all the time about sin and guilt and repentance. It was all quite beyond me but, come to think of it, he did say a seaman was involved somehow.'

'The Old Man?' Arthur Brown exhaled slowly and scratched his armpits through the sleeves of his vest. 'It's all bloody strange. What about the tobacco? I suppose it's nothing, but I can't say I've ever seen...'

'No. You have to begin with the bagpipes and all his stories about a guy who fought in the First World War. The bloke must be eighty by now. Probably dead. But the Old Man used to talk as if he was around today. And Christmas Eve, when he had me puffing and blowing for an hour, piping to him. Heaven knows what New Year will be like. He wants me to teach him to play.'

The First Mate crushed the tattered piece of newspaper into a ball and threw it out of the open porthole.

'Maybe he'll feel differently after this,' he said.

I doubt if I have ever dreaded anything more than my next watch in the wheelhouse of the *Blairskaith*. Believing, as I did, that Captain David H Sinclair bore me a malicious, though unjustified grudge, I approached my spell of duty with considerable trepidation, only to have the tables turned on me once more. Though his manner was more withdrawn than it had been of late, there was none of the truculent anger I had anticipated. Captain David H Sinclair was at work. The Old Man was in command on his bridge, carrying out his duties with characteristic, automatic, enviable precision that has led me ever since to question the frail validity of the case we had built up against him. He stood close against the windows, bracing himself against the rolling of the ship, which had become more pronounced since we changed course to 049° true. His voice was quiet, detached.

'How many revs are we doing?'

The cadet moved smartly to the engine-room telephone. 'Eighty-five, sir.'

Impassively, the Old Man's silhouette crossed the silvery patch of light and merged with the starboard wall of the wheelhouse. I stepped out after him on to the wing of the bridge, clasping the sanded handrail in the lee of the dodgers. Though his face was scarcely a shadow in the pervading blackness, I sensed instinctively that something had unsettled him. He stood for a moment, hunched in the furthest extremity of the wing then turned and came towards me.

'The wind's changed, Mister. So has the direction of the swell.'

He smiled fractionally, scarcely impeding the grinding motion of his jaws, and pushed past me into the wheelhouse. He was right. Inperceptibly at first, but with swiftly increasing violence, the wind had moved on to our port bow while the swell, surging now in great, black heaps, rolled in against our starboard quarter. The Old Man knew the score. He was busy in the chartroom with ruler and dividers long before Gospel lurched through the doorway to hand him a hastily scribbled message.

'T T T = "WILMA"

Typhoon "Wilma" now in position 23° 08 N 118° 48 E Course due N speed 10 kts. Expected to cross coast of China 40m E of Amoy and dissipate overland.'

'She's played a little trick on us, Mister Dewar. She's coming right up our bum at ten knots.'

'Indeed, sir,' said Gospel, 'there's no accounting for the ways of the Lord.'

'Or the delay in the met reports,' the Old Man retorted coldly and turned his attention to the chart.

Uncertain how to regard this remark, Gospel hung about for a few moments. Under any other circumstances, a torrent of divine justification would have flowed from the radio officer's lips, but somehow the Old Man's square, uncommunicative back quenched any spark of grace and Gospel left the chartroom with an expression of righteous indignation.

Looking over the Old Man's shoulder, I followed the twin pencil lines on the chart which indicated our course in relation to that of typhoon 'Wilma'. According to Gospel's report, the centre of the typhoon now lay somewhere in the middle of the Taiwan Banks, almost due south of our present position. Although there was no immediate danger, it was evident that on our present course, we would be relying solely on our speed to keep the ship outside the dangerous semicircle of the revolving storm. Already the ship was rolling through an arc of twenty-five degrees and as the velocity of the storm increased, our passage was sure to become even more uncomfortable. On the other hand, if the Old Man chose to alter course towards the China coast, the rolling would subside, the ship would become more stable but we would face the added danger of running into perilously shallow water with little room to manoeuvre in the limited confines of the Taiwan Strait. Before Captain Sinclair rose from the chart table, I had anticipated his orders.

'Hold her on 049 true, Mister Dewar, and ask the Chief for maximum revs, if you please.'

The Chief Engineer's voice crackled in the engine-room telephone.

'We can push her to ninety-five, Third. Ninety-eight if you're lucky.'

'Okay, Chief,' I replied. 'And hold on to your hat. Things are going to get worse before they get better.'

'Don't tell me, son. We're falling arse over tit down here already. The quicker we're out of this piece of oggin the better.'

I replaced the receiver and noted the time of the order in the book beside the 'phone. Li Sau, the quartermaster, had propped himself against the after bulkhead of the wheelhouse, legs wide apart. The glow of the compass faintly illuminated his bony arms on the wheel. Responding to the extra revs, the ship surged forward obliquely through the black, lumpy swell, buffeting and rolling as she picked up speed to fifteen-and-a-half, sixteen, seventeen knots. I glanced at the dial of the inclinometer bolted to the after bulkhead to the right of the quartermaster's head. Fifteen degrees each side of vertical.

When the cadet brought the cocoa, we cupped the warm, slopping mugs in both hands, steadied ourselves against convenient pieces of equipment and guided the scalding liquid to our lips like blind men in the darkness.

After half an hour, the Old Man left the bridge.

'Call me at the slightest sign of trouble.'

After one hour, the needle on the inclinometer dial was swinging through an arc of thirty-two degrees. After one hour and ten minutes, Roddy Hislop and I stopped talking, broke off our discussion on the merits of the nursing profession and listened to a sound that filtered through the rushing of wind and water with dull, monotonous, frightening regularity. The muffled, metallic clang came from somewhere forward of the wheelhouse. The stifled knocking of steel against steel came from the heart of the hull. The deadened, eerie thump came once every time the ship rolled to port.

'Get the Old Man, quick!'

'What's up?'

'Sounds like cargo shifting.'

The cadet and the Old Man collided in the wheelhouse door. For perhaps five minutes, Captain Sinclair stood stock still hard against the wheelhouse windows, listening to the ugly, ominous clanging, trying with every ounce of his senses to judge where it was coming from. Then he swung round, reeling off orders, spitting out instructions between mobile, grinding teeth.

'Ring half-ahead, Mister Dewar.' To the cadet, 'Get the First Mate. Tell him something's broken loose in number two tweendecks and I'd be obliged if he'd see to it at once.' To me, 'Any other traffic in the vicinity?'

'No, sir. Nothing on the screen.'

'We may have to turn her round. Get her head into the swell.'

Stability. Of course, stability. Rapidly I tried to picture what cargo was stowed in the tweendecks of number two hold. To starboard there was the tobacco, but it would never have made a sound like that. Not metal on metal. And to port it was general cargo, canned goods, crates of Hong Kong clothing, machinery. Knock... knock... knock. At every heave to port, something was crashing against the *Blairskaith*'s side and for all we knew buckling and bending her plates at every impact. The only way to prevent further damage was to lessen the rolling, to turn the ship's head directly into the swell and ride it out until the extent of the damage could be inspected and the cargo secured. But to do so now, when running before a typhoon, when every ounce of power should have been propelling us in exactly the opposite direction required immense courage, borne out by total conviction that only such a manoeuvre would ensure the safety of the ship. Captain David H Sinclair's jaw moved left to right with the motion of the ship and at every clang from the hull his yellow molars bit harder against the moistness of tobacco.

'All right, Third. We'll bring her around.'

Arthur Brown was out of his bunk and struggling into his oilskins before the breathless cadet started pounding on his cabin door. The regular, unnatural clanging had already found its way through the deck beneath his feet and brought a sinking feeling to the pit of his stomach. He was not a man to shirk responsibility, and for this very reason fought with his memory to work out why the cargo, of which he was in charge, should have broken loose. He threw open the door to admit the cadet.

'Where is it?'

'Number two tweendecks we reckon.'

'Put the bosun and the chippy on the shake and have the duty AB stand by to rig a lifeline.'

'Yes, sir.'

The cadet stumbled off along the alleyway and Arthur Brown made his way forward where the knocking sounded louder. In five minutes he was joined by the two Chinamen, silent and imperturbable as ever, and one by one they attached themselves to the lifeline and scuttled like flies across the vast, heaving foredeck to the main masthouse. Huddled against the cold, wet plates while the bosun struggled to open the heavy steel door of the masthouse, the First Mate glanced up at the windows of the wheelhouse, then at the sea breaking

high over the starboard bow and realised for the first time that
the ship was turning into the swell. Just then a huge wall of
water crashed over the starboard gunnel, lifting him bodily
and hurling him through the door after the bosun and the
chippy. Winded and soaked to the skin, Arthur Brown pressed
himself against the wall of the masthouse, fighting for breath.
His torch picked out the faces of the Chinamen close by in the
darkness.

'Rig a cluster of lights, bosun, and we'll have a look
below.'

In the narrow, vertical trunkway which led from the
masthouse to the tweendecks, the noise was louder. It rang and
echoed against the metal plates and was amplified by the
darkness until it seemed that the entire ship must be pulling
itself apart under the awful pounding of gigantic hammer
blows. The yellow beam of the First Mate's torch waved feebly
in the blackness, caressing the bulky outlines of the nearest
bales of cargo. Damn the darkness. Damn the stench of
tobacco that filled the rancid air and made you want to retch
at every heave of the ship. The bosun struggled down the
ladder, clutching a reel of power cable with four lamps, each
protected by a heavy rubber sheath. In contrast to the
torchlight, the lamps were almost dazzling, but their power
was still insufficient to penetrate the furthest corners of the
tweendecks. Slowly, methodically, Arthur Brown began to
scan every item of cargo within range of the lamps. Nothing
moved in the dancing yellow beam. Everything was in place.
Wan Lo, the chippy, joined them at the foot of the ladder and
they stood together listening; trying to pinpoint by sound, if
not by sight, the approximate location of the moving object.

'Over there, Yat-fo! Right on port side.'

The chippy dropped down and edged his way along the
wall of hogsheads, dragging the lamp cable behind him.
Cautiously the bosun followed, leaving Arthur Brown to bring
up the rear. The noise was louder. A sliding rumble ending in a
dull, echoing clang. But still nothing moved. Along the port
side of the tweendecks, the wall of wooden packing cases was as
solid as it had ever been, blank and immobile in the wavering
light. The chippy stepped round the end of the last packing

case. Suddenly there was a shout, a grinding crash and something long and low and very heavy skidded past the end of the row of cases and ploughed lazily into the farthest row of hogsheads on the starboard side. Then someone began to scream in Chinese. The First Mate yanked at the cable of his lamp. It had snagged on the corner of a packing case, but the second heave freed it and he could direct its light to the port wall of the hold. Wan Lo was lying against the side of the ship, his foot pinioned between shattered spars of dunnage and packing cases. All round him were littered crushed baulks of timber, splintered fragments of wood and thousands and thousands of broken plastic toys.

Before Arthur Brown could move, the bosun pushed past him and stumbled towards the screaming chippy. Regardless of the pain inflicted, he seized Wan Lo under the armpits, straining with all his power to free him from the grip of the timber. Before Arthur Brown could move, he remembered the object, long, low and very heavy; he remembered the two ton, twenty foot lathe loaded in London, which was now resting in a mangled bed of tobacco and splintered wood, but which at any second would begin its return journey along the track of pulverised debris to strike the hull exactly where the chippy was trapped. Then Arthur Brown moved. Ten paces brought him to the bosun's side. Beneath their combined strength, the shattered wood gave way, gouging a vicious pattern of gashes into the chippy's flesh as they pulled him clear. Then they were running, falling head over heels, dragging the chippy after them as the ship listed to port and the two ton lathe skidded past and added another clang to its symphony as it crashed against the steel plates of the hull.

A cold trickle of sweat ran down the First Mate's nose to drop into the equally distasteful saltiness of his damp beard. Two of the emergency lamps were still burning. Their wavering light reflected faintly in the moisture on the chippy's brow. Wan Lo braced himself against the wooden crates and gritted his teeth. His leg was bleeding from several deep lacerations, cuts that by rights should have been stitched immediately, but he knew that in this situation, his injuries must take second place to the safety of the ship. The lathe was still loose and, though its movement was likely to subside once the *Blairskaith*'s head was turned into the swell, until then every impact against the wall might well be the final one required to spring the plates of the hull.

'We'll have to wedge the bastard up against the wall . . .' Arthur Brown eyed the lathe warily as it once more skidded across the tweendecks into the battered, groaning row of hogsheads, '. . . then lash it up once it has stopped moving.'

Despite his injured leg, the chippy pulled himself to his feet and peered through the dancing yellow beam in the direction the First Mate was pointing. Behind the impassive mask of his face, from which even the expression of pain had disappeared, Wan Lo weighed up the situation, pictured the size and number of wedges required, speculated on how many men would be needed to drive them into place and secure the lathe before another heave of the ship could bring the two ton chunk of steel careering on top of them. He was about to make his findings known to the First Mate and ask permission to fetch two deckhands from the crew accommodation when a sudden, tremendous vibration surged the entire length of the ship, wrenching Wan Lo's feet from under him and throwing him like a rag doll against the jarring hardness of the deck.

Arthur Brown was first to get up again, clutching the ladder of the trunkway, his face drawn and taut in anticipation. When the second impact came he was ready for it and braced himself against the hard metal rungs. The noise screamed down the trunkway. The noise came slicing through metal decks and hatch covers. And this time, the sound that echoed and rang from the tweendecks walls had none of the solid reassurance of steel against steel. The sound that drained the last vestige of colour from the First Mate's cheeks was a sharp, explosive crash; exactly like the bursting of a shell. And it came from somewhere high above the *Blairskaith*'s maindeck.

'Jesus Christ!' Arthur Brown twisted in the general direction of the two startled Chinamen. 'Take charge here, bosun. I'm going to find out. . . .' And then he started to climb the ladder faster than he had ever done in his life.

Glass

When Roddy Hislop arrived back in the wheelhouse, gasping for breath after having roused the bosun and the carpenter, SS *Blairskaith* was just beginning to nose uneasily on to the track that would bring her head round into the swell and neutralise, however temporarily, the potential danger of the shifting cargo in number two tweendecks. The cadet reported and took his station behind the engine-room telegraph, leaving me free to struggle towards the radar console outlined squat and grey on the port side of the wheelhouse. In the darkness, shaded even from the faintest reflection of the pitch black sky, the greenish glow of the radar screen shone eerily from beneath the hood of the console. One glance confirmed that no other traffic was in our vicinity, that we were free to execute the long, slow arc through forty-one degrees that would bring us round to face the mountainous swell now breaking high on our starboard bow to rush in white torrents across the grey blur of the fo'c'sle. The Old Man was little more than a black shape, hard against the windows on the starboard side of the wheelhouse. Motionless except for his jaws, it was as if he was willing the ship round against the sea; edging the 14 700 tons of wood, steel and humanity under his command into the full fury of typhoon 'Wilma'. The wind, howling now past the port sidescreens of the wheelhouse, filled the air with a perpetual moan, dulling his voice as he spoke calmly to the quarter-master.

'Starboard ten the wheel, easy now.'

Answering to the helm, the white smudge that marked the *Blairskaith*'s bow swung further round, blurring the foredecks in spray, canting at a precipitous angle as she nosed into a trough between the waves. Releasing my grip on the edge of the radar set, I lurched towards the port wheelhouse windows, steadying myself against the teak rail just in time to see three tiny figures stumble through the door of the masthouse forty feet below. Through the blinding spray, transforming the armoured glass to an opaque, silvery smudge before my eyes, it was impossible to identify any of the men who had crossed the heaving foredeck. But I knew Arthur Brown was there, and the bosun and chippy, and I did not envy their task in the least.

'Starboard ten of wheel. Wheel ten degrees to starboard, sir.'

The quartermaster's voice sounded high, almost shrill in the darkness. Close against the starboard wall, Roddy Hislop pressed himself to the engine-room telegraph, his white knuckles gripping its polished handles as if, at any moment, it was likely to detach itself from the sanded wheelhouse floor. And all the time, whenever the insurmountable pressure of the waves rolled us to port, the ominous, sickening clang reverberated through the very structure of the ship, emphasising the desperate urgency to complete the manoeuvre.

'Bring her round another ten to starboard, quartermaster.'

The Old Man's voice came out of the darkness as though it no longer belonged to a body but to some other, unearthly element at one with the waves and the screaming, deafening wind. My eyes sought the polished brass shape of the inclinometer. Darkness shrouded its dial. I could only imagine our angle of list.

'Ten more to starboard. Twenty of starboard wheel on, sir.'

Cautiously, lest she should wallow at that point in the turn when she came broadside on to the swell, Captain David H Sinclair edged *Blairskaith* round inch by inch to face the waves.

'Thirty degrees of starboard wheel on, sir.'

Now it was impossible to stand upright without support. I hooked my arms round the rail and braced my knees against the forward wall as the wheelhouse canted to thirty-five degrees from the vertical. Outside, beyond the shimmering sheet of glass, the foredeck was buried beneath a seething, angry mass of white water. My thoughts leapt wildly from the Old Man, grim and silent on my right, to the men out there in the tweendecks, struggling to secure heaven knows what under that unbelievable weight of foaming water. And then, for no reason at all, four bars of *Tannhäuser* began to repeat and repeat in my head; four bars from Giles' record which, even now, was probably blaring forth in the accommodation beneath us; four bars of thunderous, cataclysmic music that synchronised exactly with the regular crash of moving cargo from our hull.

'Starboard fifteen degrees.'

'Starboard fifteen. Fifteen of starboard, sir. Forty-five degrees of wheel on, sir.'

I felt the structure shudder as we came directly into the swell and the first great sea, breaking against our bows, transmitted its vibration throughout the length of the ship. It was impossible to see through the windows now. Only the Old Man, his face pressed close to the rotating clear-view screen could possibly have picked out anything through the wall of spray that hurled itself against the front of the superstructure.

'Ease to forty ... steady as she goes.'

With a seething rush of water, the ship's bow emerged from the swell and she climbed the first wave. Windlasses, ventilators, masthouses appeared as if through a mist as foam cascaded from the foredecks. Somewhere to my right, the engine-room telephone had started ringing and I caught a glimpse of the cadet as he stumbled to answer it.

'Steady on 180°, sir. Course 180°.'

Li Sau's voice drowned out *Tannhäuser*. The quartermaster's words jolted me back to reality, to the pitching wheelhouse, steadier now that we were headed due south; to the realisation that we had just crested an enormous wave and that another was on its way. I remember relaxing a little, and the Old Man saying something like,

'They'd better lash that cargo bloody fast, Mister.'

Then I was holding on very tightly and the *Blairskaith*'s bows were down as if she was all set to drive herself straight to the bottom of the ocean. For an instant, I saw the wave rising over the fo'c'sle, black and huge and fathomless in the darkness, then it was over the foredeck and crashing against the accommodation. Even now, what followed is hazy and uncertain in my memory, though I have tried time and time again to form a logical sequence from the crazy, frenzied jumble of events. More than likely I struck my head against an upright of the wheelhouse wall, for my first memory is of totally stifling blackness followed by an overwhelming crash, as if an express train was roaring through the front of the wheelhouse. The contents of my stomach rose in my throat as a tremendous force lifted me from the ground and hurled me bodily against the wooden flag lockers in the after port corner of the wheelhouse.

When I opened my eyes, hours and hours later it seemed to me, though in reality I must have come to within a few seconds, I was cold and wet and alone. Completely alone! Instinctively I lurched towards the wheel, to the raised wooden grating where the quartermaster should have been. Already the ship was beginning to wallow. Frantically I spun the wheel, counting, praying that I could get her head round before the next wave struck. I glanced up towards the windows, to the fo'c'sle and the angry black sea stretching beyond and only then did I realise why it was so cold and wet and why the murderous roaring in my head would not stop. The starboard window just was not there. No glass. No clear-view screen. Nothing but a black, empty hole through which wind and spray gusted to the furthest corner of the wheel-house. Then someone was moving over on my right. Roddy Hislop struggled to his feet, still clutching the shattered bakelite receiver of the engine-room telephone, which emitted a faint, pathetic crackling. Painfully, noiselessly, I began to laugh. Roddy lumbered about stunned, baffled, comically unaware of his surroundings.

'Here! Take the wheel.'

Broken glass sang louder than the wind as he came up beside me. His face was white, paralysed with shock. I had to yell at him to make him understand.

'Keep her head into the swell. Hold her on one-eight-oh, d'you hear?' His mouth moved slightly in acknowledgement and he clutched the brass rim of the wheel as if it were the last thing in the world.

Blairskaith climbed obliquely up the next wave and crested it with awkward, rolling dignity. Scarcely a drop of spray penetrated the gaping hole where the starboard window had been. I watched the compass needle steady on 180°, then peered apprehensively across the blacked out wheelhouse. Not three yards away a bulky figure was wedged in the doorway. Relief was evident in my voice.

'We're holding her on 180°, sir. We'll have to block up the starboard window.'

But it was Gospel, not the Old Man who answered.

'Lord Almighty, laddie. Get some bloody lights on.'

I felt my way past him to the switchboard fixed to the after bulkhead and threw the switches of the main bridge lighting. The two five-hundred watt bulbs in the deckhead flicked to blinding, garish life casting a white, impersonal light over the chaotic scene in the wheelhouse. Between the forward wall and the after bulkhead, the entire starboard section of the floor was littered with fist-sized fragments of jagged armoured glass. The glass had peppered the spotless paintwork of the after bulkhead. The glass had stripped the grey enamel from the echo-sounder cabinet like skin from an apple.

'The quartermaster's lying in the alleyway,' Gospel informed me as he shuffled around among the debris. 'He's out cold. It must have knocked him right through the bloody door.'

Our eyes met, as if unwilling to continue searching. Why did neither of us mention his name? Footsteps resounded in the alleyway and Arthur Brown burst into the wheelhouse. Out of breath. Wet, dripping oilskins. He could not avoid the issue.

'Where's the Old Man?'

I pointed to the empty, glass strewn space where I had last seen Captain David H Sinclair. Together, the First Mate and I approached the furthest corner of the wheelhouse. We could not ignore the white, lacing deck-shoes and neat regulation socks projecting from behind the echo-sounder cabinet. We could not turn a blind eye to the dark patch of blood seeping in tiny rivulets along the joints of the sanded teak flooring. The Old Man was sitting on the floor with his back against the echo-sounder cabinet. His trousers were immaculate. His regulation shirt with four gold bars on the epaulettes left nothing to be desired. But he was not the Old Man we knew, for he no longer had a face. Beneath the tremendous pressure of water, the bursting glass had shown no mercy. It had remodelled the Old Man; smoothed him down; rounded off his rugged features to suit streamlined requirements. Fist-sized bullets of glass had carved a five inch parting in the matted hair, peeled the determination from his chin and, with surgical precision, shorn his head of those peculiar lateral impedimenta that go by the name of ears.

Before we lifted him, the First Mate claims the Old Man opened his messy, red mouth just wide enough to eject a moistened quid of chewing tobacco. I can't vouch for it. No ball of partially masticated leaves was found among the wreckage. When we laid him gently on the settee in the chartroom, it was clear that he was dead.

To say that no one mourned his passing, or was in any way affected by his death is as inaccurate as it is unkind. However, our position had become in no way less precarious, and a moment's wasted time might well have proved disastrous. Arthur Brown took command on the bridge while a party of seamen under the supervision of the Second Mate went forward to secure the lathe in number two tweendecks. The Old Man's plans always worked out. Within an hour they had completed the job and it was possible to bring the *Blairskaith* round again on to her original course. No one spoke very much during this manoeuvre, but the First Mate's seamanship proved equal to the task. At full revs once again, SS *Blairskaith* rolled lazily and ploughed on through the Taiwan Straits while typhoon 'Wilma', as predicted, headed north to bend the trees and flatten communal rice fields over the mainland of China.

My watch was over and I was no longer needed on the bridge, yet I could not tear myself away. Somewhere I found a greatcoat and stood huddled in a corner until the cold, yellow sun rose over the horizon to glare without compassion on the sparkling jewels of glass around my feet. With the dawn, the day-workers came on duty and moved about the wheelhouse in awe, while the bosun gave commands very quietly in Chinese. Someone, I think it was the Tiger, lit a joss stick and wedged it against the cover of the echo-sounder. The others brought buckets and shovels. It probably never occurred to them to give a warning or ask permission of a silent, shivering third officer whose feet were in the way. Why should it have? Under normal circumstances, I pride myself on being capable of controlling my emotions, on presenting to the outside world at least a façade of orderliness and restraint. But when the wheelhouse began to resound with the screaming of a thousand splinters of armoured glass being dropped into galvanised tin buckets; when the crashing, tinkling torture refused to stop and the sickly stench of sandalwood engulfed my throat I added my own voice to that of the glass and rushed blindly on to the port wing of the bridge to vomit into the frothing, ink-blue ocean.

When at last I pushed myself away from the rail, reeling giddily from the motion of the waves, Gospel was beside me. He reached inside his shirt and pushed an uncorked bottle under my nose.

'Drink up, son. It's Hogmanay.'

The searing, ninety-proof spirit burned my mouth. I drank, choked, and drank again until the sharp fumes filled my head and permeated my whole body with tingling warmth. I glanced at the scratched face of my wristwatch. It was seven-fifteen. At eight, I would be on duty again. Nothing breaks the routine. As Gospel and I went below for breakfast, we passed the chippy limping towards the bridge with an emergency shutter to block the wheelhouse window.

Atonement

Someone had to take the blame. In Giles St John-Browne, sullen when in company, petulant when subjected to the First Mate's inevitable questioning, we had a ready-made whipping boy who could not deny his failure to inspect the tweendecks cargo before the hatches were closed in Hong Kong. Giles did not even offer his injuries as an excuse. He was content to stare at his reflection in the polished table top as Arthur Brown's neat, round handwriting worked its way across sheet after sheet of watermarked company notepaper in preparation for the official investigation which we were bound to face on arrival in Nagasaki. Already that morning, Gospel's finger had been constantly at work filling the air with messages, copying replies, coding and decoding necessary information.

SS *Blairskaith* to Hong Kong Office: 'Master fatally injured in accident. Damage to cargo not yet ascertained. Position approx. 25° 6 N 120° 19 E. Proceeding Nagasaki as scheduled. We do not require assistance.'

Hong Kong Office to First Officer SS *Blairskaith*: 'Retain command for rest of voyage. Replacement First Officer available Kaoshiung 9th January. Marine Superintendent Far East proceeding Nagasaki forthwith. Prepare detailed report.'

Cable from Hong Kong Office, Blair Lines Limited, to Head Office, London: 'Sinclair David H No 106 Master *Blairskaith* fatally injured Taiwan Strait December 30th/31st stop full report to follow.'

Post Office Inland Telegram from Head Office to next of kin: 'It is with deep regret that we must inform you...'

Lines of communication. Lines of thought. Lines of inquiry. Arthur Brown laid down his pen and ran careworn fingers across the lines on his brow. Blame will not lie still, will seldom adhere to its target like a well-applied coat of paint. The first stone had been cast at Giles, and now its ripples were beginning to spread. Their widening circumference left no one completely undisturbed.

The Second Mate: 'I had a phone call and left the deck at least ten minutes before the hatch covers were closed. But Giles was there. ...'

And Blair Line's regulations: 'The ultimate responsibility for stowage and management of cargo lies with the First Officer. ...'

Tiny particles of dust hung in the humid airlessness of the ship's office. Arthur Brown squinted through the porthole at the round, white sun hanging in the blue-grey sky and consulted his watch. Time for lunch. Time to face up to it; to present the facts to engineers and electricians who had only heard of the Old Man's death second hand. An empty chair. A vacant place at table. Commiserations.

As I made for the door, the First Mate detained me till the others passed into the alleyway, leaving us alone. He swung the door closed with two fingers, then raised them to his breast pocket and withdrew a folded Marconigram, made out in Gospel's distinctive handwriting.

'Head Office has got off its mark quickly enough. This came ten minutes ago. Says he's not to be buried at sea. Next of kin's request. They're going to fly him home from Japan.'

'Cost a bomb, that will.'

'Indeed,' said Arthur Brown. 'But those are the orders, so I want the body sewn up in canvas and placed in number two cold-store. See to it immediately after lunch, then meet me in the master's dayroom. An inventory must be made before his things are packed ready to be sent home.'

'Yes, sir.'

I did not see the Old Man again. In the sepulchral presence of the bosun and sailmaker, I was content to leave undisturbed whatever lay beneath the rough grey blanket on the chartroom settee and make off into the wheelhouse before the Chinamen commenced their solemn task. Gospel was leaning through the hatch from the radio shack.

'Would you credit that, eh? No burial service. No funeral, and I had looked up some splendid texts too. Very tasteful, you understand. Very appropriate in this particular situation. The First Mate would have been very pleased to accept my assistance. He's never officiated at a burial at sea.'

Neither Ian Gow nor Giles St John-Browne were in the least interested in discussing the merits of shipboard funeral rites. They contented themselves by staring out across the glistening expanse of water, each trying in his own way to put the memory of the previous night to the back of his mind. Each trying to ignore the bleak, wooden shutters that blocked out part of the horizon but could not prevent the sunlight glinting on the freshly lacerated paintwork of the echo-sounder cabinet. Gospel was not to be diverted from the subject.

'Tell me boys, what is more natural than that a man whose very existence has centred on the sea should be returned to it when the Lord sees fit to extinguish the mortal flame? Cold storage, embalming and air-transportable coffins should play no part in a seaman's final journey. Five years ago, aboard the *Blairhall* between Singapore and Colombo, an old planter returning to retire in the UK died of heart failure half way across the Indian Ocean. It so happened that one of the other passengers was an Anglican missionary bishop, and he offered to say a few words before we heaved the old fellow over the wall. Now, generally speaking, the Anglican service seems to me to be perilously close to the Church of Rome and quite devoid of dignity. However, that old bishop certainly knew the ropes. Kept it simple and brief, yet very moving. After it was over, I took down as much as I could remember of what he said in case it should come in useful sometime. And now what happens? No burial. Flown home, if you please. It wouldn't surprise me if they even cremated the poor man once they got him in their clutches. No sense of tradition. No grasp of the proper things in life, eh Third?'

'Leave me out of it!' I said, and made off down the companionway to the senior officers' accommodation. The scent of joss sticks hung heavy in the humid air outside the master's dayroom and from time to time, the sharp report of a firecracker echoed along the alleyway as the Chinese set about driving off the devils whose presence threatened the wellbeing of the entire ship. Leung Wing Pa and the new Tiger were lurking near the door, their faces shining with excitement as if even being outside a room frequented by the late Captain Sinclair filled them with daring fascination. They moved closer when I approached but made no attempt to follow me into the master's dayroom.

Arthur Brown was seated at the Old Man's desk behind a pile of abstracts, manifestos and other official papers. He need not have worried. Captain David H Sinclair had left everything in perfect order. While the First Mate accustomed himself to the responsibility of command, I went over to the drawers and cupboards lining the walls and slowly set about removing their contents, listing them one by one and placing them on the day bed ready to be packed into trunks and cases for the journey home. I had seen it all before. There was absolutely nothing out of the ordinary in the narrow, wooden doored wardrobe with the mirror in front. Uniform jacket, sports jacket, tropical suit and ready-made European suit for cooler climates. Two pairs of uniform trousers, three pairs of uniform shorts in white drill. I unhooked the coathangers from the rail and laid the garments out on the bed. Despite the presence of the First Mate, despite the official inventory on the table growing longer and longer as I added details of underwear, socks and shoes, I was gripped by an unaccountable suspense, a gnawing anxiety that, at any moment, the Old Man might stroll into the cabin and demand to know why, in heaven's name, I was rifling his private accommodation. But that was silly. The Old Man was already in number two cold-store, where all the shirts and pullovers in the world would not keep him warm. Two black uniform ties, one purple silk tie, one brown and green checked tie, one blue tie. Perhaps Arthur Brown was not entirely free of the nagging guilt of trespass, for he turned to me irritably and said, 'Get a move on, Third. I want that lot out of here as soon as possible.'

The drawers and cupboards were empty. I turned my attention to the roll-topped writing cabinet. Six nautical textbooks, various; one Oxford dictionary, one sextant with case, two hundred and forty cigarettes in packets of twenty, one propelling pencil in white metal. On the green baize writing surface of the cabinet, two sheets of company note-paper projected from beneath a folded copy of the *South China Post*. What right had I to push the newspaper aside and read what had been written in a bold, angular hand beneath the full-colour imprint of the Blair Line house flag?

SS *Blairskaith*,
At sea.
30 December

Dear Cans,

I still can't stop substituting the ridiculous four letter word for your name whenever I have to put it down in black and white. But it was you, after all, who wrote it on the napkin, so you won't object, no matter how steely a glare may flash from behind Malcolm's violet-tinted spectacles. The spectacles baffled me, Eva. (There, I have used your proper name.) They disturbed me more than his pseudo-nakedness, more than the capering dwarfs, much more than the gryphon who led me to the scene. I never could make a timely exit. I have relived those hours, minutes, seconds that led to a scrap of paper and a hastily offered pen more often than any others in my life. They leap at me more vividly than the glass-cased view from a dangerously balanced plank, more frequently, my dearest Eva, than our first moment together, when our ten fingers were united by the adhesive medium of red-lead. The secret was in the spectacles, because by the fountain of life, in the company of dwarfs, gryphons, satyrs, harpies, he first presented a barrier I could not penetrate. After all, his narrow, dark brown eyes had never been a problem to a blue-eyed type like me. I had always seen through him in the past. But the spectacles were there and the eyes were not and the gryphon chose to interest himself in the Chinese lady, so I had no choice but to follow him upstairs. His muse made no effort to prevent me scribbling the address, though even then, I consciously blurred my handwriting. No matter. I lifted the pen, and because even the hottest fire cannot escape a tinted lens, I opened the first lock-gate a mere fraction to extinguish the flames. Lock-gate. What a soothing word, redolent with security and reassurance. How was I to know he'd built up a tidal wave of jealousy behind violet glass? At my first sign of weakness, it swept in to reclaim the ground I had so carefully preserved. He overwhelmed us both and at a stroke took for himself what his conceit assumed to be the essence of our existence. Your body. My self-confidence. You must have guessed by now I've seen pictures of the sculpture. For hours on end, at first, I gazed at every fibre-glass facet, at every curve and fold of waxen flesh. I pored over every angle, studied each square inch of photogravure that screamed at me in colour and black and white from shiny, cultured paper.

He almost won. Naturally, your waxen likeness grimacing from its obscene container threw me into a fit of despair. But what is done is done. Gradually I came to realise that by prolonging my anguish, by returning time after time to the squared-up photographs of his waxen abomination, I was playing into his hands. No doubt he thought that the intensity of the revulsion I had experienced at setting eyes on your duplicate bound me to despise you with equal intensity, but wax can never be flesh, no matter how expertly it has been formed. In his tawdry, sensational charade, I recognised your outward shell, but nothing more. He sought to drive me to distraction by presenting proof that he had captured your soul, but instead, he has merely perpetuated your body and by emphasising the most transient feature of your make-up, made me understand more clearly than ever before the futility of relationships based purely on attractions of the flesh. After all, your body has always belonged partly to him. Before sculptured wax there were meetings in a sanctified pine wood and a little label one inch by two inches stitched to the lining of his dusty blazer. I always knew, or thought I knew. So you see, Eva, by perpetuating the charade he has accomplished nothing. You are closer to me now than ever before.

I have come to a decision. I have been turning the matter over in my mind for some time, uncertain of making the move. How ironical that he should have supplied the final impetus! When I have finished this letter, I shall compose my resignation to Blair Lines. The words are already in my head. Perhaps the company will find it difficult to understand, but

I'm sure it's for the best. There are countless appointments available for master mariners in New Zealand, and the climate will be so good for little Maggie. You're certain to like Auckland, Eva. Accommodation will be no problem. Until we find a house, I have arranged for us to stay with ...

David Sinclair never gave up.

It would have been quite in order to pack the letter with the rest of his belongings, to slip the flimsy sheets of paper between the pages of a book and leave their discovery to chance. But Arthur Brown's back was turned and an envelope lay ready beside the newspaper. Slug Road. He had even written the address. So I folded up the letter and quietly sealed the envelope. I posted it when we reached Nagasaki, just as he would have done. Perhaps the matter will be mentioned at the inquiry. Perhaps his next of kin will have been offended at receiving a letter from a dead man, who was unable to finish it because of an appointment with a sheet of armoured glass. Who cares? I shall have my answers ready.

The First Mate rose to his feet and looked around. On every surface in the cabin, the mortal effects of Captain David H Sinclair were piled in neat, orderly rows. We could hear the two Chinamen struggling up the alleyway with an empty trunk.

'That everything?'

'Except these. ...'

I lifted the bagpipes, and as I did so a little black box slipped from beneath the bag and clattered on to the floor of the cabin. Arthur Brown stooped to pick it up.

'What's this?'

He held up the box that contained neither drawing instruments nor cuff-links, wrist-watch nor electric razor, whose maker had been so proud of it that he had added his name in tiny gold letters near the hinge. W Zakrewski, Boxmaker, Leith. I shrugged.

'One small black box, locked.'

But Arthur Brown was making an inventory. Sticking to the rules.

'Open it up, Third,' he ordered.

He handed me his pen-knife, small and flat with the name of a brewery engraved along the side. Gently I inserted the blade just above the tiny gilt lock. The box was never meant to be burglar-proof. W Zakrewski had never envisaged an assault being made on his masterpiece with cold steel. At the slightest turn of my wrist, the catch gave way and I lifted the lid. Arthur Brown leant forward to look, but said nothing. What was there to say? On a carefully constructed velvet cushion, there lay a pair of worn, leather ears fastened by a strap with a little silver buckle.